Black Tartan Slammer

By Gordon Kidd

 New Generation Publishing

Dedication

I lovingly dedicate this book to my wife Gill, for the 35 long years of loyal service shown by her.

When I retired a few years ago it became necessary for Gill to get a full-time job to supplement her then existing part-time employment, both for extra income and to cover the general day-to-day living expenses that we needed. Shortly after she started working full-time I noticed she was beginning to show her age. I usually get home from the golf club about the same time she gets home from work. Although Gill knows how hungry I am, she always says she has to rest for half-an-hour or so before she starts cooking dinner. I don't yell at her. Instead, I tell her to take her time and just wake me up when the dinner in on the table. I generally have lunch out, in the Spike Bar at the golf club, so eating out again in the evening is really not a reasonable option. She used to do the dishes as soon as we finished eating. But now it's not unusual for them to sit on the table for several hours after dinner. I do what I can by diplomatically reminding her several times each evening that they won't clean themselves. I know Gill really appreciates this, as it does seem to motivate her to get them done before she goes to bed. Another symptom of ageing is complaining, I think. As an example, Gill will say it is difficult for her to find the time to do the grocery shopping or to pay the monthly bills during her lunch hour. But I remind myself that I took Gill on "for better or for worse" all those years ago, so I just smile and offer her encouragement. I tell Gill to stretch it out over two, or even three days. That way, she won't have to rush so much. I also remind her that missing lunch completely now and then wouldn't hurt her any. I like to think tact is one of my strong points. When doing simple household tasks, Gill seems to think she needs more rest periods. She had to take a break recently when she only half-finished mowing the lawn. I try not to make a scene. I'm a fair man. I tell Gill to fix herself a nice, big, cold glass of freshly squeezed lemonade and just sit for a while. And, as long as she is making one for herself, she may as well make one for me too. I know that I probably appear like a saint in the way I support Gill. I am not saying that showing this much consideration is easy. Many men will find it difficult. Some, no doubt, will find it impossible. Nobody knows better than I do how frustrating woman get as they get older. Finally, I have to say to all good men out there – if you use a little more tact and less criticism of your ageing wife after reading this personal dedication of mine to Gill, then I will consider writing it was well worthwhile. After all, we are all put on earth to help one another.

*   *   *   *   *

PUBLISHER'S EDIT:

Gordon died suddenly on April 25 of a perforated rectum. The police report stated Gordon was found with a Callaway extra-long 50 inch Big Bertha Driver golf club jammed up his rear end, with barely five inches of grip left showing, and a sledge hammer lying nearby. His wife, Gill, was arrested and charged with murder. The all-woman jury took only ten minutes to find Gill 'Not Guilty', accepting her defence that Gordon somehow, without looking, accidentally sat down on his golf club.

Disclaimer:

All the main characters and scenarios in this publication are fictitious and any resemblance to real persons, living or dead, is purely coincidental. Although occasionally real people and places are referred to throughout the book, they are intermingled with the fictional people and events that make up the story.

Contents

"Play"

'Game, set and match to Miss Mizra 6-4, 6-7, 10-8,' bellowed the umpire, not realising that for the first time over the past hour he need not raise his voice, nor need the use of a microphone, in order to be heard.

Linda McKean, the great British hopeful, had just lost her third round match on Court No.12 at Wimbledon.

The patriotic crowd, which had displayed predictable raucous and excitable signs of favouritism towards Miss McKean over the past hour or so, was now, at best, producing only a faint, almost apologetic and half-hearted attempt to clap in the best traditions of British middle class spectator sport, this muted response being generated presumably to commiserate with Miss McKean, whilst at the same time to acknowledge their ingratitude towards Miss Mizra for being a somewhat unpopular victor.

Slumping down on her court-side chair, Linda tried hard to express publicly exaggerated signs of frustration, interchanging with some expression of annoyance, disappointment and tiredness in vaguely equal measure as the immediate realisation took hold of her that she had, yet again, gone out of Wimbledon. And, yet again, this being in the early rounds of the tournament.

Linda McKean had demonstrated from an early age a prodigious tennis talent, winning, it seemed, every junior event she entered and quickly blossomed into becoming the British No.1 ladies player with virtually everyone connected to the sport predicting a successful international future. Junior and national success initially meant lucrative sponsorship deals and ensured financial security for a limited period of time. But now, at the age of twenty-six and after sustaining all-too-frequent debilitating injuries and suffering an ever-decreasing level of self-confidence resultant from poor results on the tennis court over the past three years, inevitably this led to a plummeting official ranking and consequently sponsorship deals, including future funding, were now almost non-existent.

This was Linda's twelfth consecutive year of performing at Wimbledon, ten long years since when an extremely productive and promising second visit resulted in becoming Junior Wimbledon Champion at the age of fifteen.

The various excuses offered over subsequent years for Linda's poor performances at Wimbledon were usually supported by some convenient injury. You name it, and there was every chance that Linda had broken, strained, pulled, twisted or ruptured it. Was she a bit of a hypochondriac? Or, perhaps a highly-tuned athlete and, therefore, easily susceptible to ailments, or prone to injury? Or, was she simply unlucky?

The British press, in particular, were starting to print their ire over their own frustration and disappointment. They were now highly scathing regarding the distinct possibility of Linda never hitting the tennis jackpot and of them ever accepting her as a true British sporting champion - even though, unquestionably, she had been for several years the most accomplished British ladies tennis player.

It often seemed to Linda that the only reasonable press coverage she received was from the paparazzi who took something of a wilful interest in her non-tennis activities and natural stunning good looks, rather than her sporting prowess and minor achievements.

Linda grew up as a black girl in Troon, a sleepy but fairly affluent, white middle-class seaside town about twenty-five miles south-west of Glasgow.

Being black was highly relevant to Linda in her formative years as the only time she ever saw another black person was on the television screen or when she travelled away from Troon on holiday. There were no locals of a similar colour to Linda living in Troon, and it also seemed to Linda that neither did any visit this attractive seaside holiday town. Linda was the only non-white person to attend school at the Royal Troon Academy. She would quite possibly have had a difficult childhood had she not been able to devote most of her spare time away from school and fellow school pupils to develop a successful alternate life around tennis. Tennis was Linda's whole life. A life significantly shared with a Drew Taggart and a Gerry King, with them acting as joint mentors and confidantes. She trusted in them completely, firmly believing they were the only individuals capable of alleviating the mental torture from the disappointments and stresses and injuries sustained from her playing full-time professional tennis.

In some ways, Drew and Gerry had, rather gradually and increasingly so, assumed at the very least a part-time role of being Linda's surrogate parents. She had lost her true parents in a fatal car accident when she was only twelve years of age.

Linda had also developed into an extremely vivacious and attractive young lady. Nonetheless, she was still a bit insecure and unsure of her own sexuality, which for several years now she had questioned.

Perhaps incredibly she was still a virgin at twenty-six years of age. This almost was an unbelievable fact, but a true one nevertheless.

All the so-called tennis experts in the press and on television were certainly of one mind – Linda had a maximum of three years remaining to win a Grand

Slam event. And that presupposed she kept free of injuries.

Predictably, Linda's two best, and arguably only, real close friends in the whole world were seated in the main stand on Court 12 watching the match against Mizra.

Drew Taggart, a highly successful sports writer with the *Daily Mail* newspaper, who even at fifty-six years of age, seemed to live his life exactly in the same hyperactive style he did when he was in his late teens to early twenties. Drew had never been diagnosed by anyone in a professional capacity as an alcoholic, but it was clear to those who knew him socially that he had a serious drinking problem and one he never seemed to accept, let alone do anything about. Cocaine, as well as an endless supply of vodka, was never too far out of reach at any given time during the day or night. Drew had been married five times and all had been successful relationships according to him, justified somewhat bizarrely on the basis that he remained in contact with each of his ex-wives and was still fond of them all, even after some bitter and financially crippling divorce settlements. It was perhaps no surprise that Drew had some difficulty recounting all the extra marital affairs he had encountered during his colourful and relentless sex life. He lived in a picture-postcard cottage on the outskirts of a picturesque village near Gleneagles in the Scottish highlands, and actually perversely enjoyed the physically tiresome weekly commuter flight down to the *Daily Mail's* Head Office in East London.

Linda's only other close friend, Gerry King, frequently acknowledged to anyone sufficiently interested to listen to him that his life did not start until he was about twenty-five years of age, which probably coincided with the moment when he finally convinced himself that he was achieving little within his unfulfilled life. Avoiding further loss of time in his then meaningless existence, Gerry promptly left Glasgow for London without any forward planning, without any money, without a job and initially relied upon temporary accommodation courtesy of a friend-of-a-friend's apartment floor in Hackney, East London. These dire circumstances quickly motivated Gerry, and he soon found himself producing a false curriculum vitae that helped to secure employment at the lowest clerical level within a worldwide oil company which happened to have its European base in Knightsbridge, London. Benefiting from a newly found strong work ethic, within the next five years Gerry commanded a middle-management position which soon led to him being appointed to a succession of more senior posts that paid handsomely. This, in turn, enabled him to become more independent and entrepreneurial and profit from various private property investments and share dealings on the London Stock Exchange. At fifty-five years of age, Gerry was married with two children, and financially secure, with property in Pimlico, Central London, Dartmouth in Devon, and Santo da Serra on the island of Madeira.

In many similar ways, but also many different ways, Taggart and King both absolutely idolised Linda and, whenever or wherever they possibly could, they always tried to support Linda in person. And that backing existed, whether or not it was an attractive venue like Roland Garros in Paris in front of thousands of spectators or only a handful in some low ranking event in Kuwait City.

'Fuck me,' Drew Taggart eventually volunteered.

'Bugger, another year we'll have to wait,' acknowledged Gerry King.

They stood there absolutely motionless, now staring sightlessly at an emptying Court 12 as the crowd slowly started to disperse.

After about two or three minutes, Drew and Gerry, without having uttered any further comment to each other, started as if in automatic-pilot mode to walk down to the courtside to once again try to placate Linda in defeat.

'Hard luck,' offered Drew to Linda in what was clearly a feeble gesture of sympathy and hardly a comment doing justice to acknowledge Linda's premature exit from the most esteemed tennis event of the year.

'I should have sodding well beat her,' retorted Linda, trying to sound as genuinely angry and disappointed as she possibly could, without resorting to being altogether melodramatic about it.

'Yeah, I was sure you were going to nick it,' Gerry added, trying hard, it seemed, to at least put a positive slant on matters, and after a short pause suggested, 'The cow had so much luck, she was anointed today. Bloody bitch.'

'Maybe. But I still should have beaten her. Crumbs, I'll now have to face the press and listen to that smart-arsed Andrew Castle trying to analyse for me how I lost the match.'

There was a prolonged silence as Linda sat in the chair by the umpire's gantry. Linda was truly devastated by this defeat. The look on her face said it all.

*　*　*　*　*

'Mine's not shown up yet,' moaned Linda to Shilpa Mizra as she stood on the top outside step of Wimbledon's main foyer, clearly referring to the non-arrival of her courtesy car.

'Where you headed then? Want a lift?' offered Miss Mizra as she opened the rear door on the arrival of her own courtesy car.

'Cheers. That's kind of you, Shilpa. I'm only going a short distance to Putney. Just desperate to get out of this place a.s.a.p. You'll understand?' voiced a still somewhat dispirited Linda.

'Yeah, understand. Come on in. I'm sure Putney is on the way to Bow in East London where I'm heading. Am staying with family there.'

Shortly after the brand new Volvo V70, garishly branded in a mix of green and purple traditional Wimbledon corporate colours, sped through the main Wimbledon exit, it then took a swift detour down a side street, coming to an abrupt halt.

Within a further few seconds or so – certainly not much longer than it took Linda and Shilpa to exchange the merest glance towards each other to wonder what was occurring – one burly man had ensconced himself on the front passenger seat, whilst another man steamrollered his way to sit between the two startled young ladies in the back seat.

A gun was poked firmly into Shilpa's midriff by the man now sitting beside her. His angry looking eyes were popping out almost as much as his big belly did. A second gun was flashed on to Linda's direct eye-line by the agitated and excitable other young Asian in the front passenger seat.

Linda instantaneously screeched, 'What the hell is going on?'

The apprehension Linda felt soon morphed into full blown anxiety when the young imposter, built akin to a heavyweight boxer but who had perhaps eaten one too many curries of late, lent back from his front seat position to smack Linda across one side of her face with maximum force.

'Shut up. Another word and it'll be your last, ya black mama fucker,' he said, whilst threateningly waving his gun again directly at Linda, and then towards Shilpa. This violent act made Linda recoil in terror and she suddenly felt fear, like she never imagined possible. In fact, fear had almost blocked up her brain. The only rational thought that sprang into her head was that these two gun-swivelling maniacs looked like dead-ringers for Taliban militants she had seen recently on a television documentary. She desperately wanted to say something or other to Shilpa, absolutely anything in an attempt to release some of the massive pangs of anxiety shooting violently up and down her finely-tuned athletic body. But Linda just knew she had to keep dead quiet. There was no option. These two clearly-deranged psychopaths meant business.

What business exactly? Linda shuddered, again, at the very thought.

After about three to four minutes of driving in the car, not a single further word was spoken by anyone. The silence was not even broken when the still highly-charged-looking young man in the front passenger seat got out of the now-stationary Volvo car. He opened the back door and unceremoniously grabbed hold of Linda's hair, and dragging her out of the car and into an adjacent parked vehicle only about a foot away. Linda could just about see out of the corner of her deaden eye, swollen and filled with fear, that an equally-petrified-looking Shilpa was being subjected to a similar manoeuvre. The whole incident took no more than fifteen seconds, before they subsequently sped off in a nondescript family saloon.

Linda had no idea where they had been driven to. Nor, of course, if it was journey's end where they had just been frog-marched out of the car and into a seemingly derelict industrial unit. All she was sure of was that, given the limited time travelled, it certainly was somewhere still in South London.

Shilpa and Linda were then blindfolded and gagged, with their hands firmly tied behind their backs.

After what appeared to Linda to be about a two-or three-hour lull during which she still heard nothing except what she assumed was occasional movement from their captors. Other than that, it was all eerily and worryingly silent. The slightest noise made her stomach churn, promoting a desire to vomit her fear away.

Suddenly Linda felt a sharp pain as the heavy-duty grabber mesh tape was swiftly removed from around her eyes – stripping away, or so she thought, all her upper cheek, facial skin and eyebrows with it.

'Don't try to say a fucking word. Watch,' barked the young man as he eyeballed Linda and Shilpa, transmitting only naked hostility and was now menacingly brandishing a sub-machine gun in the direction of a nearby television set on which BBC *News 24* was being played via an old-fashioned video tape recorder.

Initially the footage showed a wholly-wrecked motor vehicle, quickly followed by the revelation that it was the same Wimbledon courtesy car Linda and Shilpa had been in earlier. The broadcast then showed an excerpt from an internet video link that the BBC were suggesting, based on informed intelligence sources, emanated from a group known to have connections with the renowned terrorist organisation al-Qaeda.

The person fronting and presenting this internet footage was proclaiming, whilst proudly boasting, that he was about to bring honour to, and retribution for, his family. From his rants, not all of which were coherent, the speculation was that this militant's action was directly linked to Miss Mirza's disappearance and probable abduction. This supposition was validated by further disclosure linking Shilpa's father, a high-ranking Indian military officer, to a recent top-secret mission by a coalition of British, American and Indian forces to eliminate an al-Qaeda fortress in the northern Afghanistan border.

Apparently, the declamatory terrorist on the video had lost all his immediate family in the particular offensive that General Mirza had co-ordinated in the outskirts of Mazar-i-Sharif, the medieval city at the northern tip of Afghanistan.

It had now become abundantly clear to Linda – presumably Shilpa too – as she continued to watch the BBC transmission, that there was little doubt that the young driver who originally picked them up from the Wimbledon foyer was one and the same as the car bomber. Tears streamed down Shilpa's face when it was conjectured that the driver was a purported member of the Pashtun Taliban. And he had driven to the largish private dwelling that Shilpa was staying at in Bow, East London, and had somehow persuaded her relatives staying there to get into the Wimbledon courtesy car. The continued speculation was that this was probably achieved on the plausible pretext that they were to join Shilpa for a celebratory meal elsewhere, and she had sent the courtesy car to transport them.

Whatever the actual detail, what was absolutely certain was that within minutes of them driving away from the house in Bow, a bomb was detonated in the car. All six passengers, including the driver, were killed instantly.

Shilpa had constantly cried and sobbed uncontrollably during the entire video showing. Linda, on the other hand, found herself far too scared of any possible ramifications to reveal the true state of her emotions.

Immediately following the conclusion of the BBC *News 24* recording, Linda and Shilpa's eyes were taped over again. Although she could see nothing now, Linda was nevertheless sure she could still smell the pent-up agitation and fury seeping from the terrorists' pores. All Linda could think was – *what the hell happens next? What the hell do these unbalanced madmen actually want? Do they plan to kill me and Shilpa?*

Linda did not have to wait long for the answer to at least some of her own questions. About an hour or so later, Linda and Shilpa were subjected to a repeat ordeal and television viewing. Only this time it was *Sky News,* clearly an update on what they had previously viewed on the BBC. There was now confirmation of a verified ransom demand being lodged with the International Lawn Tennis Association for $10 million. The terrorists had made it clear that they expected the funds to come from the Indian Government, and not from the ILTA, who they demanded only act as intermediaries.

The initial reaction to these two broadcasts, almost perversely, left Linda feeling somewhat relieved. At least this ransom demand offered some hope that she might well get out of this nightmare alive. As she momentarily thought of Shilpa still sobbing and snivelling beside her, whilst simultaneously glancing at one of the terrorists, Linda was decidedly less optimistic about her colleague's own chance of survival.

*　*　*　*　*

'Fucking bastards.'

'Cunts. Absolute fucking cunts,' spat Drew, joining in with Gerry's swearing upon watching Linda and Shilpa being paraded on a pre-recorded video on the popular Arab Al Jazeera television network.

'Shit! Linda looks shit, man.'

'Shaking like a shiting dog. Clearly petrified stiff.'

It had now been some three weeks since Linda and Shilpa had been taken hostage. Deadlines being set by the kidnappers kept being re-negotiated by Special Branch negotiators who were having to stall for time due to the lack of common ground with less than unequivocal and full agreement between various UK Police Forces and high-ranking UK Government Foreign Office officials. And they were certainly not helped by the Indian Government's belligerent stance and reluctance to get involved in negotiating directly with hostage takers.

Until now, Gerry and Drew were more than happy to leave matters in the hands of experienced police officers working with government officials and the likes of MI5. However, they were now for the very first time having doubts if any real progress was being made. Certainly press conferences were becoming few and far between and what little information was being released to the general public offered little evidence that there existed anything other than a worryingly protracted impasse between the various authorities and the kidnappers.

Gerry and Drew exchanged profound anxieties as to how much longer these terrorists-cum-kidnappers would be prepared to accept one excuse and subsequent delay after another.

'You know all those Asian punters you once had to work with at Texaco Oil Company?'

'What, all the Pakis and Indians working in the petrol stations in the East End?' interrupted Gerry.

'Yeah. Them. Would there be any point putting the word out?'

'What, within the Asian community?'

'Yeah. Offer them a substantial reward for providing any information.'

'Great idea, mate. Well worth a try.'

'Remember, we know important detail from an original eyewitness about the second hostage car used. And don't forget that detail has never previously been put into the public domain, just in case it prompted the bastards to destroy the getaway car. If they haven't already done so by now, of course.'

'Okay, mate. Gotta be worth a shot. I'll see what I can do,' promised Gerry enthusiastically.

Gerry had worked with Texaco Oil Company, assigned specifically to London's East End area, for about two years. Although that was some time ago, he still thought he had established a rapport with many resident Asians, as he personally had been responsible for recruiting quite a number into jobs which, most probably, they still held. Added to that, Gerry had been instrumental in negotiating commercial business loan deals on highly advantageous financial terms to certain Asian individuals. The more he thought on it, the more Gerry was confident they would not have forgotten him. He optimistically hoped they would see this as an opportunity to help and repay him in kind.

Quickly revisiting some of his old East London Asian haunts, Gerry organised a few meetings with about a dozen individuals in total, a mix of Asians from different countries. Some he met in small groups. Some of them Gerry openly referred to, almost affectionately, as the Patel Mafia. They all, to a man, welcomed him with open arms and, in a display of false confidence, they were all ultra positive that they could provide some assistance, and that the £10,000 reward monies on offer was not a consideration. They would all lie directly into Gerry's eyes about the reward money being unimportant. And, done in a way so as if being so very genuine and sincere. It was almost a bit of a charade. It always made Gerry laugh inwardly to himself. He had experienced this Asian trait on so many occasions over the years. He sometimes mused to himself that they all must have been successful politicians in a previous life.

Gerry had high hopes that these meetings would lead to something constructive. He had a feeling in his waters. Or maybe that was because he desperately wanted it to be the case, that some local Asian would get lucky by spotting something suspicious or relevant. Or hit the jackpot and caught sight of the car of which he had now circulated the details.

'Fuck me Drew, but I've just been given an address from a curry-cruncher contact of mine where the hostage car is presently parked.'

'Can he be trusted?'

'No, not really. But what have we got to lose? Should you and I go check out this address first?'

Gerry and Drew debated the pros and cons of whether or not to check the address for themselves in the first instance, as opposed to giving it straight to the police. They decided to have a look first and then consider later as to what to do next.

The address given led them to a run-down small block of industrial units in Camberwell, South London. Initially they had some difficulty finding the car in question, as it was located well away from the roadside, at the rear of a derelict garage, which looked as if it had been once a small, old-fashioned, one-pump island petrol filling station from a bygone era.

When Drew and Gerry first clapped eyes on the vehicle's registration plate they broadly smirked at one other. It was probably the first time either of them had smiled in the past three weeks.

Within hours, the Flying Squad, led by a Brummie by the name of Chief Superintendent Phil Hickin, masterminded a swift and successful rescue with the aid of one of the biggest armed raids ever carried out in the United Kingdom.

Both Drew and Gerry, especially Gerry, had previously expressed their doubts about Hickin's ability. He always appeared to them to be all smarmy talk and no action. He also dressed swanky, as Gerry often observed, but without the 's'. However, to Hickin's credit, the end-game operation resulted in a remarkably straightforward, well-planned and well-executed rescue, lasting in total what could have been no more than a four-hour time span.

Linda was freed.

So too was Shilpa. Both seemed physically unscathed. However, it was surely a matter of how much, not if, they had been mentally traumatised by their horrendous, almost month-long ordeal.

The sheer volume of relief on everyone's emotionally-tired-looking faces and minds was almost transparent. Except that Gerry felt he had a little something extra to celebrate. Or, so he kept reminding himself. Without him, Linda might well have been killed by the kidnappers, who were nothing less than terrorists prepared to kill. That hypothetical theory assumed, of course, that Gerry continued conveniently to overlook the fact that it was Drew who actually suggested, in the first place, that Gerry contact his so-called Patel Mafia contacts.

The conclusion of the only scheduled press conference presented Drew with the opportunity to do what he likely did more than anything else in this life – drink alcohol.

'Let's have a drink to celebrate your freedom to play tennis again.'

There appeared a distinct lack of enthusiasm judging by Linda's exhausted-looking and bloodshot eyes.

*   *   *   *   *

Gerry sat waiting for Drew and Linda in the early evening at the Paxton's Head - a pseudo British 'spit & sawdust' pub located in a wholly untypical part of London where only the rich and famous could afford to live. The pub was reliant almost entirely upon tourist trade with its location benefiting from being opposite the ostentatious and elite Knightsbridge department store of Harrods. Gerry was dressed as he always dressed – in nondescript casual clothes, usually purchased at Marks & Spencer (or substituting the popularly known St Michael brand name for the make-believe designer label of Sainte Michelle as he was often fond of repeating to appear, and fail, to be humorous with). He used to work nearby in Knightsbridge Green and it was his suggestion to meet at the Paxton's Head with the expressed prior agreement that they would all get blind drunk to somehow console each other over Linda's kidnapping ordeal. Or, celebration that she had survived. Whatever.

Gerry knew only too well that his dear chum Drew never needed an invite, nor an excuse to get drunk.

Almost an hour had passed by. No sign of Drew. Nor Linda.

Fortunately for Gerry he liked his own company. He was a patient individual; patient with a relaxed, easy-going attitude to most matters in life, particularly now that he had effectively retired early to enjoy a perceived simpler and slower pace of life in the idyllic Devon countryside. It was a far cry from his Glasgow roots and the council estate slum, which he called the 'war zone' in recognition of all the gangs and drugs and general crime. This being several decades prior to such criminal activity becoming commonplace in many other inner cities throughout Britain.

Gerry continued to use the waiting time, on his own, to drink a couple of bottles of Mexican lager whilst he reminisced with himself to alleviate any possible boredom. He recounted how he had known Drew for what must be half a century, practically ever since they were born and grew up living in the same street in Auldhouse, South Glasgow. The late 1950s was his earliest memory of a shared enthusiasm with Drew - playing football in the street with a tennis ball when they were between five and seven years of age. Generally playing in the streets in those days was less dangerous as motor cars were few and far between. That was definitely true of the council estate Drew and Gerry grew up in, where even some 'auld banger' of a motor vehicle was a luxury very few could afford.

This early childhood bonding between Drew and Gerry was probably helped by the fact that they went to different denomination schools located in far-flung areas of the city and therefore never saw each other during the school day. Gerry wondered, in retrospect, if this separation only increased the sense of two young lads looking forward to meeting each other at the end of the boring school day to play football in the street together. Gerry laughed to himself as he remembered some of the football related banter, and even the odd typically childish argument he had with Drew over many years as they both actively supported different football clubs, Drew's love affair with Partick Thistle being partially matched by Gerry's passion for Glasgow Celtic.

Just about the one and only regret that Gerry moaned about was Drew had been the beneficiary of a far better education than he had. Gerry was somewhat envious that Drew was educated in the north centre of the city at a fee-paying Protestant school with an excellent academic reputation. Whereas Gerry went to a Catholic school, in the once notorious gangland Gorbals area east of the city that struggled to get a reasonable percentage of its pupils to even attend the classrooms on a regular basis, let alone become academically disciplined or challenged.

Their friendship and attraction to sport further developed into a real enjoyment for playing tennis in their early teens and they were soon active members of Hillpark Tennis Club, a friendly and unpretentious club situated in a relatively affluent area about a twenty-five minute walk away from where they both then lived in Auldhouse. Gerry's father was an active committee member of the bowling section of the club and he introduced and encouraged Drew and Gerry's membership.

Eventually Drew ended Gerry's private trip down memory lane when he arrived at the Paxton's Head pub (a 'spit & fart shit hole' Drew often referred to it as, if only to wind Gerry up who, he knew full well, was fond of the place) and much later than arranged, looking rather dishevelled having adorned his expensive Ralph Lauren polo shirt with a couple of blobs of sauce courtesy of some fast food consumed en-route. He was perspiring profusely, probably as a consequence of his known high blood pressure, and being already half drunk having consumed the best part of a bottle of expensive Black Label vodka back at his hotel room.

Linda also arrived much later than expected at the pub, looking radiant as ever and every bit the fit and attractive sportswoman, and in marked contrast to her recent 'guest appearance' on Al Jazeera television.

'Sorry guys, got badly held up,' offered Linda as if by way of some sort of lame excuse or apology and then quickly spluttered out, 'Look, I've got some bad news for you guys. I'm jacking it in.'

'Jacking what in?' queried Gerry immediately.

'The tennis.'

'Come again, hen?' requested Drew, appearing to momentarily sober up at the very thought of Linda retiring from tennis.

'Look,' stressed Linda, sounding unusually stern, 'I'm pretty sure I'm going to lose my main sponsorship deal with Colegate and I've earlier today been offered a job to coach down in the Algarve at Roger Taylor's Centre. Maybe it's finally time to call it a day, eh? I think I've lost my appetite for competitive tennis. All this business with Shilpa has completely drained me dry of any enthusiasm for the tennis lifestyle and being constantly on tour.'

These comments created a couple of minutes embarrassing silence as the three of them exchanged rapid-fire eye contact with one another as if to gauge any initial reaction to this dramatic and unexpected suggestion from Linda that her professional tennis playing career was effectively at an end.

'Shit,' was Drew's eventual considered response, immediately followed by a sudden movement towards the bar to shout in a rather aggressive and impolite tone to a startled barman an order for another half pint of bitter and a large vodka chaser.

They all then discussed at length their own highly personal views on Linda's career path and what the future could and/or should hold for her. They did not reach a consensus, only talked and then increasingly argued around the subject in ever decreasing circles.

'This is crazy...... we must have an agreed plan of action,' drawled Gerry.

'That's what we've been trying to do for the past two hours, you arsehole,' replied Drew tartly.

'Yeah, well maybes we'd have got somewhere if you hadn't got so pissed so quickly. So pissed as per usual,' retorted Gerry.

'Come on guys, let's not argue amongst ourselves. I'm quite happy accepting that job down in the Algarve. I can think of far worse jobs.'

'You ain't working on any fucking tennis ranch and that's final,' snapped Drew in a dismissive manner. 'I thought we had at least agreed on that, yes?'

'Okay, my fine feathered friends, I'll listen to any sensible alternate suggestion.'

'Well, I have a hypothesis,' responded Drew, belying his likely inebriated state of mind.

'Does it hurt?'

'Shut the fuck up, ye eejit. And listen to me, pal. Look, I interviewed for my paper recently a sport psychologist. She's a bit of an odd ball character with some wacky, cranky ideas, but it's worth a shot, eh?'

'What, *me* see a shrink?'

'What have you got to lose, Linda?' reasoned Gerry.

'Okay. Okay,' conceded Linda, sounding only somewhat reluctant.

'Linda, are you about next week?'

'Yip, I'd agreed yonks ago to spend a week down at Roehampton helping my coach with some school kids on a residential course.'

'Okay, I'll try and organise a session with Dr Keegan as soon as. So, why don't the three of us get together at the end of next week and discuss this whole matter of your future, properly and soberly this time?'

'That'd be a first,' moaned Gerry. 'How many empty glasses of whisky do I see in front of you?'

'At least I'm no paranoid neurotic with a glass half empty approach. Now, do us all a favour and shut the fuck up, pal. You and I need to meet tomorrow and see if we can put our hands in our pockets and come up with the money Linda's gonna need.'

'Are you going to be sober tomorrow then?' Gerry asked patronisingly as he turned to walk away to hail a taxi.

'Shut the fuck up, pal,' shouted Drew again in a typical, if slightly exaggerated, sounding Glaswegian accent that he was known to perfect from time to time to make him sound aggressive, presumably in the belief then nobody would then continue to argue with him.

'One of these days someone's gonna deck you, pal. That motor mouth of yours only seems to manifest itself when you're pissed,' lectured Gerry in a half-jest, half-serious sardonic tone of voice as he affectionately put his arm around his dear old friend as they both staggered along Brompton Road, in the middle of Knightsbridge, without realising several vacant cabs drove straight past them.

*   *   *   *   *

At the very earliest opportunity Gerry and Drew did meet up to discuss Linda's financial predicament. It was duly convened at Gerry's small pied-à-terre flat in Pimlico.

Gerry, possessing an educated if not altogether astute business mind regarding investment opportunities, had gradually built up a small property portfolio over the past thirty years. He had his main residence in Devon. But he enjoyed the luxury of a Central London base.

'This flat seems to get smaller every time I come here,' muttered Drew.

Gerry ignored this remark, believing that Drew was merely envious of him owning any flat of any size in Central London.

'Have you got any idea as to how we can raise the money Linda needs?' Gerry asked whilst pouring Drew a watered down glass of cheap supermarket own brand labelled whisky.

'How much does she need then?'

'Weren't you bloody listening last night?' groaned Gerry.

'Of course. Of course. Don't get your knickers in a twist – ye miserable auld toad. £50,000 wasn't it?'

'I wish it was. It was £250,000 not £50,000, she reckons.'

'Shit. That much, eh?'

'Yip. 'fraid so mate.'

'What £125k each?'

'Yip.'

'Bollocks man. She shouldn't need that much, surely? Shit, that's what five grand a friggin' week?'

'I know, but that's what she said. Elana Baltacha's now got herself into the Top 100, but she still has to work in an Edinburgh sport shop during some of the winter months to help make ends meet. Anyway, I suspect Linda was thinking an additional 250 grand would cover her expenses for a slightly longer period than a year though. Guess there's all those expensive air fares to the Middle and Far East. Then, there's that tosspot of a feckless part-time coach.'

'How much does he get?'

'Dunno exactly but I think it's something like £35,000 plus expenses.'

'For the amount of time he puts in, we should call him Dick Turpin from now on.'

'Okay, let's cut to the chase Drew. Can you raise £125,000?'

'Yes. I guess so. Possibly. Probably, like,' said Drew sounding somewhat unconvinced that he could.

'Can I ask how?'

'How what?'

'How you plan to raise the £125k?'

'Well, I've got £75,000 odd in various savings accounts and odds and sods. Some I'll need to give some notice on, mind.'

'And the rest?'

'Not sure. Perhaps an endowment policy I could cash in by redeeming early.'

Gerry thought this showed a typical lack of Drew's business acumen that needed to be highlighted in Gerry's particular own brand of sarcasm, 'Bet your bank manager just loves receiving an overdraft request facility from you.'

'Awe right, smart arse – bet you ain't got any better ideas.'

Gerry knew he had though. And, he could not wait to be given the opportunity to impress.

'If it helps you any, mate, I know of a company listed on the Alternative Investment Market whose share value is likely to double over the next few weeks.'

'What's the Alternative Investment Market when it's at home, then?' enquired Drew, sounding a tad cynical of what his friend was suggesting, as well as intimating he was being about as interesting as a railway ticket.

'It's higher risk than say the FTSE 100 Top UK Company shares that trade on the main London Stock Exchange,' responded Gerry authoritatively, full of his own self-importance.

'What d'ya mean by higher risk?'

'Exactly what it implies. But the higher the risk, the higher the reward.'

'*Mmmm*' Drew's lips made a noise to match suitably his facial expression as if to imply he was becoming interested, but still less than convinced, 'You'll need to tell me a helluva lot more before I invest, and whilst you're at it, pal, how's about you put some more whisky into this damn thimble of a glass and less water this time, eh?'

'Fair enough,' laughed Gerry, revelling in his friend being beholden to him, no matter how temporarily.

Gerry was addicted to buying and selling shares on the London Stock Market. A daily habit. His drug. It was akin to gambling. He loved the buzz of picking a winning stock, just like others enjoy picking a winning horse at the races.

Over the years, Gerry had made a limited number of shrewd and profitable deals directly within the general residential property market. But these same investments required little else other than a long-term strategy. If Gerry was, for once, to be honest with himself, then he would have to concede some of his more impetuous and poorly-researched share investments had cost him dearly. More than he would ever care to admit. And certainly not, ever, to the likes of Drew, for fear of much likely ridicule.

To supplement this investment activity, Gerry was an avid follower and participant on a particular financial bulletin board on the internet. Like-minded people would post comments on message boards, usually anonymously by way of a pseudonym, bulletin boards being a valuable research aid to potential stock market investors where facts and issues can be stated and debated to a world-wide internet audience. Gerry was keenly aware that a major problematic aspect of these internet bulletin boards can occur when a minority abuse these financial threads. Such as, the posting of falsehoods by inveterate liars in the hope those same untruths would be believed by gullible and inexperienced private investors. These devious and unscrupulous characters would invest themselves, then pump the stock up by encouraging others to invest their money based on lies and false rumours. And then shortly afterwards, sometimes within minutes or hours, dump their own shareholding by selling it and banking a small but quick profit.

'Pump and Dump merchants', as they were commonly known.

Gerry felt he could never be so stupid so as to fall for such blatant and deceitful malpractice, which to his mind was morally indefensible.

Ramping bastards, Gerry hated them all with a passion.

'So, come on tell me all about this investment idea before you're forced to pour me another whisky, ya miserable tight git,' mocked Drew.

'It's called Think Kids Entertainment plc.'

'What sort of a fucking company is that to get involved in? Is it run by paedophiles?'

33

'Stop yer mocking, mate. The company has enormous potential, particularly within the merchandising field for games and videos and toys based on the innovative and unique characters the company hold the intellectual licence to.'

'Like fucking what?'

'Well, there's one particularly interesting intellectual property in the company's portfolio known as BUMs to any five-to-seven-year-old who ever watches children's television, or as Butt Ugly Martians to give it its proper full name.'

'Tell me you're not being serious, are you, pal?'

'Well, over 40,000 shareholders who have invested in the company can't all be investment retards,' protested Gerry.

'Sure you ain't wearing your rose-tinted specs? So, where does the company income come from then?'

'This is potentially another modern day Mutant Ninja Turtles. Remember, mate, that was once an enormous worldwide money-spinner and success story for another company and its respective shareholders,' declared Gerry, before adding as he looked at his computer screen, 'and the share price is currently about 6 pence per share to buy. There's enormous short-term potential for it to double in value over the next few weeks.'

'Why so, arse ho?'

'It's a volatile share, but has wide market appeal. I say again, it has forty-odd thousand individual shareholders. There's even talk of a film deal with Universal.'

'Okay, okay, you're starting to interest me at long last, you boring tosser. Can you show me anything on your laptop?' asked Drew.

'Sure. Let's have a butcher's right now, mate.'

Gerry got his laptop out and went straight to the Global Private Investor website, a specialist support service company to the financial markets.

'Look, Drew, the price has gone up over twenty per cent just this morning alone. It's now 7.25 pence to buy these shares at this precise moment.'

'Bloody hell, a twenty per cent increase in one day - that's impressive man,' nodded Drew in agreement.

'Shit. Look. It's just this very second gone up, again! Now 7.5 pence to buy.'

'Screw me, mate. Licence to print money, eh? What else can you tell me about Think Kids then?'

'Okay, let's visit one of the Think Kids Entertainment's threads on the bulletin board, shall we?'

'Go on then,' barked Drew as he spilt some of his whisky whilst raising his hand holding the glass as if gesturing that Gerry should exercise some urgency.

'There's two threads currently open. One started by the username of ABarclayman and one under the nickname of Slimeball Smithy. Now, ABarclayman strikes me as being a bit of a toss pot who is a master ramper. He'd tell you his granny's horse was running in the 2.30 at Doncaster and was a dead cert winner. Trouble is, he has less brain cells than a dead rat. He's probably an exceptional traffic warden in real life. Slimeball Smithy, on the other hand, claims he's an extremely successful businessman and holds, so he claims, shares in this stock to the value of a quarter of a million pounds. Unfortunately, I have good reason to suspect he's a bullshitter too,' spat Gerry indignantly.

'There's even one other very sad bampot who regularly posts on these threads who never actually buys nor sells any shares. Incredible, I know. Some just treat it like a social network site. Spiteful losers in life, generally, with no friends, who are effectively social misfits with nothing better to do with their time. Anyway, let's not give a tinker's cuss about those two ramping fuckwits. Now, I suggest we ignore the bulletin board altogether, and instead let's look at Think Kids Entertainment's website whilst we're online, mate.' Gerry continued to semi-lecture Drew as if he was the fountain of all knowledge when it came to share dealing.

'Just as I thought, there's apparently been a press announcement made earlier today. Wonder what it states. Let's look and see, eh? The Company has issued a trading statement and look it says they're "trading ahead of expectations".'

'That's got to be good news, isn't it, Gerry?'

'Yip, it sure is, mate. And look, they're also saying that a film contract has all but been signed with BUMs.'

'Does it say who with?'

'Yeah, with Universal. Now that *is* brilliant. Absolutely brilliant, man.'

'Anything else of significance?'

'Blimey. Yes. It goes on to say that they expect revenues to exceed £8 million over the next twelve months just from the BUMs intellectual property alone, and they are taking legal action against some professional advisers for gross misconduct and corporate negligence. Jesus, it says they're suing for £30 million.'

'That must be a misprint, huh?'

'Probably not, as it says £30 million elsewhere in the release, look down there, so it ain't no misprint,' confirmed Gerry. 'Well, bugger me. Now that explains why the share price has gone up so sharply today.'

'Have we missed the boat here, Gerry? What d'ya think?'

'Methinks there is plenty of mileage still left in this stock. In fact, I think it has the potential to be 30 pence by the month end. £1 a share by the year end. Honestly.'

'15 pence would suit me just dandy – double me money,' laughed Drew, still sounding nervous, but nothing like as much as twenty minutes previous.

'Well, you'd better be quick, mate. It'll be 15 pence before you know it.'

Gerry was in his element. Drew would now have to ask him how to buy shares.

After a few moments of silence Drew did indeed ask Gerry, 'So just how do I go about investing in this Think Kiddies thingy Company then?'

'It's easy, mate. Leave it to me. We can set up an account on the internet via a stockbroker for you right here and now.'

'Let's not waste any more time, let's do it right now, pal,' breezed Drew, whose enthusiasm and confidence in Gerry had seemingly overtaken any earlier doubts now with the prospect that he could conceivably make some quick money after all.

Gerry just loved Drew being beholden to him. He was clearly in his element.

As Gerry and Drew were leaving Gerry's property in Pimlico they bumped into a balding, obese, middle-aged man in the common hallway. Gerry had got to know this neighbour of his - Hugo Summerfield - reasonably well over the past couple of years.

Summerfield was an accountant with his own practice in Brighton, as well as Belgravia, and an associate branch in Santa Barbara, Los Angeles where he retained several clients who were well connected to the general movie and film entertainment industry based nearby at Hollywood. His main residence was a large country house, set in over twenty acres straddling the counties of Sussex and Kent. He also owned a small leasehold flat in the same building as Gerry in Pimlico.

Summerfield knew of Gerry's shareholding in Think Kids Entertainment as they had discussed it previously, and this presumably prompted him to enquire, 'How's your shares doing in Think?' whilst managing to sound genuinely interested as he did so.

'Not bad at all. They're up about twenty per cent today. In fact Drew here has just bought thirty grand's worth only fifteen minutes or so ago.'

'Hello, Drew, pleased to meet you. But I wouldn't buy shares in that heap of a crap company.'

'Oh, why is that then?' countered Gerry sharply before Drew had an opportunity to respond to Summerfield.

'Cause it's all hype and fashion. Here today – gone tomorrow. No financial fundamentals whatsoever. Did you see the last set of profit and loss accounts? They show minimal revenues. No profit in sight, yet have somehow managed to burn best part of £18 million over the past couple of years.'

'Is that right?' pitched in Drew, a frown appearing on his forehead.

'That's not what you said, Hugo, when we last spoke. You thought it was a great investment,' retorted Gerry, trying to sound as dismissive as he could.

'Well, we'll see, won't we, sooner or later? Anyway, how's that girl of yours doing?' Summerfield asked with a smirk.

'Which one?' asked Gerry, knowing full well exactly to whom Summerfield was referring.

'You know the one,' bellowed Summerfield, whilst grinning from ear to ear, with some saliva starting to show on his lips, 'Linda – the fit one with the enormous knockers.'

Gerry thought to himself that only *a complete and utter twat* like Summerfield could make such a crass and vulgar comment about Linda. *Why is Summerfield so far up his own arse? I'd tell him where to shove it but his head is already up there.*

'She needs sponsorship,' quipped Drew.

Gerry immediately kicked Drew playfully as he interjected, 'Look we've really gotta shoot. See you around sometime Hugo, eh?'

'Yeah, nice meeting you,' concluded Drew as he and Gerry departed.

Walking down to Victoria Tube Station Drew turned to Gerry and snarled, 'Who was that tosspot then?'

'The one you've just lied to, saying how nice it was meeting him? You're losing your touch, you two-faced arsehole!'

'Why does he speak with marbles in his mouth?'

'Oh, he apparently went to Eton and then Cambridge Uni.'

'What, educated way beyond his own intelligence?'

'Yeah, something like that pal,' cackled Gerry. Followed by loud chuckling and rolling of the shoulders by Drew.

Later that same day, when Gerry returned back to his Pimlico pied-à-terre, the first thing he did was to check out the Think share price on his computer. He could not believe his eyes. The price had dropped back to 5 pence per share from the price it had been earlier in the day. Gerry immediately felt depressed. That converted into a mild state of panic as to whether or not he should tell Drew of this unexpected and seriously disappointing development. He decided against doing so. He then went on to the internet bulletin boards to see if he could find out what was going on, and why the alarming drop back in price.

The bulletin boards could not shed any light on the matter, except it confirmed there had been an unusually high volume of dealing in Think's stock that particular trading day. On further investigation, Gerry was horrified to see there had been a whole series of sell transactions just prior to close of that day's business on the London Stock Exchange. He was now starting to get deeply concerned.

Gerry's doorbell rang. It was Hugo Summerfield.

'Look, I'm sorry about earlier, Gerry. Did I say something I shouldn't have?'

'Not really. But, I wish you hadn't made that negative comment to Drew about the Think shares. He's nervous enough as it is after buying all those shares today.'

'Sorry,' responded Summerfield, without sounding the slightest bit sorry.

'What's done is done, I guess. Now, was there anything else, Hugo?'

'Yes, can we have a chat about Linda McKean? I was interested in what you had to say about her wanting sponsorship.'

'I didn't.'

'Didn't what?'

'Say anything about Linda wanting sponsorship,' said Gerry frostily, trying his utmost with body language to make Summerfield feel he was about as welcome as an estate agent with body odour.

'Yeah, sorry, it was your friend Daniel said that.'

'Drew. You mean Drew, I take it? So, what about it?'

'How much is she looking for?'

'That's none of your business,' hissed Gerry, who by now was getting extremely irritated that

40

Summerfield was still talking to him, let alone on such a private matter as Linda's finances. He was not about to explain, nor justify, the many reasons to Summerfield why he was considered an unsuitable sponsor for Linda. He would spare them both that particular embarrassment.

'Well, I'd like to make it my business. I know you and her are joined at the hip,' Summerfield added sarcastically, 'All I want to do is discuss with you broad brushed terms and conditions to enable me to make a sensible and realistic formal offer in writing to her.'

'As I say, Hugo, I don't want to appear rude here, but it truly is none of your business. End of. Now, if you don't mind I've got other things I'd like to be getting on with.'

Conniving fat lump of a crooked accountant.

Gerry did not sleep particularly soundly that night.

He was then 'live' on his laptop at about 7.50am ready for the opening session when the Stock Market started trading at 8am. He was actually talking to, and having wholly meaningless conversations with, his own computer monitor.

Gerry's worst fears were realised when the opening price for Think Kids Entertainment had been marked down another whole penny to 4 pence per share.

Fuck. Fuck. Fuck, shouted Gerry hysterically to himself, over and over again.

Should he do the decent thing and phone Drew? No, he decided he would keep his nerve and see how the morning's trading panned out. He was glued to his computer screen for the next three hours or so, watching every single trade as it was electronically transmitted on to the Global Private Investor trading system and simultaneously on to Gerry's computer screen.

Gerry could not believe his eyes. It was one sell after another sell. Nobody, it seemed, was buying any shares in Think.

There were now rumours starting to circulate via the Global Private Investor chat-room that the film deal with Universal Inc had been withdrawn and that Think had serious cash flow problems.

The share price continued to bomb at a rate that Gerry had never witnessed before with Think or any other share, for that matter. The price was now down to just over one penny per share.

Gerry was, without doubt, deeply troubled now. Not exclusively, nor especially for Drew, but now for himself. His questionable knowledge of, and expertise in, share dealing and general confidence in his own ability was momentarily absolutely shattered. He had, after all, invested several times in Think over the past six months to a total of approximately £85,000 and had arguably financially over-extended himself in that regard.

Gerry's body managed an icy cold sweat as he saw the letter 'A' appear on his lap top screen against Think - 'A' meant an official Announcement to the Stock Exchange. It usually meant there was either major good news or major bad news to statutorily report to the financial markets.

The statement read -

"Think Kids Entertainment plc is now considered to be trading insolvent and the Board of Directors have called in the liquidators.

Accordingly, shares have been suspended from trading on the LSE."

This was Gerry's worst nightmare, financial disaster staring him straight between his own two eyes, courtesy of his own computer screen. Effectively he had just lost £85,000 in a momentary flash. He instantly knew that he would never see a single penny of this investment in Think recouped now that some liquidator had been reported as having control of the company.

Gerry felt isolated by his inability to rationalise how he was going to impart this disastrous news on to Drew. He would now simply have to tell Drew. He had no choice if to avoid the worst case scenario and that would be for Drew to find out for himself from elsewhere. *My God. What am I going to tell Drew? And how? Face-to-face? Fuck. I'm no coward. Fuck, fuck, fuck. What a complete dick I've been. Shite, Drew's never gonna forgive me for this. Fuck, fuck, fuck, I'm going straight to hell in a hand basket of stale black pudding and a can of flat Irn Bru.* Gerry picked up his mobile phone and punched in Drew's number.

'Hello, Drew, are you in London today?'

'Yes, mate. I'm at the *Daily Mail*'s office in Wapping. Why?'

'Can we meet up for a drink tonight after you finish work?'

'Sure. Where do you fancy?'

'Is the Sportman's Inn in Victoria okay with you?'

'Yeah, but isn't that where you always suggest we meet when you've got some duff news to tell?'

'See you at seven and don't be your usual over an hour late or turn up half pissed.'

Gerry put the receiver down, a cold shiver still intermittently running through his body. He had found himself in some tight and uncomfortable spots before. This was as personally embarrassing as it got, he thought. Drew meant the world to him even though they mercilessly bickered and wound each other up.

For once Drew arrived on time, seven o'clock in the evening, at the Sportsman's Inn, already suspecting Gerry had some bad news to impart and he was anxious to know precisely what. Gerry had his faults. Drew always highlighted those faults at every opportunity, but Gerry was never a drama queen. And for once, Drew arrived sober but, as always, expensively dressed, on this occasion in his Tommy Hilfiger padded jacket co-ordinating well with his Armani tweed trousers, which in turn complemented his Timberland roll top boots – all purchased just the previous day in one of Drew's frequent shopping excursions.

'There's been a right mare with those Think shares,' Gerry spurted out before Drew even had time to order either of them a drink.

'What, has the share price dropped again, then? Don't worry, I checked on the internet this afternoon and saw that it had dropped down to 1.75 pence. It's still early doors, mate. I only bought the shares like five minutes ago, right? Shares go up and down like a whore's knickers. Everyone knows that. Even me.'

'Drew, me auld mucker - the shares have been suspended from trading on the Stock Exchange.'

'What exactly does this mean then?'

'Well,' sighed Gerry, 'it's too early to say for sure, but it don't look good, mate. It appears the company is bankrupt and unable to trade solvent, which is illegal if you try. I believe Official Receivers have been appointed.'

'For fuck's sake, Gerry, tell me you're pulling ma plonker here?'

'City accountants KPGB have been mentioned and once they get their teeth into things they take no prisoners. They're just corporate sharks. They'll sell the company or its assets and try and pay off as many creditors as they reasonably can. Shareholders will be bottom of any creditors' list. Sorry, but I think we've got to be realistic and prepare for the worst here. I think we've both lost the whole lot of our investment.'

'But, I've lost £30,000.'

'I know, and I've lost £85,000.'

'I can't afford to lose £30,000.'

'I can't afford to lose £85,000.'

Drew and Gerry stared at each other in disbelief.

Gerry had had a bit of time to rationalise matters, but the gravity of the situation was obviously just dawning on Drew.

'That well and truly fucks up our plans with Linda now, doesn't it? What a stupid fuckwit I've been listening to your investment advice.' Entirely out of character, Drew stared long and hard at his glass rather than drink from it before he felt able to continue. 'Thanks a lot, pal, for that piece of shit investment advice,' snarled Drew, 'you clearly know absolutely fuck all about share investments, you lying shitebag. Trying to impress me the other day, were you?'

'I wasn't to know that the company would one minute say they were trading ahead of expectations and then soon afterwards be declared insolvent by their creditors,' protested Gerry.

'I knew I shouldn't have listened to you,' said Drew, 'I just fuck'n well knew it.'

Just as Drew was likely to go off on one with his predictable put-on aggressive sounding Glaswegian accents and give Gerry a right verbal ear bashing, Gerry tried to take the initiative away from his irate friend by volunteering, 'Drew, what if I as a gesture of goodwill somehow get at least £25,000 refunded to you? I'm feeling mighty guilty about things. Honest, mate.'

'Where are you goin' to get that kinda spare dosh from?' queried Drew. 'You're already down £85k, you said.'

'Don't *you* worry about where I'll get the money from, pal.'

'Yes, well okay, Gerry. I appreciate that. A £5,000 loss, I suppose I can live with that.'

'Okay then, mate, that's settled. Somehow I'll get the £25,000 put into your bank account as soon as I can arrange it. It'll take a wee bit of time, mind. A good few weeks at least. I'll have to sort a few things out.'

Drew would have been blind not to notice some signs of sheer relief etched on Gerry's otherwise troubled-looking face.

Gerry and Drew formally shook hands at this point and spent the next four hours or so getting drunk and forgetting all about shares in Think.

No doubts, though, Drew would have been asking himself, would Gerry actually come up with that much dosh? And if so, how exactly?

Gerry took himself off on a low-cost flight from Exeter Airport to Funchal to spend a couple of days quality thinking time on his own in the hope he would be able to manufacture a plan of action to resolve the current financial plight affecting not only himself, but also directly Drew and indirectly Linda.

He owned a small and fairly dilapidated ex-farmer's cottage near Santo da Serra on the island of Madeira. The cottage was as remote as it was dilapidated, but its one redeeming feature, for Gerry, was the fact that it was relatively nearby to a testing golf course; a course considered by him to be just about as good as anywhere he had ever played in his entire life. And, he had played hundreds all over the world.

If Gerry was ever to hatch an action plan, he felt the solitude of playing golf on his own on his beloved Santo da Serra course surrounded by the breathtaking landscape might just conceivably inspire him. It did.

The master financial recovery plan that Gerry conceived on the golf course was to sell a residential investment property that he had bought about ten years before purely as a regular rental income. The flat benefited from being adjacent to the University of Strathclyde in the heart of the city of Glasgow. It had proved to be a nice little earner for Gerry and, although the property deeds were jointly held in his and his wife's name, he personally received the revenue as it was paid direct into his private bank account from the management agent.

It was eminently logical and sensible, given his current predicament, that he sold this flat and use the proceeds from the sale to subsidise the loss he had made on the Think share fiasco. Funds raised from the sale could also be used in conjunction with Drew, to sponsor Linda, as well as repay Drew for Drew's own unfortunate loss in Think. One major obstacle kept surfacing in Gerry's mind and that was this property was held jointly with his wife. And would his wife, Ann, go along with this asset disposal proposal? Gerry did not have to give that a single moment of further thought. Her answer, Gerry was certain, would be an emphatic, 'Never.'

However, the more Gerry thought on it, the more he was convinced it was the one and only answer to his financial difficulties, especially when allied with any plan to invest in Linda.

The flat must be worth at least £250,000 surely? No outstanding mortgage on it. I'll have to pay some Capital Gains Tax on the profits. I should still net about £200,000. If only I could sell without Ann finding out. Maybe the witch has forgotten all about that flat? Don't think she's ever been to it. Maybe after ten years it's been erased from her thick mind. Is this plan possible? It's risky. If I get caught in the act, what would Ann's reaction be? The deception would be the straw that'd break the camel's back as far as our marriage was concerned. Good. Maybes.

Gerry enjoyed his life, and his lifestyle, and the personal freedom he had to do what, when and where he wanted more or less within reason and without question or exception, whilst Ann could be relied upon to fulfil the role of full-time housekeeper. This arrangement suited Gerry just fine. Conversely, he would freely concede that he knew his general attitude towards his wife of nearly thirty years standing probably left Ann so frustrated and unfulfilled and getting more bitter and twisted as time passed by. There was always the strong suspicion in Gerry's mind that Ann often thought she would prefer a divorce, but always stopped just short of asking for, or demanding, one.

Before leaving the 19th hole at the charmingly rustic Santo de Serra clubhouse, Gerry had convinced himself that he could, after all, sell the flat without Ann ever being aware of it. He would have to execute this plan by concealing the property sale transaction from his wife, and not encounter any unforeseen circumstances or have any downright bad luck. It would necessitate having to practise forging Ann's signature, which would be required on any legal documentation that had to be ratified. It would also mean he would have to make sure his lawyer telegraphically transferred the proceeds from the sale into an account that Ann had no access to, and preferably not even any limited knowledge of.

Yes, brilliant plan. Absolutely brilliant. The more Gerry thought on it, the more convinced he became that certainly, in theory at least, it was plausible he could pull this scam off. Sure, he reminded himself, he would need a small slice of good luck, but it was something he felt was well worth taking the risk on.

Gerry could not wait to share the detail of his perceived master plan with Drew and needed no motivation to pick up his mobile and contact his old friend.

'Hi, mate. Better sit yourself down. I've got some brill news for you, for once.'

'Oh yeah, now this I want to hear. Will I believe you, though?'

'It's how I'm gonna get the money. For you. For me. For Linda. So, do you want to hear more, eh?'

'Yeah, yeah, of course I do, pal. Why don't we get together for a drink when you return to Blighty and you can entertain me with every single soddin' detail.'

'Give me a bit of credit for once, Drew, and hear out my wonder plans.'

'Aristotle once said that it is the mark of an educated mind to be able to entertain a thought without accepting it.'

'Fuck off.......pal.'

*   *   *   *   *

'Why the sunglasses indoors, Linda?' enquired Linda's coach as he approached whilst she sat on a luxurious couch in the equally luxurious lounge of the Bank of England Sports Club at Roehampton, South London.

'I've a thumping headache.'

'How comes?'

'Was out on the raz last night with Drew and Gerry.'

'What, again! They're a bad influence on you.'

'They're not a bad influence on me. Anyway, I enjoy their company.'

'Sorry, Linda, but for me they're both assholes.'

'Well, I may need them more than ever now, Emilio.'

'Why?'

'I've lost my sponsorship with Colegate and frankly I don't think I can continue with the expense of playing the circuit full-time. Not solely with my current winnings from tournament play, at any rate.'

'My parents might be willing to help with your finances.'

Emilio Fazzi had been Linda's part-time tennis coach for the past five or six years.

Although born in Virginia Water, Surrey he came from Italian parentage, both of whom were independently extremely wealthy. It amused Linda to recount how often Drew and Gerry made reference to Emilio being a 'tennis gigolo' probably evidenced by his natural Italian good looks inherited from his mother, who had been in earlier life a famous Hollywood film actress. Linda genuinely liked Emilio, although there was nothing like the strong bond that existed with Drew and Gerry. Linda knew that Emilio was a reasonable, if not an outstanding, coach and had all the coaching certificates the Lawn Tennis Association ever produced. And Linda never quite saw the 'drain-pipe' personality in Fazzi that Drew, in particular, frequently referred to. There again, she often had difficulty winning the argument that, with Emilio's coaching methods, her game had not improved to any significant level over the past few years.

'Thanks for the offer of talking to your parents about sponsoring me, but I've held some initial discussions with Drew and Gerry about my finances. They seem to think they can come up with something.'

'But they're both clowns, Linda. A right pair of jokers.'

'I owe them so much. They deserve the right to any first refusal.'

'Why's that then, Linda? We've worked together for a few years now, but you've never really fully explained to me why the close relationship with them.'

'I'm sure I've told you this before, that my mum and dad died in a car crash when I was twelve. They originally moved over to Scotland from Dallas to enable my father to take up a senior lecturer position at Glasgow Uni.'

'Yeah, but where do Gerry and Drew fit in?' interrupted Emilio.

'I joined Hillpark Tennis Club and got to know them there. Then after my mum and dad's death I had to live with my mum's best friend in Troon, about a whole hour's drive away in those days. There weren't any direct public transport links. I initially kept up with the tennis at Troon, but somehow I found it hard to fit in there. Both at school and the local tennis club. About nine months after leaving Glasgow I came back to play in a competitive match at Hillpark. Drew and Gerry just happened to be there. We got talking. We became friends, regardless of our age differences. I then managed to persuade my guardian that I could rejoin Hillpark on the basis Drew and Gerry provided a door-to-door chauffeur service. Which, bless them, they duly did for several years and until I was fully mobile of my own accord. The friendship just blossomed, slowly but surely, over those years. They've become like big brothers to me. I owe them a lot.'

'I see. But that doesn't mean after all these years that they now would be the best people to invest in your tennis future,' argued Fazzi.

'Maybe. Maybe not. But, like I say, I owe them first refusal after all they have done for me over the years. Goodness, they even saved my life only a couple of weeks back - when I was kidnapped by those raving loonies.'

'Just be careful, Linda. Butch Cassidy and the Sundance Kid were less of a liability than Drew and Gerry.'

Linda withdrew her dark glasses, at the same time expressing a more typical radiant smile that complemented her whiter-than-white near perfect teeth glowing against her dark skin, 'C'mon then, let's not hang about here blathering, let's go and get some practice in on the tennis court. I need to get away sharpish to see a sports psychologist this afternoon. See if she can help me improve my game.'

It was the most pronounced put-down she could spontaneously think of without being noticeably professionally (or unprofessionally) disrespectful towards her coach.

Drew had, in fact, managed to arrange with Dr Keegan to meet up with Linda, helped somewhat by her consulting room being conveniently based in Fulham only five minutes distance between Putney, and from Linda. A late cancellation by another patient also helped.

Dr Eileen Keegan was a short-tempered lady in her mid-to-late fifties, devoid of any natural female beauty or charm, and so unlike anything Linda had been expecting. Keegan was forthright, almost to the point of being uncivil. Initially, Linda did not take to Dr Keegan's evident lack of personality, however it quickly became obvious Keegan had a major redeeming feature in that she was sincere in trying to offer constructive comment and, although unorthodox in approach and manner, she at least seemed to Linda professional enough to know exactly what she was doing.

The upshot of the meeting was that Dr Keegan recommended a short session of hypnosis in conjunction with further counselling sessions.

Keegan had diagnosed that perhaps Linda had led too sheltered an existence since her parents died. Certainly in the material sense. She evidently wanted materially for nothing, according to Keegan. Even her emotional needs were satisfied by all the sympathy and encouragement that had been bestowed upon her by others. Keegan acknowledged the fact that Linda did not like losing tennis matches, but the prognosis was that it had become just like most other aspects of Linda's life – it was something Linda could all too easily deal with. And that was plain wrong and unprofessional. It was time Linda felt some real emotional pain and distress over losing. She also had to manage her mental skills more effectively.

On making her way back to Putney by taxi, Linda caught up with Drew on her mobile.

'God, she's a bit of an auld battle-axe, but I'm glad I went for the consultation. She hypnotised me and she reckons she instilled into me something that will trigger a nasty or unpleasant reaction when I lose matches.'

'What, like Paul McKenna does to stop someone smoking?'

'Yeah, guess so, or something similar. She went through the type of stuff you'd expect from a sports' psychologist. Things like learning to relax, having self-belief, embracing the competitive struggle, dealing with the fear of failure, de dah, de dah. But I think Dr Keegan may have hit upon something when she emphasised the need to develop and maintain proper mental training techniques to help me improve my focus. She's given me a set of tapes and complementary exercises.'

'That's interesting, hen. Be even more interesting to see if it actually works. See you later on in the week.'

'Thanks. And thanks for suggesting Dr Keegan to me.'

Linda was also intrigued to find out if the hypnosis would actually work or not. Intrigued, but still somewhat sceptical.

Linda sent Drew and Gerry a simultaneous email which relayed the fact that she had received a formal letter of a sponsorship offer from a solicitor acting for and on behalf of a Hugo Summerfield. This letter proposing to fully fund all her expenses for the next twenty years in return for a 50-50 split on all income that Linda generated – both on court and off.

Linda indicated that it seemed a great offer, but wondered if Gerry or Drew knew of this Hugo Summerfield, as she did not. Gerry quickly replied that Summerfield was a neighbour of his in Pimlico. He further volunteered to Linda that Summerfield had been asking loads of questions recently about her, so he was not entirely surprised to hear of this unsolicited approach.

Drew emailed Linda advising 'no deal' and to simply ignore Summerfield and they would somehow, as agreed, raise the money privately between themselves.

When Drew contacted Gerry a little later to let him know in no uncertain terms what he thought of Hugo

Summerfield, particularly Summerfield's action of going behind their backs to try and do some sort of a deal with Linda without their knowledge or consent, he suggested to Gerry, 'Give him a call, pal. Sort the geezer out. If not, I'll do it. Now, do I have to do everything?'

Gerry agreed to confront Summerfield and telephoned him at the first opportunity.

'Hugo, I thought I told you the other day that Linda was none of your business?'

'I'm making it my business.'

'Why?'

'I am far more wealthy and successful than you'll ever be. I can help Linda become a champion.'

'That's highly debatable. Anyway, what's in it for you, pal? You know sod all about tennis.'

'That's actually not strictly true. Ask my wife. We are both keen followers of the game.'

'Bet you don't play?'

'So what? Anyway, why ask such a banal question?'

'How's about - because you're an ugly, fat bastard. And you're a slimey accountant. In fact, I'd tell you where to shove your offer to Linda, but your head's already up there blocking the way.'

Gerry's failure with Summerfield prompted Drew to insist he was the only one qualified to go and tell Summerfield the facts of life face-to-face.

'You just leave Summerfield to me to sort out. He's history. Watch and learn. Watch and learn, pal.'

*   *   *   *   *

Drew rang the door bell of the imposing manor house near Bodiam on the Sussex/Kent border to be greeted

55

by an attractive middle-aged woman, looking a dead ringer for Joan Collins, the famous film actress, circa fifty years of age.

'Can I help you?'

You certainly could, was Drew's immediate thought, quickly followed by him responding, 'I'm looking for Mr Summerfield.'

'Sorry, he's at work. Have you tried phoning him?'

'Yes, and I've left several messages which haven't been returned,' lied Drew.

'Sorry, who exactly are you?'

'My apologies. I'm Drew Taggart. A longstanding and suffering friend of Gerry King. You know Gerry, I believe?'

'Ah yes. Gerry's a fabulous guy,' gushed Mrs Summerfield. 'Come in, please do come in.'

'Don't mind if I do.'

'What's this all about then? Shall I phone Hugo now for you?'

'Well, if you wouldn't mind. I'm here to talk him out of his wee scam to invest in my best friend's future.'

'Sorry, I don't follow?'

'Your husband has effectively agreed to write a blank cheque out for Linda McKean, to sponsor her tennis career into planet infinity. And that husband of yours wants to control Linda's career and earnings potential even after she's long retired from playing tennis. And I ain't happy about that. Not happy at all, in fact,' Drew said, sounding very convincing with, for once, an unintended pronounced Glaswegian accent and ever so slightly threatening tone to his voice making an automatic guest appearance for some effect.

'I see. I know nothing about this. A blank cheque you say?'

'Aye, well, me and Gerry have been working very hard to put a financial package together for Linda. We've known her since she was a wee lass up in Glasgow and we know Linda is comfortable with our proposals. Indeed Linda has more or less agreed them. Yet your husband continually tries behind our back to stitch us up,' exaggerated Drew somewhat.

'How comes?'

'By writing direct to Linda with all sorts of formal letters of offer that she never asked your husband for in the first place,' exaggerated Drew yet again.

'So, what exactly is the problem then? Am I being slow on the uptake?'

'The problem is your husband simply won't take no for an answer and the point of my trip here today was to make sure he did. Once and for all.'

'I see.'

'Sorry to lumber you with this problem. And, so sorry I've forgotten my manners now - what's your name again, hen?'

'Sandra.'

'Hello, Sandra, pleased to meet you, I'm sure,' said Drew in his very best effort of substituting his hitherto slightly aggressive tone for a deep sexy voice as he dipped his eyes downwards towards Sandra's considerable cleavage.

'Would you like a drink whilst you're here, Drew?'

'Ah, yes please,' responded Drew. *Yes, a drink would be splendid. Quite, quite splendid. So would a shag.* Then he noticed that Sandra appeared to be wearing a nippleless bra. The signs were there, he thought. Then Drew had further immediate thoughts and feelings in his groin region in particular.

'Can I level with you, Sandra?' and without waiting for any response continued, in his best Sean Connery Scottish accent, 'I think you're classy and drop dead gorgeous and I want to make love to you like you've never experienced from that miserable drip of a fat bastard of a husband of yours.'

'My, my, you're such a charmer, Mr Taggart, aren't you?' grinned Sandra coquettishly as she sat herself down on the huge luxurious soft-fabric sofa, and in so doing only managed to sexually arouse Drew to extremes by revealing much of her attractive legs as her silk dress automatically slid up her body on impact with the sofa.

Drew accepted, even by his standards, he was chancing his arm by acting so directly, so quickly, but Sandra's behaviour was transmitting a clear and positive signal and it was now or never and he was never one to turn down even the remotest opportunity of having sex.

He immediately joined Sandra on the sofa and within seconds they were both at a fever pitch of lust and excitement. They proceeded to have sex right there and then on the sitting room floor, falling off the sofa, and breaking in the process an expensive-looking chess set displayed prominently on a nearby table.

About five long minutes later they both laughed loudly at each other, quickly but passionately kissed each other full on the lips and then Drew lit up the obligatory joint as he sat up.

'Hey, that was magical. Absolute magic. All too short, mind, but every second a quality one,' reasoned Drew, still in his best Sean Connery accent. 'Thank you for that.'

'It was all my pleasure,' insisted Sandra lewdly.

After a few minutes of self-satisfying, mutual smug silence, Sandra broke the quiet by asking if Drew still wanted to speak to her husband.

'Do I have to? I suppose I do really,' sighed Drew. It was the last conceivable thought on his mind.

'Why don't you leave Hugo to me?' suggested Sandra, winking mischievously. 'Well, I don't think I like the sound of what he's doing with Miss McKean. Hugo won't spoil your plans. I can guarantee it.'

'Sounds champion to me,' winked back Drew, 'I'll leave that self-indulgent twat of a husband of yours all to you, then.'

They stared at each other for no more than a couple of seconds longer before breaking out again into loud and sustained laughter.

Sandra then got a bottle of champagne out from the fridge and they both moved upstairs and spent the next couple of hours in one of the many bedrooms.

*   *   *   *   *

Drew and Gerry met up again a couple of days later to discuss their respective progress on outstanding matters over a liquid lunch on the Quarter Deck Balcony of The Old Ship moored on the River Thames by Hammersmith Bridge.

Drew confirmed he had "sorted Summerfield out" and that he could still get his hands on £95,000 through a variety of means, some of which would necessitate extending his current overdraft facility with his bank and also rescheduling his mortgage repayments.

Gerry, in turn, agreed to put in the balance required of £155,000.

This informal treaty meant that Gerry would get his £155,000 back first from any profits Linda made, Drew the next £95,000. For what at first appeared an inequitable arrangement they would nonetheless be equal partners. Simple as that. Thereafter, they would enjoy a further 25% between them from whatever

Linda made from the rest of her full-time tennis career on the tournament circuit. They would sign a ten year legal contract between all three of them to that effect.

Gerry felt he simply had to let Drew in on the devious and somewhat fraudulent and illegal means by which he intended to raise this finance. He also felt, on balance, he had little choice as he was sure Drew would soon enough start to question the actual detail of his perceived master plan and perhaps more importantly unwittingly make a comment in front of Ann which would give the whole sordid game away. When told the basis and detail of Gerry's plan, Drew made it known that he was sceptical that it would even work. Almost to the point of being critical, although he conceded it clearly solved a major problem for all three of them in almost equal measure and furthermore in one timely and convenient fell swoop.

In any event, the whole issue was now practically past the point of no return. Gerry had already received not only a property valuation and estate agents duly appointed, but within twenty-four hours a formal offer was made of £245,000 for the flat. And it was a condition of this sale that the transaction be completed within thirty days.

Three weeks later and Gerry was perspiring profusely as he tried various specimen signatures of his wife's before forging her signature on to the actual legal documents agreeing to transfer the ownership of the flat in Glasgow. Maybe it was the perspiration created from the heat wave the country was enjoying. Maybe it was the guilt, knowing he was committing a criminal act. His face was noticeably damp all over, almost as if he had quickly washed without a towel aid.

After a full hour of wholly differing practice attempts at perfecting his wife's specimen signature -

some of which he thought were just about passable and some were downright nothing like Ann's signature even if it had been a quick scribbled one - Gerry finally signed the original legal contract document for and on behalf of Ann only. He was reasonably content with the signature, if not the pangs of guilt that were shooting through his whole system.

The next step for Gerry in his now master-cum-forgery plan of action was to get his wife's signature witnessed preferably with a 'genuine' signature. As Drew was the only one to ever get to know the precise detail behind this fraudulent transaction, Gerry thought it reasonable and sensible to ask Drew to witness Ann's signature, and called upon him to facilitate this straightforward requisition.

'No fucking way. No! No! No! I'll go along with your scam and will take its secrecy to my grave, but don't you fucking dare ask me to be directly involved or implicated in a criminal act.'

Gerry was dumbfounded at Drew's unexpected reaction, or as Gerry tried hard to see it – overreaction.

'Are you absolutely sure? You can't see your way clear to sign it?'

'Positive, and don't ask me again. Got it?' Then, after a few moments Drew continued, 'I won't be an accessory to any unlawful act. Can't believe you'd ask that of me. Shite, man.'

This was indeed a dilemma, or an obstacle, that Gerry had not given any thought to previously on the Santo da Serra golf course, as he simply never considered it to be a potential problem. Now, he was starting to panic. Especially as time was in short supply.

Fortuitously, Gerry was due to play tennis that evening with someone he knew worked as a legal assistant in a big City law firm and was well used to signing and witnessing agreements. Following on from the game of tennis and in the bar afterwards Gerry signed the contract there and then with his own signature and it was witnessed in the traditional manner by his friend, the legal assistant. Gerry then confidently proceeded without creating any suspicion, 'Oh, do you mind awfully witnessing Ann's signature, just there, the stupid cow signed it not realising it had to be witnessed.'

With deductions for various fees etc, £230,000 was now as good as in Gerry's personal bank account. *Job done. Phew!*

The only matter he would now have to take account of was to make sure HMRC did not at any time in the future make any reference to it in any contact or correspondence with Ann in any subsequent tax returns to The Revenue. But as Ann was never requested to complete a tax return, Gerry did not expect that to ever create a problem for him. Although Drew's earlier condemnation of 'how d'ya sleep at night, pal' was ringing in Gerry's still slightly moist ears which were also suffering from his continuing mild, but unsightly state of perspiration.

*   *   *   *   *

'Hello, Linda. I have some fantastic news, lass. All the money is now in place between Drew and me and we're ready to ask you to sign that legal contract between the three of us.'

'That's braw. Ready whenever you are,' Linda said sounding, not unreasonably, genuinely grateful.

'What are you up to next week, Linda?'

'Nothing really. Bit of serious training before heading off to The States – that's all.'

'Have you got any tournament play or other commitments?'

'Not that I recall. Nope. Pretty sure I haven't.'

'How's about if I enter you into a tournament down in my home town of Dartmouth? You've never been there, have you?'

'Yes and no,' responded Linda not sounding altogether sure if she fancied the idea.

Gerry eagerly explained that once a year there was a Royal Regatta at the Port of Dartmouth, a historic Devon seaside town where Gerry lived part of the year and his wife lived all of the year. The thought greatly appealed to Gerry to have Linda visit and stay at his home. It presented the opportunity to show off his impressive house overlooking the estuary. And Linda was far better company than his wife. Not to overlook the fact of being far younger and more sexy and attractive than Ann.

'Are you still at the Bank of England sports ground in Roehampton coaching those kids and doing some training sessions?'

'Yeah.'

'Then, why don't Drew and I come down there tomorrow and I'll fill you in on Dartmouth? Anyway, there's the outstanding matter of Mr Fazzi to sort out.'

'What's to sort out?' enquired Linda.

'Well, Drew and I have decided he's frankly an unaffordable luxury. In other words we - and that now means all three of us - can't afford him.'

'That's a pity. I like the guy.'

'But think about it, Linda, what's Fazzi achieved for you? I think, if anything, there's a strong argument that you're over-coached. The bottom line is we simply can't afford to pay his wages. Come on, you know that.

We've no option but to part company with him. That needs to be done ideally as soon as.'

'Okay, okay,' agreed Linda, if only managing to sound a trifle reluctant. 'Am I to tell Emilio the decision then?'

'Drew and I can do that for you if you'd rather?' offered Gerry with a conspiratorial grin on his face whilst starting to sense the sheer warped pleasure this opportunity would present him and Drew in return for all the years of having to suffer Fazzi's company as part of their tennis entourage.

'Yes, okay then, you tell Emilio but please make sure you're pleasant about it and *please* emphasise that it's only because of the current shortage of funding.'

'He isn't by chance down there in Roehampton with you, is he?'

'Yip, he's here.'

'All right, Drew and I will kill or do something or other with two birds tomorrow then.'

'Was that meant to be funny?'

'No, sorry, nothing intended by that. Honest.'

Linda a bird? Boy did Gerry fancy Linda. He found it easy to delude himself that he felt like thirty-five years of age. If only he could summons up the courage to trying something on with Linda. Then what? He would bottle it. Without question. Always.

'Where's Emilio?' asked Drew, sounding impatient.

'He's over there, I think, waiting for his next pupil,' helped Linda.

Drew and Gerry then walked briskly across the immaculate croquet lawn and crept up behind the bench where Emilio Fazzi was sitting, just by the tennis courts.

'Fazzi,' barked Drew in synthetic rage, 'you're fired,' in an American accent as if probably trying to imitate Donald Trump.

'Fired?' spluttered Fazzi, looking decidedly startled as he turned round and recognised immediately the clear warning signs of two pumped guys in front of him.

'You, pal, will no longer be Linda's coach. Understand? You're fired, man,' continued Drew, now trying on his aggressive Billy Connolly-type voice.

'What does Linda have to say about this?'

'Linda's now under our personal management. We can't afford a lazy arsehole like you, got it? You're about as useful as a chocolate teapot to our Linda. And, just as well you ain't made of chocolate. You love yourself so much, you'd have eaten yourself by now.'

From both Drew and Gerry's pronounced agitated body language it would have been obvious even to Fazzi that there was absolutely no point trying to have a rational discussion, so his only sensible option was to walk away without making any further comment. Drew and Gerry, too, saw this as being their cue to walk in the opposite direction and in doing so Drew turned to Gerry to proclaim, 'He's got less personality than that fitba coach Sven-Goran Eriksson.'

'C'mon, be fair. Nobody, but nobody, has less personality than Eriksson,' smirked Gerry. 'Didn't you say there's a new biography just published about that muppet?'

'Aye, "*England 2001 to 2006 – The Glory Years*" ghost written by A. Pisstaker.'

*　　*　　*　　*　　*

'Okay, I'll come down to Devon after all. What about accommodation then? Will you book something for me?' asked Linda.

'Why not stay with us, if you like?' insisted Gerry.

'Fine by me. What about Ann, though?'

'Oh, she'll whinge about it to me, and smile and laugh with you as if you're her best friend come to stay,' laughed Gerry.

'Is she still a bit of a dragon?'

'Yip. And she still wears white clothing most of the time.'

'Eh? You what?'

'Well, she still likes to wear plain white clothing to blend in perfectly with the kitchen's white goods. You know, with the washing machine, tumble drier, fridge, cooker and such likes.' Gerry's attempted humour was probably again lost on Linda.

After Gerry put the phone down he began to fret about getting Linda registered for the Regatta Tournament, which was due to start within the next seven days or so. Gerry telephoned for an official tournament entry form on Linda's behalf, only to be advised by the Tournament Secretary that the closing date for applications had just passed.

'But I'm asking on behalf of Linda McKean.'

'I don't care. Entries are now closed.'

'Has the draw been made yet?'

'Nope.'

'Well then, surely to God, man, you can still grant her a wild card entry, or find some way to fit Linda in?'

'Nope.'

Gerry had this one major grievance about Dartmouth in that many born and bred locals made it patently obvious they looked down their noses at people who had come to live there, many as second home owners. Just like Gerry, in fact.

Consequently, Gerry had easily convinced himself that this Tournament Referee was only being obstinate for the sheer fact he could not accept Gerry as being a bona fide Dartmouthian.

'Do you actually know who Linda McKean is?'

'Yip.'

'Who is she then?' demanded Gerry starting to lose his temper.

'She's the top ladies tennis player in the country, I believe.'

'Exactly. So don't you think loads of tennis enthusiasts both local and grockles visiting Dartmouth for the Regatta would love to see Linda in action?'

'I'm sure they would.'

'Well, can she be slotted in then?' Gerry said with a long sigh as if to signal he was maybe getting somewhere.

'Nope.'

'Is that your final word?'

'Yip.'

'Well, I'm gonna make it a point of mine to let the *Dartmouth Chronicle* know and everyone else for that matter,' growled Gerry, 'just how friggin' inflexible you've been on this.'

'There's no need for that. Perhaps we could, after all, fit the girl into one of the handicap events if there's a cancellation between now and the tournament starting.'

'Bugger off, you certified half-wit,' shouted Gerry as he slammed the phone down into its socket.

Gerry picked Linda up from Totnes rail station, about a thirty minute drive away from Dartmouth. He thought Linda got more seductive every time he saw her and as she sat beside him, in the passenger seat of his car was no exception, confirmed by the erection he could feel grow, as did the level of personal embarrassment he was starting to feel. All he could see and concentrate on was Linda's long, long dark legs, enhanced by the fact she was wearing a white mini skirt.

'Well, what's this Dartmouth place like then, Gerry?'

'Ah, it's lovely. Am sure you'll like it. But I must tell you right away there's a wee bit of a problem with the tournament itself.'

'What, it's been cancelled?' guessed Linda.

'No, not quite. They wouldn't accept your entry. Too late, apparently.'

'No possibility of a wild card entry then?'

'No. The dickhead of an organiser to the tournament said he might be able to fit you in to one of the lesser categories. Of course, I told him where to stick it.'

'Did he know who I was?'

'As the prize tosser was fond of saying, "Yip".'

'Oh dear, what happens now? I hope this isn't a wasted trip for me, Gerry.'

'Nay worries, sunshine. I've arranged for Frank Haffey - the professional at Torquay - to come over and give you some rigorous practice sessions for a couple of days. Plus, Drew is coming down tomorrow and will stay the weekend. We'll have the ideal opportunity to finally all sign those contracts and legal paperwork of yours. Anyway, it'll be the last chance we'll have to see you before you go and win the US Open in six weeks.'

Drew duly arrived that weekend in Dartmouth. Sometimes, usually when drunk, he conceded that he always enjoyed visiting this attractive spot on the English Riviera, whilst also admitting to being envious of Gerry having a stunning house in this undeniably lovely part of South Devon.

Gerry was in his element, acting host to his two best friends. Quite possibly his only real friends. He, pretty much, now considered Dartmouth to be his home town in practical terms - although, Glasgow always remained home in his heart. And partly because Dartmouth was now home to Gerry he was particularly enjoying being seen out and about in Dartmouth with Linda by his side. Not only did she stand out - she was black - but she turned heads with a mixture of her stunning natural beauty and the fact that many passers by recognised her from media exposure, particularly television.

Dartmouth, being a small seaside town, relied heavily on tourism and The Royal Regatta week was the main event on the social calendar for most of its 2,000 residents when the population of Dartmouth amplified to around 30,000 odd during Regatta week.

The Regatta week was not quite in the same league as, say, Cowes on the Isle of Wight, but it still benefited from a long tradition with the first Regatta being held back in 1822. In 1856 Queen Victoria visited Dartmouth during the Regatta along with Prince Albert, ever since when it became – somewhat dubiously – known as the Royal Regatta.

Rowing, sailing, craft exhibitions, road races, tug-of-war competitions and a whole variety of the more mainstream sports like golf and tennis held official tournaments. The Royal Air Force always sent their legendary Red Arrows formation to put on a thrilling display of dare devil flying, allegedly because the River Dart estuary was one of their favourite places to visit and perform. This being justified, by popular rumour, to be because the landscape of the many steep hillsides bordering the estuary and town helped create a spectacular and dramatic aerobatic display for their supersonic machines.

Gerry felt sensationally proud of himself whilst walking through the old town with Linda by his side - and as often as he reasonably could arrange it without it appearing embarrassingly obvious - in some form of embrace or other.

Do people wonder why she is with me? Do they think she is my lover? he flattered himself.

For Gerry it had been a highly successful few days during the Regatta.

Both Linda and Drew seemed to enjoy themselves immensely and it had been a relaxing and fun time for all three of them. Gerry convinced himself that was all his doing. It had also been a productive get-together as Linda had actually at long last signed a ten year deal with Gerry and Drew.

Linda still had absolutely no idea whatsoever regarding any of the background detail or problems relating to the actual manner by which the funding had been procured, being blissfully unaware of the all the trials and tribulations it had presented Drew and Gerry with.

On the drive back to Totnes train station Drew and Linda were effusive towards their host about how much they had enjoyed their trip to Dartmouth.

'Thanks, guys, but you know what I enjoyed most?' asked Gerry then answering his own question, 'Reading the *Dartmouth Chronicle* today and seeing the damning article about you being here, Linda, and being prevented from playing in the tournament by some tosser so far up his own arse he wouldn't be able to enjoy your exceptional skill and craft even if you paid him a bucket full of money. Jesus, there was even more spectators watching many of your practice sessions with Frank Haffey than there was actually watched the sodding Ladies Final of the damn Regatta tournament itself.'

'Yes, I know. It was a missed opportunity, wasn't it? There's always next year, huh? You know me, I like putting on exhibitions for the spectators when I know I'll win even with one hand tied behind my back. I do hope that tournament organiser feels deeply embarrassed about his inflexibility,' suggested Linda coldly.

'Oh, I do very much hope so, too. The last Royal Regatta tournament he ever organises in Dartmouth, methinks,' crowed Gerry.

'I see Ann's still a bit of a dragon then,' declared Linda, altering the topic of conversation, at which point Gerry immediately turned up the volume control on the car CD player which was playing Jeff Beck's *'Hi Ho Silver Lining'* and this in turn prompted high decibel communal signing, well out of tune, from all three of them.

The car they were in was now noticeably rocking as well as travelling at 35 mph along a typically quiet and narrow Devon country lane.

Exactly where this journey would ultimately lead over the ensuing months was perhaps not too far distant from each of their innermost private thoughts.

'Game, set and match to Miss McKean 6-3, 6-1,' confirmed the umpire in a soft, almost bored voice as if he had just endured, rather than enjoyed, officiating this particularly uneventful match, which had turned out to be little more than a practice session for Linda. From Linda's perspective she was simply content with a solid performance, if unspectacular victory, against Miss Czink from Hungary and was not the slightest bit concerned that this not unimportant match was an unexpectedly one-sided affair.

By beating Miss Czink, Linda was through to the last sixty-four of the U.S. Open and was feeling a touch pleased with herself.

Perhaps more significantly, Linda was starting to believe that she was playing as well as she could remember. Maybe Dr Keegan's psychological remedies were actually starting to pay dividends? Although Linda would prefer to accept the improvement was due in no small part to the full-time training and support she was receiving from Frank Haffey over the previous couple of weeks. Linda was really enjoying working with Frank since the 'new management team' of Gerry and Drew, whilst they met in Dartmouth, had sold Frank to her on the pretext that they both work together strictly on a temporary basis during Grand Slam events only.

After their brief introduction to each other at Dartmouth, Frank went over to get to know Linda better during the pre-US Open tournament at Forest Hills. It gave Frank a chance, particularly during practice sessions, to work on and improve upon some known and accepted weaknesses to Linda's game.

Haffey possessed a completely different personality to Fazzi. Frank's CV certainly highlighted the fact that he had more varied experience of coaching than Fazzi and hopefully had the right man-management skills and motivational techniques that Gerry and Drew believed Fazzi sorely lacked.

Linda readily acknowledged that Frank was bringing a new dimension to her whole approach to tournament match play as well as an entirely different training regime and preparation programme, both physical and mental, which she found more varied, enjoyable and stimulating than anything she had been used to. But, would it bring any rewards?

'That's my girl,' enthused Frank. 'Your concentration was spot-on out there and you never let Czink get into any sort of rhythm. Your shot-making selection is definitely getting smarter and more productive. Those outright winning drop shots were brilliantly disguised. Absolutely brilliant. You're the best player in this event.'

'Steady on, Frank,' beamed Linda, enjoying this extreme show of enthusiasm. 'You're almost in danger of making a black girl blush.'

'Don't make me laugh, pet. Seriously, you continue to play like that and you're as good as US Open champion. Bring on Zerova. I hope she wins her match today, then you'll be as good as through to the last thirty-two,' predicted Frank.

'Remember, she's given me a good thumping on two flipping occasions in recent years at Wimbledon!' protested Linda, but still smiling as she said it.

'Did she? So what? You're a miles better player than she'll ever be.'

'Okay, I buy that.' Linda was feeling more optimistic than she had done for quite some considerable time. *Zerova doesn't frighten me. Not one jot. Bring it on.*

'Hi, Linda, Drew and I will be arriving tomorrow. When's your match scheduled with Zerova?'

'It's at 2.30pm local time. Jeeees, I sure hope you're gonna make it!' exclaimed Linda excitedly.

'Yeah, Drew's checked out the travel schedule, the intention being to get to Flushing Meadows well in time for your game with Zerova. That'll happen unless something unforeseen delays us.'

'Great stuff. Can't wait to see you guys again.'

Court 10 at Flushing Meadows was the venue for Linda's match against Cathy Zerova, and Zerova had, just like Linda, won her own previous match rather easily.

So Zerova, too, was clearly in a reasonable vein of form, it seemed to Linda.

Linda was nervous. There again, she was always nervous before a match, but on this occasion slightly more so, as this one had a distinct edge to it for her. Not only did it offer the opportunity of revenge for previous Wimbledon defeats, also if she won then it meant she would be through to the last thirty-two of a Slam event and that was something she probably would have accepted at the start of the tournament. It certainly would be a tangible, if minor, show of some progress being made. And particularly timely and encouraging so soon after Gerry and Drew had invested so much money in her.

As Frank and Drew and Gerry sat together watching Linda and Cathy Zerova knock-up, they all looked tense and anxious, evidenced by the lack of conversation between the three of them.

Drew and Gerry only briefly conversed the once that they were both surprised, yet suitably impressed, by what they were witnessing. Even whilst knocking-up Linda looked more positive and confident than they had seen for quite some time and appeared to have added a bit more power and zip to her ground strokes, as well as moving and reacting that tiny bit quicker and sharper as well.

They were undoubtedly even more impressed once the match got under way and Linda broke Zerova's service twice to lead 5-0 in the first set.

'Blimeeeeey,' exaggerated Drew. 'Can't remember when I last saw Linda play this well. She's confidently hitting the feck out of the ball. What have you been doing to her, you sly auld fox, Frank?'

'Absolutely nowt. Well, nowt really. She has all the talent, it just needs channelling properly. Remember, guys, she was desperately short of self-confidence.'

'Yeah, thanks in no small part to that feckless coach, Fazzi,' Gerry added.

Linda continued to dominate Zerova and eventually ran out an easy victor by the score line 6-1, 6-3. A place secured in the last thirty-two of the US Open.

Drew and Gerry and Frank now had permanent wide grins on their respective faces. So, too, did Linda.

Certainly, it was one happy looking little tennis entourage. For now, at least.

*   *   *   *   *

Drew and Gerry were sitting at an outside café table on Broadway Avenue enjoying the early morning sunshine, both reading the newspapers in the hope they might find some mention of Linda's progress in *The Open* (as most Americans arrogantly referred to it). Disappointedly, but hardly surprisingly, there was no mention whatsoever, but from the classified results coverage they could see that Linda would now have to play Martina Bondarenko who was seeded No.18 and who Linda had never previously beaten in any competitive match, to the best of their recollection. The one minor additional attraction of this draw was that they thought this match would be scheduled for one of the show courts. Drew and Gerry both preferred that, if for no other reason than they personally enjoyed the atmosphere of the show courts, and with Miss Bondarenko being American, it almost guaranteed a predominantly charged and partisan American crowd expecting, if not demanding, Miss Bondarenko to win.

Drew and Gerry spent the next half an hour or so exchanging typically inane banter, mockingly deriding each other over complete and utter trivia. There was usually never any need to mention any detail about Linda. It had all been said before, time and again, from years gone by. They simply could see no wrong in Linda as a person, and did not possess enough technical nous to make any constructive comment regarding her tennis play or strategy. They predominantly saved any verbal contribution by endless predictable displays of sheer enthusiasm and commitment. No more, no less.

'So, what do ya make of Martina Bondarenko then?' queried Drew.

'Not sure, mate. Let's just hope Linda does us proud and puts in a good performance, that's the main thing really, isn't it?'

'Bollocks,' retorted Drew in his own inimitable style, 'absolute bollocks. Good performance – the main thing? You talk so much crap at times, tosser. Our girl must win. Got it? That's the only attitude to have, man.'

'Okay,' replied Gerry, as he hid behind his newspaper as if to sulk at being lectured at. Or, perhaps it was a case of, once again, feeling isolated by his own inability, or lack of wit, to finish off the banter in his favour.

'This is *it*, pet,' said Frank in an assertive tone of voice. 'This is only the start of something special. Go out there and show those arrogant yanks that their girl is a second class citizen. She'll be as nervous as hell in front of all those yankie idiots shouting and spitting their greasy burgers and hot dogs all over the place. Shut them up. Do it quickly. Get an early break of service, if you can. Go for your winners early on. Take reasonable calculated risks. Be aggressive. You're technically playing well enough to make those shots happen. Put her on the back foot, and don't let her get back into the game. Just like you did with Zerova - got it? And remember, she's got a slightly weakish temperament, so if the crowd go quiet and anxious I reckon there's every chance she will, too. Got it?'

'I hear you, Frank. Wish me luck.'

'You don't need luck, pet. Relax. Be positive. Go out and enjoy the moment.'

Linda lost her opening service game, not helped by serving two double faults. *This is crazy. Why am I nervous? What on earth have I got to be nervous about?*

Linda won the next four games with almost flawless tennis. Aggressive, but controlled, play. All the increased confidence and execution and penetration of shot quickly returned. As Linda sat beside the umpire chair with a comfortable 4-1 lead at a change-of-end she momentarily looked up at Drew and Gerry and Frank and saw them all looking extremely pleased with her, and presumably themselves, too.

Linda thought she could relax and start to enjoy the party time atmosphere with them and help forget about the unappreciative crowd and slightly hostile atmosphere in the stadium. Linda thought wrong.

'Miss Bondarenko leads 5-4, having won the first set 7-6,' confirmed the umpire, struggling to be heard over the increasingly noisy and excited and biased American capacity audience of 23,000 within the Arthur Ashe Stadium (the largest permanently dedicated tennis arena in the world).

Linda wondered where the past forty minutes or so had disappeared to. She was serving to stay not only in the set, but also in the match. Potentially only four points away from defeat. What had gone wrong? She was pretty sure she was still playing as well as when she started the match.

Right, she thought, maybe she had not pushed herself hard enough to find that tiny extra bit of inspiration needed. She momentarily thought of Dr Keegan and having that bit of ultra-determination and guilt trip over any probable defeat. That extra bit of risk taking was what was called for. As Linda walked out to receive the balls from one of the ball girls she looked up in the general direction of Drew and Gerry and Frank and gave an exaggerated wink as if to say, 'Don't worry.'

As the ball girl placed four tennis balls on to Linda's outstretched racket, the ball girl then gave Linda a pronounced wink to which Linda responded with a slightly giggly reaction.

The ball girl then winked, for a second time, to which Linda thought, *how odd. How very odd.*

Maybe the ball girl simply had mistakenly thought Linda's original exaggerated wink a few seconds earlier was intended for her.

Linda smashed down two clean aces in that service game along with one service that was virtually unreturnable. It gave Linda just that little instantaneous and significant lift that made all the difference. Then, her game went immediately up into a top gear with minimal response from Miss Bondarenko, who was starting to make more mistakes as the expectant crowd became progressively nervous and agitated as increased unforced errors crept into Bondarenko's game. Linda, deliberately and wisely, kept the rallies longer and longer, patiently waiting for an increasingly likely unforced error from the racket of her now less than confident opponent.

There was little doubt that Linda was now, at twenty-six years of age, a mature match player and had learned the hard way from bitter past experiences that once an opponent was showing signs of inconsistency, she must capitalise on it.

Linda beat Martina Bondarenko just about deservedly so, 6-7, 7-6, 6-3.

It was hardly a vintage performance, although the result would be viewed by some tennis pundits as the biggest upset of the tournament so far.

Gerry flung his arms around Linda. He once told Drew there was no nicer smell than the pungent aroma of perspiration from Linda's damp body after a competitive match.

'Gee, that was awesome, honey,' he proclaimed in the worst American accent imaginable.

'Well, thanks, young man,' Linda said at the same time offering Drew a high five.

All three then engaged in a communal celebration huddle together.

'Did anyone see the antics of that young ball girl?' asked Linda, immediately changing her mood as she broke away from Drew and Gerry's joint embrace.

Frank, Drew and Gerry all shook their heads in unison.

'Maybe I'm mistaken, but she seemed to be giving me some strange looks.'

'Probably in awe of you, Linda,' offered Gerry.

'Yeah, maybe. But I'm not so sure. She almost looked as if she was coming on to me.'

'Good grief,' snapped Frank, 'get a grip, pet. She must be only what, barely twelve or thirteen years of age?'

'Yeah,' said Drew, clearly wanting to change the subject, 'I think it's about time Gerry and I hit the Manhattan bars. This is thirsty work watching you, Linda,' he cackled.

*   *   *   *   *

Gerry and Drew agreed that it was never too early to celebrate anything that Linda achieved. And Linda getting through to the last thirty-two of the US Open was in their minds a definite achievement.

Drew, in particular, was in his element. He was in a dynamic city full of energetic people who shared his preferred fast-moving lifestyle. Officially in New York working for his employers the *Daily Mail,* it was hardly arduous work given that he had only to produce a couple of feature articles for his newspaper which, with Drew's journalistic talents, was simply a bread and butter task. This, in turn, afforded him plenty of spare time to spend with Linda and Gerry, as well as enjoy the attractions of New York. After the obligatory quick snort of cocaine and half a bottle of vodka to maximise his desired feelings, he went down to the lobby area to rendezvous with Gerry.

'Let's hit this city running,' proclaimed Drew, acting as if he had ants in his pants.

Gerry, transparently less than enthusiastic, replied, 'Okay, but not a late one eh, please? I'm kinda tired after all the travel and excitement of the match today.'

'Ya big woose, man. What are ye? A big woose,' snapped Drew, the cocaine in his system ensuring he looked twitchy and wired.

Off the two of them went into the busy streets of Manhattan to sample whatever came their way. The more bars visited, the better, appeared to be the uncomplicated itinerary. Well, that was clearly Drew's intention, at any rate. And, he succeeded in double quick time.

'How many friggin' bars have we been to now?' protested Gerry.

'Stop yer whinging, man. Enjoy yerself. Or piss off.'

'You been on the coke tonight? Or the wacky baccy?'

'So, what if I have?'

'You're so unpredictable when you're as high as a kite, and tedious, and boring. Not the least bit funny. Nor good company.'

'Well, fuck off then. See if I care.'

'Okay, chum, I will. Anyway, I'm tired,' said Gerry in a pathetic tone of voice.

'Well, go then. Sourpuss. You're like a stale fart following me around in any event. The quicker you go, the quicker I start to enjoy myself again. Go back to your hotel room for a ham shank. Go on. Piss off.'

'Be careful, my friend. This is a dangerous city – no matter what the Mayor of New York says to the contrary in the glossy travel brochures.'

Gerry was probably right to issue the warning.

No sooner, it seemed, had Gerry returned to his hotel room and fallen into a deep sleep when he was awoken by his mobile phone. His first reaction was to ignore it as it would be almost certainly Drew being drunk and acting silly but when he noticed that there had been eight missed calls his conscience got the better of him and he decided to answer it just in case it was a genuine emergency.

'Who's that?' barked Gerry angrily.

'Who's that?' came the response from a mysterious and unrecognisable voice.

'Fuck off whoever you are, pal,' snapped Gerry and just as he was about to press the *off* button the response at the other end was an extremely loud and clearly panic-stricken tone of voice.

'Whoever you are, don't hang up. I'm here at the Bellevue Hospital with someone I think you know.'

Gerry could tell from the accent it was a probably a New Yorker and also someone who was starting to sound more and more genuine and well meaning by the second.

'Sorry? Who exactly are you then?' drawled Gerry slowly, beginning to feel wide awake and almost alert again.

'It doesn't matter who I am. I'm with your brother, man, at the hospital. He's been lynched by some low life punk. Get off yer fat arse and get down here to the hospital's casualty department straightaway. This geezer looks in a bad way, man. He needs a friend.'

'Is this some kind of hoax? How'd you get my number to contact me?' demanded Gerry.

'Fuck me, man. How'd I get your poxy number? Fuck me. Is *that* important? I just pressed the 'resend' button from the last number on this fucking cell phone. To get any fucking message to any fucker who knows this poor sucker here. Now get your fat fucking arse down to 462 First Avenue, pronto. Now!'

*　　*　　*　　*　　*

'How the heck is Drew?' enquired Linda, managing to both sound and look every bit as concerned for Drew's health and welfare as she actually truly and genuinely was.

'Effing awful. Well, he looks awful at any rate. His face is badly bruised and smashed up. Those fuckers must have taken some warped pleasure in beating the crap out of him,' spat Gerry. 'It was sadistic and gratuitous violence.'

'We *will* be allowed to go and see him after the match?' insisted Linda.

'Of course. I'm sure Drew will be really delighted to see you, especially if you win today,' Gerry said, trying to force a half-smile on to his face, as well as Linda's.

'Of course I'll win today. Not for me - but for Drew.'

'That's the spirit, pet,' enthused Frank, 'but, forget about Drew for a couple of hours and concentrate on one thing, and one thing only, your tennis. Got it?'

'Gotcha, coach.'

Linda's next opponent was Georgina Walsh, again from the U.S.A., and again someone who should on paper be good enough to beat Linda without needing to perform to her maximum. But Linda felt strangely ultra-confident of beating anyone at the minute, especially on the fast-paced cement court, which the Louis Armstrong arena certainly was. Fast. Very fast. However, thinking of how precisely she planned to actually beat Miss Walsh, Linda had some difficulty removing the thought of poor Drew's beating from her mind. Linda wished she had been able to at least visit Drew as then she could assess for herself just how bad a condition he was in.

Georgina Walsh was seeded No.4 and was, arguably, the fittest and the most stubborn of players on the women's tour – outside China, that is. Walsh rarely made any unforced errors and would endlessly chase and chase from all sides and from all conceivable angles of the court. She was not Linda's favourite type of opponent as Walsh had a knack of frustrating even the most positive and patient of players. Linda knew that to beat Walsh she would need to concentrate and be patient to a level that she had rarely achieved in the past.

Why-oh-why did Drew have to end up in hospital? She could well do without that worry, she thought. But there again, Linda recalled one of Dr Keegan's theories, and Keegan would have approved of having Drew at the forefront of her thoughts and presenting that special extra personal motivational drive and reason for winning. For Drew.

The match in the early games was intriguing but hardly a classic with the only notable feature of the contest being that both Linda and Miss Walsh kept the unforced errors down to a bare minimum. That came more naturally for Walsh, less so for Linda. 'Chess Tennis' Linda often called it, disapprovingly.

With the score line standing at 6-6 in the first set - a tie break - clearly it was a critical stage in the match.

Linda remained focused and quietly pleased with her patient and controlled performance. However, she knew only too well that tie-breaks were a bit of a lottery, not helped by the fact she suspected Walsh would continue to play her predictable game and absolutely nothing would change. One point here, or there, would make *all* the difference to the outcome of the set. And Linda knew her Achilles heel: sometimes she got the dreaded elbow at truly ultra critical points, particularly in a cautious, conservatively played, tight match. Linda decided she needed to suddenly change her whole approach in the belief it would come as a major surprise to her opponent and she could, therefore, hopefully profit from an unexpected change of tactic and strategy. High risk, but Linda considered it was calculated and worthwhile.

It worked a treat for Linda, helped by executing a couple of huge serves and making two highly adventurous and high risk winning volleys resultant from attacking Miss Walsh's own serves.

Linda won the tie-break by the remarkable score line of 7-0.

That was a massive psychological boost to Linda's confidence and helped take it to a new level. It also made the crowd, who had predominantly been supporting Walsh, less of a negative factor for Linda and more importantly, for once, Miss Walsh went completely to pieces.

Linda ran out a fairly comfortable winner in the end 7-6, 6-2.

After shaking Miss Walsh's hand, Linda looked up at the television gantry and waved as if to draw their attention to her. She then blew a big kiss towards the television cameras and mouthed, 'That was for you, Drew.'

Linda was so excited that she thought she could play her forthcoming match there and then, so pumped up with adrenaline was she.

*   *   *   *   *

Drew fidgeted constantly as he lay in his hospital bed. He was feeling somewhat clinically depressed. But, this was only because he could not quite recall when he last had a vodka and tonic. He wanted one, desperately.

'Someone said you had been badly bashed up. Blimey, to me you still look the handsome auld devil you always were,' beamed Linda.

'Don't make me laugh, hen. I've got nine fuck'n fractured ribs, apparently. Anyway, the important thing is you won today. Great stuff. Give an auld man a kiss,' demanded Drew.

'With pleasure.'

'How's you feeling, matey? You look a lot chirpier than you did this morning,' Gerry breezed into the conversation.

'Well, I was able to watch the match on the telly. It's made all the difference, man. Don't even feel the pain any more. Yeah, well if you believe that, you'll believe anything, I guess,' he grimaced.

'So, what actually happened then, Drew?' asked Linda. 'Gerry says you got beaten up by a wee gang of local hoodlums.'

'Well, I'm not sure, Linz - it all happened in a flash, like. I was walking, okay staggering, along some street or other and I'll admit it probably looked to anyone and everyone that I was a helpless lost soul with tourist stamped across my forehead. Yeah, yeah, and I know what you're all thinking. Yes, I was well pissed. Think one of my drinks had been spiked.'

'You mean you'd taken some coke before leaving the hotel?' remarked Gerry, sounding extremely unsympathetic.

Why does Gerry have to be always so boringly practical and predictable? Why can't he just relax and enjoy what little is left of his life? Drew thought to himself.

'Okay, yeah, I was blootered. These couple of seriously hackit looking thugs who wouldn't have looked out of place in the front row for Harlequins Rugby Club, started to take the piss out of my accent.

They then asked if I was interested in some 'action'. I thought they were trying to flog me some dope. When I asked how much, they asked how much I wanted and how much cash had I on me - next thing I know I'd been frog-marched down into some dark alleyway and had the shit beaten out of me. I don't think they liked me, for whatever reason. There was no need to have given me the beating that they did.'

'Black bastards,' interjected Gerry with a scornful look on his face.

'No. Actually they were white,' whispered Drew, as if embarrassed and disappointed to confirm this fact. 'I, too, always thought it was only blacks who did this kinda thing.'

There was a moment or two of slightly awkward silence, only broken by Linda volunteering, 'Well, that was a bit of a conversation-stopper then.'

'Come on, guys, cheer me up for Christ's sake,' requested Drew.

'Thought I'd done that already,' responded Linda.

'Of course. And you have, ma dear. You did us proud out on court today,' confirmed a grateful Drew, albeit continuing to feel decidedly sorry for himself, because of being extremely stiff and uncomfortable and in quite a bit of agony even allowing for the pain-killing injections.

'No chance, I suppose, of getting me a G&T smuggled in here then?'

Drew's plea was ignored.

'This'll make you laugh. Guess who I bumped into today?' asked Gerry before answering his own question. 'Emilio Fazzi. And I sent him your best wishes.'

'Tell me you didn't?' coughed Drew in some physical distress.

'No way. I told him Linda had learned more from Frank in the past few weeks than she ever learned from him in six years.'

'Good man. He's such an arse that guy. Born without any personality. Tell me, Linz, who have we got in the last sixteen? My bet is it'll be Na Zheng from China?'

*　　*　　*　　*　　*

Linda was relaxing in the plush interior competitors' lounge just next to the huge players' restaurant within Flushing Meadows' impressive complex. However impressive Flushing Meadows was on the inside, it was undeniably a concrete monstrosity on the exterior and without doubt the least aesthetically pleasing to the eye of the four Grand Slam venues.

Flushing Meadows, as America's National Tennis Centre, was synonymous with three things in almost equal proportion – the first being the tennis itself, secondly, countless extremely busy fast food outlets frequented by the voracious hordes of slurping, belching and chomping local spectators and thirdly the ugly, hugely unimpressive concrete exterior surround.

Linda was enjoying reading some of the newspapers from back home in the UK which were starting to show an interest particularly now that she had reached the latter stages of such a prestigious tournament. The broadsheets in particular were giving quite a bit of coverage, although the tabloids were picking up on the proceedings as well in their own inimitable style with Linda featuring more as photographic detail, rather than actual tennis playing content. Still, Linda was no different from any other sports person in that it was never a chore to read positive and complimentary things being written about you.

Out of the corner of her eye Linda was aware that someone was hovering just behind her, so much so it was irritating her enough to turn round to see.

It was the ball girl who had unnerved her during her match with Bondarenko.

'Yes, can I help you?' enquired Linda.

'Can I have your autograph please?'

'Sure. Nay problem,' obliged Linda.

'Thank ya,' drawled the young girl. She was dressed as if she were a prostitute with fishnet stockings and an extremely short skirt with a tight fitting top that was at least a couple of sizes too small, but helped show off an extremely well developed upper body.

'Can I have a photograph, too, please, Miss?'

'Sure thing.'

At which point, in a synchronized manner someone appeared in front of Linda with a camera. The young ball girl had at the very same time sat down beside Linda and a photograph was instantaneously taken. What Linda had not expected was the kiss that this girl smacked on her lips.

'Sorry,' said the young girl, 'but you're my heroine. I just *love* ya, sugar.'

Startled, and not amused, Linda tried to recover her composure, 'That's enough of that – now be off with you,' she growled.

She could not help but look at the person holding the camera. He sent a shiver down her spine. He looked one mean dude she thought and his crooked smile just as he walked away did little to alleviate Linda's feeling of unease.

Later that day, Linda found out that she was indeed scheduled to play Miss Zheng in the last sixteen. The tournament favourite. The defending U.S. Open champion.

Linda had never played against Na Zheng except on a couple of occasions in a doubles match. She had a built-in mentality from an early age not to fear anyone on the tennis court, but Na Zheng was as near to utter respect before becoming fear as it got for Linda.

Na Zheng was yet another product from the Chinese 'boot' camp, which had over the past two to three years been responsible for a constant production line of potentially world class players. Na Zheng just happened to be the first to become hugely successful. Nobody doubted Zheng was the first of many from that country.

Still, Linda knew she simply had to beat the likes of Zheng if she was ever to win any Slam event and, she also knew, Frank would never allow her to feel inferior to anyone on a tennis court.

He telephoned her just to enquire if she was in the right mental frame of mind and having a quiet, restful night in.

'No, Gerry's not leading me astray. In fact, I think he's gone off to visit Drew at the hospital. And, yes, Frank, I will get to bed soon, and try and have an early and good long sleep tonight,' Linda reassured him.

Just after finishing the conversation with Frank, Linda received a text message on her mobile. It read – *'u r in big trouble'*.

How strange, Linda thought, not quite being able to dismiss it as a bit of a crank message, much as initially she tried to.

Then, as Linda got into bed, her mobile buzzed again. It showed a photo of her and that ball girl. It looked almost pornographic.

Bloody heck. What exactly is going on here?

Linda stared at the image, trying hard to remain calm whilst quickly rationalise what was going on. Before she had time to give the matter any further detailed thought another text message was received - *'$100k or we go to press'.*

'Gerry, it's me, Linda. Can you come over to the hotel straight away? Fully realise it's late, but crikey, I think I'm being blackmailed,' said Linda. 'Can you come over right away, Gerry, *please?'*

* * * * *

Linda had a restless night with not much more than two hours sleep.

That morning she went out to Flushing Meadows' practice courts with Frank to prepare for her match in the afternoon against Na Zheng.

What should have been a really exciting day for her was now more likely to be one full of trepidation until this blackmail matter could be sorted out.

Gerry agreed, if a little reluctantly, to take charge of this nasty business. Any reluctance on Gerry's part was only due to him being apprehensive as to what lay behind these threats, and a profound lack of inspiration as to what to do next for the best.

Being on his own did not help: no Drew, who was still in hospital, no Linda, as obviously she now had to try and prepare for her match and no Frank as his expertise and time would be needed more than ever to get Linda into the right frame of mind for her match against arguably the world's current best tennis player.

Gerry considered his initial port of call should be to Brigadier Mitch Jones, a prominent tour official, who he had at least some limited rapport with, having briefly met the Brigadier on two or three prior occasions when in Linda's company. The Brigadier was English, which Gerry thought might somehow help him.

Brigadier Jones was less than helpful. In fact, he did not seem to give a jot as to the predicament that Linda was facing, instead taking the line that it was no more than a childish prank, and in his opinion one that would go away as quickly as it had arrived.

How covenient for the Brigadier to take this view, thought Gerry, realising that the Brigadier was clearly highly stressed out himself, his duties as joint tournament referee being his one and only priority.

Just as Gerry was pondering his next move, he got a call on his mobile from Frank, who informed him that Linda had received yet another text saying she had only one hour remaining to make a decision on the blackmail demand.

Frank also told Gerry that he had ordered Linda to switch off her phone, and at the first opportunity after the match she would replace her mobile with a new one and a new number.

Well, at least, this crystalised matters somewhat for Gerry.

For one, it seemed that all this was to somehow coincide and take advantage of the forthcoming match in the common belief that if Linda lost she would almost certainly be on the earliest available plane out of the country. For two, there would not be the opportunity right now to involve the police in any meaningful investigation, given the time constraints and the likelihood that the text sender was using a stolen, pay-as-you-go mobile phone that could not be traced back to them.

Gerry was starting to panic; he did not know what his next best move should be for Linda's benefit. Just for good measure, Gerry's paranoid mind was starting to wonder if this was part of a bigger conspiracy involving Drew and the yobs who attacked him just to make everyone either directly or indirectly involved feel even more vulnerable. *Why had Drew been beaten up so badly for what amounted to little more than a few sodding green bucks?*

Gerry then wondered if the British press would in any event take any real interest in this photograph of Linda. With that in mind, Gerry made a quick call to Drew in hospital. Drew insisted that he would contact his own Sports Editor at the *Mail* back in London.

The clock was ticking. And ticking fast. Some fifteen minutes later, Drew confirmed to Gerry that it was bad news from his Sports Editor, who was already aware that the photograph was being touted around most of the tabloid newspapers, being offered to the highest bidder.

Gerry decided that there was no more he could do. A dispiriting feeling of 'Que sera' came over him.

As he went over to the practice courts, Gerry decided, that it might be preferable to lie to Linda, or at least mislead her. He even tried to further reassure himself, as he attempted to ease his conscience a touch, that there was no option but ensure her mind was relocated solely to a tennis agenda.

'Linz, it's all okay. It was, after all, a childish prank. The police have interviewed the ball girl and she's admitted it,' lied Gerry, trying to sound genuinely relieved and convincing that the saga was at an end.

'What a stupid young girl. How could she ever have imagined she would get away with it?' shrugged Linda.

'I know. But forget about her and just concentrate on playing well this afternoon. Let's just put it all behind us now,' pleaded Gerry. 'The match against Zheng is all that matters right now.'

'Amen,' sniffed Frank.

Much as Linda tried, she simply could not find her 'A' game – achieving her 'B' or 'C' game seemed at certain times even to be a struggle. This was the worst she had played all tournament and she was simply not causing any serious problem for Na Zheng on court, with what amounted to a wholly uninspired performance.

The traumatic events over the past 24 to 48 hours, it appeared, had finally caught up with Linda and some signs of mental exhaustion were evident. Her physical condition, too, was perhaps not helped by the lack of proper sleep the previous night, as well as the searing New York late summer heat on court doing little to make her feel nor look comfortable. Certainly her body language, Frank noted, was not what he wanted to see.

Gerry watched the match in virtual silence, without having any notable verbal exchange with Frank sat beside him. Even Drew back at the hospital was wishing to himself that in some perverse way Linda would lose so that they could all pack their bags and get the hell out of New York City. He was finding it impossible to put any positive slant on being confined to a hospital bed, without access to any alcohol, whilst Linda was almost certainly hours away from a media frenzy and being accused of behaving inappropriately with a twelve year old.

For the record, Linda was beaten 6-1, 6-3 and her highly eventful US Open was at an end.

Or, so she thought.

*   *   *   *   *

A cab had been called to take all three of them to the airport in forty-five minutes time. Whilst Linda waited in the hotel lobby area having a coffee by herself to kill some time, Gerry was helping Drew pack his bags, having discharged himself prematurely from hospital earlier that morning.

'You're Linda McKean, aren't you?' murmured a man in a lilting Welsh voice as he sat down on the large sofa beside Linda.

'Yes,' said Linda. For a split second wondered if she should follow that up by asking if he had come to blackmail her. But thought better of it.

'Sorry, I'm Neil Patterson from *The Sun* newspaper. Have you seen this? I was wondering if you cared to make any comment?'

Linda could not believe her own eyes.

This Neil Patterson person had just shown her the back page of *The Sun* which had Linda congratulating Na Zheng at the end of her match the previous day and then an adjoining photograph of her kissing *that* ball girl, with the bold article heading:-

ALLEGED SEX WITH MINOR – KNOCKED OUT OF MAJOR

The picture of Linda shaking hands with Miss Zheng had the heading:-

KNOCKED OUT OF MAJOR

The caption kissing the ball girl:-

ALLEGED SEX WITH MINOR

Linda stared long and hard at the newspaper, before eventually furiously responding to Patterson, 'No! I have no fucking comment to make whatsoever. Now, just fuck off.'

Did I just swear? Hell's teeth, this is really getting to me now.

Sure, Linda was perhaps half-expecting some negative backlash from the British press in particular, but what was printed in *The Sun* was as damaging as she could have ever imagined it being.

When Gerry and Drew arrived down in the hotel reception area about ten minutes later she was still visibly shaking.

Gerry retrieved the copy of the newspaper conspicuously hanging half-way out of the adjacent waste bin into which Linda had thrown it.

'Excuse me Gerry,' said Linda. 'Thought you promised this had all been sorted?'

'W.. e.. l.. l,' stuttered Gerry, 'I kinda thought it had.'

'What kinda shit talk is that?' interrupted Drew.

'Sorry, Linda. I did what I thought was for the best. For you. There was no way there could have been a conclusion one way or the other before your match, so I thought it best you went out there on court believing it was all a childish prank and the matter was finished with. Honest, I *did* speak to Brigadier Jones and he said to forget about it.'

'What do you want to do now, Linz?' asked Drew, shaking his head in Gerry's direction in mock disbelief at Gerry's lamentable display of decision making and poor judgement.

'Drew, we'll go tell the cops that it ain't true of course and we must assist them in anyway we can to catch the perpetrator of this crime. It *is* a crime you know! Blackmail *is* a crime I hope in this country too, isn't it? Not reporting it will make my situation even worse once those nasty sods from the press start digging deeper.'

'But, we'll miss our flight back to London,' Gerry reminded them.

'To hell with that. I want this sorted before it escalates out of all control,' objected Linda, over-ruling Gerry's trivial reasoning.

All three of them then headed off to hail a cab to the nearest police station.

The desk sergeant acknowledged straight away that he recognised Linda and was extremely helpful and sympathetic, seemingly appreciating the embarrassing predicament she was in. He presumably also knew only too well what twelve-year-old New Yorkers were capable of getting involved in, and that perhaps also explained the constant look of disgusted decency he expressed throughout note-taking and conversation, particularly with Linda.

Much to Gerry, Linda and Drew's surprise the ball girl was picked up and being interviewed back at the police station within the hour. But that was not the only development.

The ball girl maintained that she, too, had been blackmailed and used against her will by others to perform this stunt on Linda. It was an elaborate and less than convincing tale that the girl was spinning, but one the police ultimately would need time to investigate before deciding if any further action could, or should, be taken.

It was now apparent that nothing was going to be achieved by Linda, Drew and Gerry staying in New York one minute longer, and in any event the damage to Linda's reputation had already been done. A plan of action was unlikely to be successful through litigation against a twelve-year-old hard-nosed New York minor.

Only a specialist public relations or media expert would likely get Linda out of this public embarrassment unscathed. Or, by pleading mitigating circumstances.

'I can't wait to get back home,' Linda sighed as she turned towards Gerry and Drew on boarding the *Virgin Atlantic* aeroplane at La Guardia International Airport.

However, on arriving back at London Heathrow it was a case of out of the frying pan and into the fire as all three of them could hardly believe the posse of photographers and newspaper hacks awaiting them. It was a scrum to get past.

All three of them appeared shaken up by the experience of this unwanted reception committee of reporters and photographers, but Linda, in particular, was distraught. This, surely, was indeed another living nightmare for her.

First, the kidnapping in London. Now, being accused of having a relationship in New York with a minor.

The questions just kept getting hurled at Linda :-

'Did you have sex with a twelve-year-old?'

'Are you a lesbian?'

'Can you explain what happened?'

'Were you being blackmailed?'

'Why didn't you report it to the police?'

'Are you going to sue *The Sun*?'

It was bedlam. Sheer bedlam. All Linda could shout back in her defence as she tried to jog and reach the exit signs as quickly as possible was, 'I've done nothing wrong. I have nothing further to say.'

'Shit. That was an effing nightmare,' snarled Drew as they all sat uncomfortably in the taxi on the drive into Central London from Heathrow Airport, 'but there is *one* positive to come out of this, you know?'

'Oh yeah?' asked Linda, in disbelief.

'Yeah. Two can play at this game. You, too, can offer your side of the story to the press. And, at least there is the small consolation that your version will be the truth, the whole truth and nothing but the truth - eh?'

'Yeah,' agreed Gerry. 'Eh, guys, I like the sound of that. I really do. Damage limitation, at the very least.'

'I'll have a word with my editor at the first opportunity.'

Drew managed to speak with his editor first thing the following morning. But it was not initially the word or support he had been expecting. Drew's editor wanted to run the story as an exclusive, which Drew did not have a problem with. What Drew did have a problem with was his editor also wanted any article to be as juicy and as interesting and as controversial as was possible, for which he was more than prepared to pay Linda handsomely for the rights to exclusivity in respect of such private and personal revelations. Drew protested that all Linda wanted was the truth to be printed and her name publicly cleared, particularly for the alleged under-age sex angle and for that she was happy to not receive a single penny or, at least, have any fee paid to a children's charity. He suggested Great Ormond Street Hospital.

So, Drew and his editor ended up compromising and a more serious and less sensationalist story went to the printers. Pictures of Linda showed her looking thoughtful, if not slightly distraught, rather than sexy and glamorous, and there was a picture and a statement attributed to the ball girl denying that Linda had been guilty of any wrong doing.

Linda was able to read the following day just how successful Drew had actually been, as a two-page spread in the *Daily Mail* exonerated Linda vis-à-vis the New York ball girl farce and the article was all positive publicity from start to finish. Unfortunately, she started reading some of the other newspapers and they appeared to have every conceivable sexy historic picture ever taken of her from every angle. The extremely limited lineage and old quotes attributed to Linda were taken entirely out of context and portrayed her as one seedy and controversial character.

'No smoke without fire,' it generally seemed to read in most newspapers.

Linda began to wonder whatever was the point of agreeing to an exclusive story when most other newspapers just printed whatever it was that took their fancy, regardless of whether it was accurate or not. As long as it sold copies, that was all that was at stake.

Hardly a day passed by over the ensuing few weeks that did not result in Linda being reminded in some form or another of the events that had taken place in New York, in the guise of a television interview, newspaper article or magazine feature. Reporters and photographers persistently harassed her. If not the media, it would be someone from the general public trying to be kind and thoughtful by saying a few encouraging words whenever and wherever she happened to be. Linda found it impossible to accept any words from anyone she had never previously met as being something she encouraged, or respected, so it was all quite pathetic and futile.

The one consolation was that the WTA Tour was moving on to Asia, which was an area of the world fairly distant from the British media circus as far as television, radio, and press coverage went. Linda wondered if a couple of months playing on the hard courts of Bali, Jakarta, Beijing, Seoul and Manila would have the benefit of effectively ensuring the British press would quietly forget all about their apparent obsession with her and a certain New York ball girl.

It was to be a huge relief, almost like being on holiday, when she arrived in Jakarta. It was like a throw-back in time. No British press, and no interest from elsewhere being shown in her. She was able to concentrate, once again, on her tennis. And her tennis benefited accordingly.

Although Linda failed to win any of the tournaments she entered on the Asian Tour, she played well enough to reach two finals. She narrowly lost in both, but did not have a single major disappointing tournament. As a consequence her world ranking rose to No. 23, the best it had been for quite some considerable time.

*　　*　　*　　*　　*

It was now time to decide whether or not to return home to Scotland for a Christmas break. Linda was in two minds whether or not this was a smart idea.

On one hand she was simply looking forward to being home for Christmas, but at the same time she wondered if the British press were lying in wait to regurgitate all the under-age sex allegations and insinuations again.

Her own worst fears were soon realised after she booked into a small hotel room in the West Kensington area of London following a long flight from Seoul via Cairo to London Heathrow.

No sooner had she half unpacked her suitcase when she received a call from the *Daily Express* newspaper requesting an interview.

The following day there was a procession of various journalists and others trying to invade her privacy.

Some Christmas this is going to be, she thought.

For that very evening Linda had prearranged to meet up with Drew prior to her making an appearance live on the BBC's *Sports Personality of the Year* award show. Linda was wondering why she had ever agreed to go on this programme; it was not as if she had really achieved anything throughout the year and was certainly not going to be nominated for any award, let alone be presented with winning one. Then she remembered being pleaded with by Sue Barker back in the summertime at Wimbledon to do so on the pretext that Ms Barker always felt passionate that tennis, woman's tennis in particular, never got the promotion or publicity she felt it needed. Especially once the annual Wimbledon fortnight was concluded.

Drew had to fight his way through a throng of bodies on the hotel porch. When he and Linda exited the hotel to enter the BBC courtesy limousine to transport them to the BBC conference centre, it was obvious that the waiting twenty to thirty journalists and photographers still believed there was indeed a story to be told regarding Linda - even if the absurd under-age sex allegations had been publicly refuted and, moreover, proven to be false.

The scale of this unexpected and overwhelming invasion of her privacy completely blew Linda's mind, just as it had on returning to Heathrow from New York those few months before. It unnerved her to such an extent that immediately once through the scrum of photographers into the limousine, all she then truly wanted to do was get as far away from London as quickly as was humanly possible.

Drew tried hard to persuade her otherwise and suggested they stop off en-route for a drink and to chat things through. This they did. They certainly did.

Several large vodkas were drunk in record time for Linda, as well as her helping herself to a small quantity of Drew's cocaine supply.

Linda never drank vodka, never mind five or six large measured glasses in less than forty-five minutes. She had never snorted cocaine before, either. Would this sudden behavioural change of partaking of a vodka and coke mix help her endure the boredom of being a member of the audience of this rather predictable TV show of nearly three hours in length? Would it generally alleviate the sudden bout of depression she was suffering from, courtesy of the British press?

'Can I just say, ladies and gentlemen, that it has not been the most successful year for British tennis. However, the one bright spark was Linda McKean's brilliant performances in New York a few months back at the US Open. Absolutely treeeemendous stuff,' offered Sue Barker in her ultra enthusiastic style. 'And I'm pleased to say Linda is with us here tonight. Hello, Linda, nice to see you again.'

'Nay probs at awe,' replied Linda in an uncharacteristic put-on heavy duty Scottish accent.

'It's been quite a good year for you, Linda, hasn't it?'

'Has it?' snapped Linda defensively. 'What's been good about it then?'

'Well, *hum, er...*' stuttered Barker, 'like I said, your performance in New York for one?'

'Are you taking the piss?' hissed Linda. As she said this then the audience both in person and on television could see Barker's complexion go an even deeper shade of reddish-brown than normal.

The cameras immediately switched away to the other side of the studio area to a more flustered looking than usual Gary Lineker whose professional life, it was rumoured, always required either an auto-cue or, at the very least, a prepared script.

Linda's brief performance on the show, of course, only re-kindled the general press interest in her, to such an extent that she seriously thought of taking a few weeks break over Christmas on some deserted island where she could be left alone in peace.

If only that were possible. Of course, she knew full well it was not, and she also knew that wherever she tried to escape to, then the British press, if they felt so inclined, usually had ways and means of locating her in no time at all.

On the return journey to Kensington, Drew reminded her that she had agreed to be his escort the following evening at the plush Grosvenor House in London's Park Lane where the annual dinner, dance and awards ceremony for journalists was being held.

'Into the lions' den, eh?' mocked Linda.

'Yes, I guess it will be, hen. But I'm afraid you're down on the guest list with me on the seating placement. So, for you now not to turn up will only be playing into the media's hands. If you don't show up it will be seen as a weakness on your part. It'll only demonstrate that you are influenced by what they say and print about you. Don't give them that satisfaction. Anyway, I need to be there. In fact, I want to be there. I'm up for a nomination in one of the categories and that's the first time that's happened to me in my long journalistic career.'

'Would you *really* like me to be there, Drew?'

'I most certainly would, ma dear. It would be an absolute honour to have you sat beside me. Nothing would give me more pleasure.'

'And what will all your work colleagues think?'

'I don't give a stuff what they think. Neither should you.'

The highly rated and popular television personality Jonathan Ross was the award's presenter that evening. He tried to be true to his usual form by introducing some stand-up comedy repertoire to make traditionally staid individual award ceremonies interesting and entertaining for the majority of the 1,200 guests present.

'And now we come to a very special award for this evening and that is in recognition for twenty-five long years dedicated to sports journalism, especially tennis, a game I myself particularly enjoy playing and watching, but Drew, I believe, sees it in a different light to me, whether it be through alcohol abuse or drug abuse or helping to sort out seedy incidents of under-age sexual relationships. Frankly, I am in complete awe of his versatility and talent. Would you please acknowledge the undoubted achievements of that mad, wacky, Scotsman. It's the one, the only Drew Mac Taggart. Sorry, Drew Taggart, ladies and gentlemen, Mr Drew Taggart.'

It seemed that Mr Ross was one of very few in the huge ballroom who thought this was in the slightest bit funny, judging by the embarrassingly slow and sporadic show of muffled hand clapping, mixed with loud murmurs vibrating around the 120 dining tables.

That seemed to be a cue for Drew. 'Time to go sunshine,' he said, then turned to the guests at his table to apologise for a sudden and rapid departure. And whilst making his way briskly to the exit he turned round and shouted back up to the main stage area in his best, his loudest, his most angry put-on Glaswegian accent, 'Fuck you, pal - ya big sassenach poofter.'

This short act of defiance probably made Drew feel about ten feet tall and much prouder of himself than he would have felt even on receiving the long-serving journalistic award.

It was likely only to be a momentary joint of pleasure. And one he would regret in the morning when it was inevitable that even his friends and work colleagues would incessantly take the proverbial piss out of him for being so stupid as to publicly over-react in front of so many distinguished media dignitaries.

It was even more inevitable that the Executive Board at the *Daily Mail* would have something to say to Drew, and not something he would enjoy hearing.

Perhaps, most important of all, this was just another sort of incident that would do Linda no favours whatsoever, and would only inflame an already increasingly hostile press against her.

Christmas could not come and pass quickly enough for Linda. Then, at least, straight after Christmas six continuous weeks in New Zealand and Australia on the other side of the globe seemed a joyous prospect.

She, quite literally, could not wait for the next Gland Slam event down in sunny Melbourne, which somehow seemed light years away from the dark, wet, cold and miserable atmosphere in the United Kingdom pre-Christmas.

And Linda was not even thinking of the weather.

'Game, set and match to Miss McKean 6-1, 6-1,' confirmed the umpire to a relatively small crowd of about 800 on an outside court and which seemed comprised mainly of English and Scottish expatriates, judging by the periodic display and waving of the many St Andrew's flags and the odd Union flag.

Linda had easily won her opening round match of the Australian Open.

Frank confirmed he could now see tangible evidence that Linda was concentrating better on her match tactics and her consistency levels were almost something to no longer worry about. Nonetheless, there was some general mounting concern over Linda's demeanour off-court.

This behavioural change manifested itself in conversation. Linda seemed guarded, almost laboured in her verbal exchanges with everyone, including Frank, but particularly with the press, whereas before there had been nobody more approachable and easy to talk to than Linda around the Tour. Where had the sunny disposition disappeared to?

'Well played, Linda,' gushed Frank.

'Ta.'

'You seem a bit subdued today, pet.'

'Am I? Sorry, don't mean to give that impression.'

'There's no way either Drew or Gerry is joining us here then?'

'No, none whatsoever,' sighed Linda.

Frank mentioned that he was intrigued to see how she performed in a major event without any distractions from Gerry and Drew. He quickly qualified that by blatantly trying to emphasise that he liked and trusted them both and accepted their intentions towards Linda were completely genuine, however, he wondered if they were sometimes an unnecessary and unwanted distraction.

'Ah well, I'm sure they are with you in spirit and watching every match on the Sky channel back home,' Frank reassured her.

'Yeah, suppose so.'

Whilst on a well earned break after a full hour's session in the gym, Linda remembered that she had forgotten to ask Frank if he had experienced any problems with the security gate attendants whilst getting into Flinders Park earlier that morning.

'No more than the usual frisking, that's all. Why do you ask?'

'Ah, it's probably nowt, but it took two white guards fully ten minutes rifling through my bags and everything. Thought for one minute they were going to strip search me!'

'Why'd you make that comment about them being white, out of interest?' enquired Frank with a slight frown showing up on his forehead.

'Did I? Sorry - must have said it without thinking. Or, maybe I'm being overly suspicious, but as they were searching through my stuff someone nearby shouted out "fucking pommie nigger" which kind of took my breath away momentarily.'

'You're not being a tad paranoid, pet?'

Paranoia? Linda would start to worry now about being paranoid.

'Did the security guards actually say anything to you?' asked Frank.

'No. That's the more annoying part – they just laughed.'

'Probably some juvenile Aussie sense of humour.'

'Possibly,' conceded Linda, sounding less than convinced.

'Do you know yet who we've got in the next round?' Frank asked.

'No. Do you?'

'Yip, it's Helen Ritchie,' confirmed Frank. 'Nice and easy one then.'

'Oh yeah? She's local. Do you know if we are on one of the main courts?'

'Don't know, pet, but I suspect so. It'll be a fantastic atmosphere. You prefer that, yes?'

'I guess I do, as long as it's not late at night and half packed with jeering half-sozzled Aussies,' smirked Linda. 'It often amuses me to see the number of fans sitting in the stands swigging their 'tinnies'. You never see that at Wimbledon or Queens Club, do you?'

The following day Linda happened to be paying partial attention to the television in her hotel room as she pottered about to pass away some spare time. The main news story of the day particularly caught her attention as it showed some graphic footage of protestors rioting in the centre of Canberra. It seemed, to Linda more than a bit surprising as it was being reported as being solely a result of racial tensions that had slowly but surely become an issue in Australian society, with many longstanding Australian citizens having serious reservations about the government's current immigration policy, and the consequential effect it was starting to have on crime, unemployment and general living standards.

The reason Linda thought this to be surprising was she had always been hugely impressed from previous visits to Australia by just how friendly, cosmopolitan and carefree a people they generally appeared - a multi-cultural, integrated society fully at ease with itself. *Perhaps the mood of the nation is changing somewhat?*

It prompted Linda to recall the incident earlier that day with the security guard and the abusive and probably racist comment that she suspected was for her benefit.

An hour or so later, Linda turned up for her preceding match practice session with Frank and to work on a strategy for the game scheduled for the following day with Helen Ritchie.

A small group of people behind the netting on the practice court seemed to be showing an oblique interest in them. Without making a particular issue of it, Linda soon felt compelled to find herself within a few yards and staring directly at the crowd, perhaps eight or nine in total. She smiled deliberately to gauge a reaction. There was not one. All just looked back with a cold, emotionless demeanour, save for their steely-eyed stares; most certainly there were no responding smiles. Needless to say, this was definitely not the reaction Linda was hoping for, and it unnerved her more than a little.

Maybe they're all enthusiastic and loyal supporters of Helen Ritchie? Linda unconvincingly tried to justify their strange behaviour.

The group stayed around to continue to watch Linda and Frank go through their routine knock-up-cum-practice-cum-training session.

Linda could not help herself by eventually mentioning the group to Frank.

'I'll quietly have a word shall I?' offered Frank.

'Would you mind? Cheers, Frankie.'

Frank sauntered over in the general direction of the group picking up some stray tennis balls on the way, as if trying hard to make his purpose seem unintentional.

'Are you trying to find some weaknesses in Linda's game for Helen then?' asked Frank in a jovial, light-hearted manner.

'Why are you working with a dyke of a nigger?' countered an aggressive young man in a broad Aussie accent.

There was a silence. Frank clearly struggled to find a suitable reply, and before he did so the abuse continued. 'And she's a Pom as well, fuck me, cobber, the golliwog ain't got much going for her, eh?'

Frank did not engage in any further conversation with these foul-mouthed youths as presumably it would take up too much time away from Linda and might prompt Linda to come over, which he probably assessed was the last thing that she should do.

Linda was sitting by a court-side seat taking in some more liquid and on Frank's return instantly asked what the small crowd were about.

'Absolutely nothing,' Frank assured her. 'They are just enthusiastic tennis fans and, like you say, probably fans of Helen Ritchie, being local lads. Right, that's enough practice for today. Let's get you back to the hotel for some rest. We'll talk about tactics for the match tomorrow over a light lunch.'

'I think the only way Ritchie can beat you tomorrow, Linda, is if she gets so pumped up by the home crowd and that helps raise her game to a level that she has not achieved before. But, remember, Linda, that scenario is still possible and you have to be prepared for that eventuality,' warned Frank.

'Okay, I will.'

'Will what?' snapped Frank.

'Be prepared,' snapped Linda back, believing it was a rather trite comment for Frank to make. *Of course I'll be prepared – I'm a professional.*

'How exactly, will you be prepared?' enquired Frank.

'Eeerrrrrr, okay, coach, please remind me,' said Linda, trying to make light of the conversation and realising she might have been too judgmental, too quickly.

'Come on, Linda. Concentrate. *Please!* You might, as a last resort, have to consider a bit of gamesmanship. To break up her concentration. Disrupt her rhythm, too.'

'I hear what you say, Frank, but you should know me well enough by now that I don't like deliberate gamesmanship of any sort.'

'Okay then – what do you propose to do to counteract if she hits a purple patch, feeding directly off the adrenaline from a highly-charged, partisan crowd? And get her to revert to her normal level of play?'

'Okay,' conceded Linda. 'I take your point. What'd you suggest then?'

'Well, you could try the predictable and dispute some line calls, I suppose. That might work and break her concentration. And momentum.'

'Or, it'll just encourage her even more and make her think she's got me well rattled,' said Linda, with a shrug of her shoulders.

'Perhaps. Maybe you say something mildly derogatory to her, then? Wind her up maybe? She strikes me as the fiery type. After all, she does have red hair. Anyway, it's just a thought for tomorrow or whenever. You know what, Linda, you're just far too nice.' Frank shook his head, laughing.

The following day the weather was unusually overcast for the time of year and it looked like rain, or more likely a thunderstorm, was not too far away. Linda got the same treatment again from the security guards on entry to Flinders Park. It was now most definitely starting to niggle her.

The match with Helen Ritchie was scheduled for the Rod Laver arena and programmed to be the third match on that court.

After a warm-up session with Frank, Linda agreed to give a short interview with ABC, the regional television network. She had not quite realised just how popular Helen Ritchie was in New South Wales. In fact, she was a bit of celebrity, as she was currently the girlfriend of Harry Matheson, the famous Hollywood actor, who was also Australian-born, again a fact Linda was unaware of until the television interviewer mentioned it.

Play began about six that evening in front of a jam-packed Rod Laver arena and Linda was impressed with just how vocal the crowd was.

She was even more impressed to see Kylie Monogue sitting in the visitors' VIP Box, beside Harry Matheson as it so happened. Despite Linda's personal adulation for the mega star, the attraction soon became a distraction as Kylie started to make it pretty obvious with over-the-top enthusiastic participation that she wanted Ritchie to win the match. This also seemed to not go unnoticed with the majority of the spectators. It was quite a tidal-wave of noise and, although initially Linda appreciated such a raucous atmosphere, it soon bordered on what she perceived as being irritatingly hostile. Although she was disappointed at the general reaction that Ms Monogue's presence had created, she was not altogether surprised given the level of hero worship Kylie enjoyed, especially in Australia where her status was that of a 'national treasure'.

If only that had been all Linda had to contend with, outside of the actual playing of the game, but it was not to be. Linda noticed a couple of unpleasant and crude hand-written small placards occasionally going up making derogatory comments. One placard displayed the word 'pom', with another nearby placard 'nigger' and a third in the same row, 'dyke'.

Why me? Why the hell me? Linda wrestled with her emotions. Unpleasant memories of New York came flooding back. *Those childish bigots and hecklers can shove it where the sun don't shine. Must remain strong.* Linda was arguably just about a strong enough character to be able dismiss this from her mind as she focused that bit deeper and told herself to refuse to look in the direction of the placards again. But, to compound matters, as the general crowd noise levels abated, then there was the isolated shout just at the very point when Linda was about to serve. Linda never quite understood precisely what the shout was saying exactly, however deduced enough from the timing and tone to be sure they were not words of encouragement. The tone particularly sounded rather threatening. It seemed to her that nearly every point, especially after any rally, that Helen Ritchie won was acknowledged like Ritchie had just won the final point to become a Slam champion. Whereas Linda's were greeted with almost silence, not even some begrudged applause – no great surprise in that, except, Linda always expected some sporadic vocal support, albeit disproportionate, if only from the ex-pat community. But it was not in evidence that evening.

Linda could not believe the standard that Ritchie was performing to. Ritchie had managed to get the crowd into a state of extreme frenzy and expectation with her exciting and assertive nothing to lose shot making. Helen Ritchie won the first set 6-3 but, in truth, the margin of difference between their respective performances was greater than the score line actually suggested. Linda was heading for an unexpected defeat unless she did something dramatic. Matters then went from bad to worse when Helen Ritchie raced into a 4-1 lead in the second set, the one consolation being that it was only one service break. Notwithstanding that fact, Linda was facing defeat in the next ten minutes or so unless there was to be a major turnaround. Without giving the matter a great deal of forethought, Linda complained to the umpire about the unpleasant and distracting placards which she felt were a nuisance and unsettling, and requested to have them removed, along with the owners. This was perhaps the last opportunity to exercise her growing frustration and annoyance at these individuals. The umpire duly phoned through to the tournament referee. The ensuing protracted interlude caused a reaction that Linda had not expected, let alone planned for. This delay inevitably got Ms Ritchie's attention, and equally the crowd's attention, who were now beginning to whistle and jeer and slow hand-clap their disapproval to the delay. They probably, not unreasonably, suspected whatever Linda was doing - she was complaining simply for the sake of it, in a feeble and pathetic last minute attempt at gamesmanship.

Certainly Ms Ritchie was transparently irritated by the delay, possibly frustrated by not knowing what precisely was going on, as she came storming over to join Linda by the umpire's chair.

'What the hell is going on here?'

Linda, displeased by Ritchie's tone of voice, retorted, 'None of your beeswax,' which, more than likely, did little for Ritchie's escalating bad temper.

'Are you trying hard to be a bad loser or does it come naturally?' hissed Ritchie.

'No, but I hate losing to a bigot with bigoted supporters.'

'What do'ya say? Take that back, you black cow.'

'What, a nigger and a dyke, do you mean?'

'Well, if the cap fits.'

'Ms McKean, I can tell you that a steward will have the offending placards removed,' the umpire confirmed.

'Thanks,' acknowledged Linda without sounding at all grateful.

'God, you're a sore loser. Typical whinging pom,' shouted Ritchie, before walking back to the service line whilst at the same time gesturing and encouraging with the use of her arms to the spectators to show their continued appreciation and support for her. It was hardly necessary as the atmosphere was already electric helped in no small part by the whooping and hollering from the partisan crowd, and now with the added spice of considerable animosity developing between the two players themselves.

Linda narrowly won the next two games, much to the howling disapproval of the vast majority of the crowd. They were behaving more like a raucous Aussie Rules Football crowd rather than a typical tennis one.

The players changed ends at 4-3, and as Linda and Ms Ritchie sat down in their respective chairs at this changeover the jet black sky above produced torrential rain within literally seconds.

In the players' locker room Helen Ritchie made it known to Linda that she was still far from happy, believing Linda had falsely and maliciously accused her of being a racist.

'But you are, and so are your blinking anti-social and unsporting supporters,' insisted Linda.

'Take that back!' fumed Ritchie.

'Why should I? It's true, isn't it?' Linda spat, not quite believing how angry and vindictive she had become all of a sudden. Was Dr Keegan's hypnosis having far too strong an effect on her losing mentality?

'Just because I haven't got a boy friend like Harry Matheson doesn't mean every black girl on the tennis court is a dyke,' snarled Linda. 'Do you have to give him a blow job every night to ensure you keep him as a boyfriend?'

At which point Helen Ritchie, within less than the next four seconds, had hurled one of her many tennis rackets at Linda, shouting, 'You fucking pommie bitch!' as she did so.

Also, in doing so, Ritchie was naïve and foolhardy, to say the least, especially in an area that contained many casual observers and witnesses. It was, therefore, inevitable that the incident soon came to the attention of tournament officials who were compelled to take immediate disciplinary action for such a violent act.

Helen Ritchie maintained later to the tournament officials that she had not meant to hit Linda on the head, nor cause her any physical harm. But, by then, her protestations were all in vain. Her act of temper had left Linda needing medical attention and also requiring two stitches to a nasty-looking cut on the side of her forehead.

As a consequence, Ms Ritchie was automatically disqualified from the tournament, even though Linda did half-heartedly try and have the match completed by requesting Ritchie's disqualification be overturned.

This all did little to endear Linda to the local populous. It was a main news headline on all the television networks, and the sports sections of the newspapers. Additionally, it was hyped up out of proportion in the local media as Linda having deliberately manufactured the incident for her own benefit, regardless of how strongly she protested her innocence by showing the evidence of her injury or making it known her desire for Ms Ritchie not to be disqualified.

After all the shenanigans surrounding New York, this was absolutely the last thing Linda wanted in the proceeding Grand Slam event. It only offered yet another excuse for the media to hound and persecute her. This time it was not so much the English press, although they too were lapping this incident up, but the Australian press who were, it seemed, determined to give Linda as much negative coverage as possible.

The phrase Linda had used in the heat of the moment with Helen Ritchie by calling her a white whore was haunting her particularly as she could not deny having said it. Matters were compounded by Linda receiving a Court Summons from Harry Matheson the following morning in respect of alleged defamatory and slanderous remarks she had made to Ritchie about her performing a daily oral sex act on Matheson.

Linda was beginning to wonder if trouble followed her. How was she going to get out this particular predicament? She truly did not have the faintest. Neither did Frank.

When Linda telephoned both Gerry and Drew back in the UK, they could only suggest she go see a local lawyer for professional advice.

Linda did go and see a local lawyer. Fortunately it turned out, resultant from rapid email exchange between the respective solicitors, that all Harry Matheson wanted on careful further considered reflection, as did Helen Ritchie, was a full and unambiguous public apology. Linda was more than happy to oblige with this request.

With some trepidation, immediately after the meeting with her lawyer, Linda contacted Helen

Ritchie by telephone to apologise to her with all the sincere fervour that she could muster.

Much to Linda's surprise, the reception she received from Ms Ritchie was not the anticipated one. Helen Ritchie was, in fact, equally contrite. It transpired Helen had no prior knowledge of the racial abuse that Linda felt she was being subjected to, especially immediately before their match with the security guards, and then during the match itself with the spectator placards. Helen wanted no association whatsoever with racism and it was made clear by her that neither did Harry Matheson.

Linda found Helen continuously attempting to reassure her that any racism was strictly a local issue resultant from high unemployment. And that the local inhabitants in the area were venting their anger and disapproval to an unpopular government policy on immigration controls, blamed by many for the unacceptable unemployment levels in the region. Furthermore, Helen was at pains to make it known she was convinced these racists were limited to a few lunatic activists only looking for any and every opportunity to vent their frustration and anger. They were not tennis fans. Finally, how important it was for Linda to believe that Helen was being genuine and sincere whilst expressing these sentiments.

Helen suggested a press conference to clear the air in public and one was hastily convened by Harry Matheson's lawyer for later that very day.

Hardly a word was spoken by Linda during the ten minute or so staged session before the television cameras and press.

Helen, on the other hand, went to great verbal lengths to exonerate Linda entirely and explain that Linda was the one who had suffered mentally and physically from the whole incident. Helen articulated quite convincingly that she had only herself to blame for being disqualified from the tournament and she fervently wished that the Aussie public would enthusiastically support Linda. Helen's final comment was that she sincerely hoped that Linda would go on to win the Australian Open after stressing, yet again, that she and Harry Matheson abhorred the antics of a limited number of extremists who she was confident would be dealt with by the police.

Helen and Linda kissed each other on the cheeks and then hugged one another in what appeared a mutual show of genuine affection and reconciliation.

It was a highly convincing performance by Helen Ritchie, and one that seemed to convince most, if not all, of the many sceptics assembled in the Press Room.

* * * * *

'How's the head, Linda?' enquired Frank.

'Still thumping like crazy,' groaned Linda. 'I'll live. It was only a couple of stitches required. Just don't feel up to a full practice session today.'

'Okay - I understand, let's do the bare minimum. Let's just hit a few balls for say half-an-hour and loosen up the muscles and then have the rest of the day away from tennis, eh? Anything you fancy doing particularly?'

'I've been given this address by an uncle of mine who suggested I might like to pay a visit to a cousin that I've never met before. She lives somewhere called Warrnambool. Apparently it's only a couple of hours or so drive out of town along the coast. Sounds quite an appealing diversion away from the media circus here. I was thinking of hiring an open-top car. Drive along the coast and see if it helps my throbbing headache and reduces the swelling on my forehead a little,' drawled Linda.

'Want any company?'

'No offence, Frank, but probably best I go alone. Anyway, you'd only be bored with any family reunion talking about distant relatives that probably mean little to me, so it'd surely bore the pants off you.'

Linda was rather enjoying the lingering, dallying drive along the beautiful coastal road between Melbourne and Adelaide. It was rather invigorating driving with an open-top car and she felt she could almost be completely relaxed, if it was not for the flashback memories from events of the past few days. Also, not to forget, the stitches in her wounded head were stiffening against the strong coastal breeze with its salty sea air.

Warrnambool, a seaside tourist destination if ever there was one, looked not to dissimilar to her native Troon, probably bigger and for sure the sun shone warmly considerably more often, she suspected.

To say Linda was initially shocked when she eventually met up face-to-face with her cousin would be an understatement. The address, as it so turned out, looked like a monastery and her cousin was in fact a Catholic nun and had taken her religious vow about ten years ago. *Uncle Robert never mentioned anything about that. Nothing whatsoever.* Was Linda in a monastery? A convent? A nunnery? *What, exactly*, she wondered? Not that precise classification mattered.

Her cousin's name was Margaret McDonald, Sister Margaret, and Linda's immediate impression was an extremely favourable one. After the initial awkward moments of self-introduction pleasantries, it became clear to Linda over the next couple of hours that Sister Margaret was an immensely likeable person. She appeared genuinely warm and friendly. She also appeared open and trusting, which was hardly a surprise given her occupation, or more accurately her vocation. Although it was early doors still, what soon became an added delight to Linda was Sister Margaret's sense of humour. Without doubt, Linda also could see that Margaret was strikingly attractive, even without make-up, or with the handicap of her religious robes.

'You must remember to call me Maggie, wont you? I'll be offended if you don't,' insisted Sister Margaret.

'Sure thing, but you'll forgive me if it takes me a wee while to get used to it?' Linda asked, as she and Maggie giggled simultaneously.

The two of them soon built up a rapport that had Linda wondering why she had never made the effort to find out about Sister Margaret before. Within the next couple of hours there was an outward display suggesting they had known each other all their lives. Although, privately, Linda still had a little difficulty coming to terms with this newly found friend-cum-family member being so devoted to religion. Religion had certainly never featured in Linda's life to any degree. Not so far. Whatever - Sister Margaret sure lifted Linda's spirits no end.

As they hugged each other goodbye Sister Margaret hinted to Linda that she must pay another visit before leaving Australia.

'If I'm still in the tournament and staying in Melbourne, then I'd absolutely love to come back here. On second thoughts, I'd like to come even if I lose my match tomorrow,' blurted out Linda in nervous excitement. 'I enjoy being here at the convent. It's so relaxing and different from what I'm used to, and, of course, there's your company too, Maggie.'

'Stay for the weekend if you like. There is always a spare bedroom for welcome visitors to the convent. And you, my dear, are more than welcome.'

'You know what – I might just do that. Yes, Maggie, I just might.'

*   *   *   *   *

Next round of the Australian Open saw Linda drawn against Viktoriya Kutuzova from Russia.

It was to be a relatively uneventful match played on Court No.5 in front of a subdued half-filled arena. What little vocal support existed was spread thinly between a small group of British expats applauding fairly loudly, but without showing any real enthusiasm except when Linda played a particularly good shot; otherwise they remained fairly passive. Maybe Linda was still being a paranoid android, believing that the remaining spectators were quietly wanting to see Ms Kutuzova win with what perhaps was favouritism based on the lesser of two unpopular players. It was not exactly what Linda had hoped for given the recent plea by Helen Ritchie at the press conference, however, she nonetheless felt somewhat relieved to see no signs of any backlash or of any racial elements from what few spectators there were present around Court 5. It was as if many original ticket holders had taken the opportunity to go elsewhere for a lunch or drinks break after the conclusion of the preceding match on that particular court.

Linda won in an uninspired fashion by the score line 6-3, 7-5.

Vikotoriya Kutuzova kissed Linda at the end of the match in the customary Russian style. Given Linda's recent exploits, she felt a little uncomfortable with the gesture, but at the same time also appreciated it was the custom from that part of the old Soviet Union.

Back in the changing rooms, Linda had her usual shower and was generally doing all the normal things she did post-match. She noticed, but tried hard to ignore, the fact that Vikotoriya Kutuzova was giving her long stares without making any comment or conversation. This was embarrassing Linda somewhat and enough for her to break the silence and tension that she felt was building up.

'You okay, Viky?' enquired Linda.

'Ya, I am good. Thank you so much for asking. You are so very kind,' responded Kutuzova.

A few further awkward moments of silence later, Kutuzova continued with just the very kind of remark that Linda had been dreading.

'You have a beautiful body, Leendah. You know, yes?'

'Thanks,' replied Linda, whilst at the same time not wanting to prolong the conversation she wished now she had not initiated and was thinking only of how quickly she could get dressed and packed and leave the changing room.

Kutuzova then went into one of the shower cubicles.

Thank heavens for that. Right, let's get out of here. Fast.

But, no sooner had Kutuzova gone under the shower than she was out again and was standing literally only a couple of yards directly in front of Linda; dripping wet and with only a towel round her waist.

'So sorry, do I embarrass you, Leendah?'

'No,' said Linda, still not looking in Kutuzova's direction, pretending instead to be concentrating on getting dressed and organising her stuff.

'I really like you, Leendah,' Kutuzova added as she concurrently took a couple of steps forward and then put her hand on Linda's cheek as an apparent act of affection.

Absolutely mortified, Linda protested, 'Look Viky – you have got me all wrong. You seem to think because of all the publicity I got at the US Open that I'm a lesbian?'

'Ya, I am sure,' simpered Kutuzova, unabashed.

'No! Watch my lips. I am *not* into women. Okay? Got it? Understand? I'm no rug muncher. I have a boy friend,' Linda lied to a suddenly startled and bemused looking Kutuzova.

Linda went from being mortified to furious and grabbed her bag and stormed out of the changing room.

Linda had dinner with Frank that evening and unsurprisingly it was a rather subdued affair. She was thinking that Frank was probably, in turn, thinking that she had once again unprofessionally got herself into the wrong frame of mind. Did Frank not have some sympathy that situations seemed to conspire against her and were not necessarily of her own making?

'You've got the Italian Antonella Zanetti in the next round, did you know that?' enquired Frank, as if trying to start up a conversation.

'Yeah, I know,' confirmed Linda, without sounding particularly interested.

'What's the matter now, pet? I thought after that visit to see your cousin you'd be in a positive and jolly frame of mind,' moaned Frank.

'Oh yes, I really enjoyed my visit to see my cousin. In fact I'm going to stay with her over the weekend.' Linda considered whether or not to tell Frank that her cousin was a Catholic nun, but then thought better of it.

She simply was not in the mood to have even a half-hearted discussion about it.

'Well, if you win tomorrow then you'll have most of the weekend without any scheduled matches. The last sixteen doesn't begin until Monday. I think a complete break away from tennis for forty-eight hours might actually do you some good, you know, as long as you promise to do some exercise, especially some distance running to keep your fitness and stamina levels up. But let's win the match today first, eh? That's what we are here for after all. Heard from Drew or Gerry?'

'Nope.'

Mrs Zanetti was one of the few tennis players ranked in the Top 50 who was married. Linda knew her quite well as they had played some doubles events together a few seasons back. Linda was jokingly confident at least Zanetti would not try and proposition her either before or after the match, which was a mild consolation factor, given the antics of Kutuzova which were still preying on Linda's current fragile mind.

The match, as Linda fully expected, was played in a friendly and sporting manner, which suited her just fine. What suited her even more was that she was winning the match comfortably, as she was playing particularly relaxed and fine tennis – possibly in no small part due to the pleasant atmosphere on court between the two players. So well was Linda playing it started to resemble an exhibition match and she found herself successfully executing some outrageous shots. And, as she did so, it became obvious that the crowd were responding favourably to this. Any appreciative applause was absolute music to Linda's ears. She was eager to please the crowd at every opportunity, and this only led to an unprofessional error of judgement. She over-stretched herself going for a shot that her chances of making under normal circumstances would have been very unlikely. But, such was her temporary high confidence level that she went for it anyway. It resulted in her straining a thigh muscle. It also resulted in restricting fluent movement even after an injury time-out and the attentions courtside of the physiotherapist.

Linda ultimately managed to hold on and beat Mrs Zenetti 6-2, 7-6, probably only because she held such a commanding lead prior to the injury. Surely few spectators doubted that had it gone to a third set this would have resulted in Linda being knocked out of the Australian Open.

The injury made any proposed weekend retreat to the convent a difficult decision. Frank earnestly proposed it was more sensible to stay in Melbourne and have regular phyiso treatment over the weekend as opposed to Linda's simple, but probably flawed, theory that with some rest the injury would clear itself up. Linda simply could not wait to get herself away from the claustrophobic Melbourne tennis scene to the relative peace and quiet of the Warrnambool convent with her cousin, Sister Margaret.

*   *   *   *   *

'Tell me, what would you really like to do over the weekend?' gushed Maggie to Linda.

'Dinay ken,' replied Linda in a rare show of her faint but proud Scottish brogue.

'You seem a bit troubled underneath the external show of confidence if you don't mind me saying so, Linda.'

'Yes,' she confirmed with a heavy sigh. 'You're dead right. It's been quite a troublesome six months or so for me professionally and personally. But I should be grateful, I guess, as I have my health and enjoy what I do for a living. Though I have this strong belief I am missing out on something in life.'

'Look, no pressure – but there's a day retreat at the convent tomorrow. It may help you understand for yourself what you want out of life. A detox of the soul, if you will,' suggested Sister Margaret.

'Will you be there, Maggie?'

'Sure. Why don't we take a walk around the lovely, peaceful grounds here and you can tell me all about what's been troubling you. Unlikely I will be able to offer any specific advice, but I am more than willing to listen.'

Linda liked the sound of this suggestion, if for no other reason Maggie was the first person she felt she could confide all her troubles to with confidentiality and trust being as assured as assured could be. Sure, Linda respected Drew and Gerry implicitly as friends, but even with them there were certain highly personal issues that Linda did not feel entirely comfortable discussing.

'You know what, Maggie. Here is a tester for you. How about we discuss my sexuality?'

'Not a problem at all,' replied Maggie, positively. 'But, what exactly is the problem?'

'Well, for starters I'm twenty-six and *still* a virgin,' exclaimed Linda in a self-mocking tone of voice. She just knew her anxiety was not that she fancied women in preference to men; she was ultra-confident that was not the case. But, after all the nonsense with the ball-girl and then the Viky Kutuzova come-on incident and the inescapable fact she had never experienced sex full stop, the issue was simply making Linda feel anxious about the whole subject.

'And?' Maggie asked.

'And that is not normal is it - surely?'

'I'm still a virgin, too,' said Maggie with a straight face, before breaking the slight tension by laughing and saying, 'but I guess that is normal for a Catholic nun.'

Linda laughed too, 'Well, I don't know of too many nymphomaniac nuns for sure.'

'Fortunately I don't know of any at all,' howled Maggie.

'Do you want to get married some time and start a family?' enquired Maggie.

'Yes, I think so. Yes, I'm sure I do.'

'Well then, I'm sure it will happen.'

'Yeah, but sex is different from marriage,' Linda replied with a cynical raised eyebrow.

'I must tell you that the Catholic doctrine prohibits any sexual act until two people are joined together in holy matrimony before the eyes of God.'

'I just feel as if I'm missing out on something and it's not helped by the constant jibes I hear or read suggesting I might be a lesbian.'

'Are you?' enquired Maggie.

'That's just it – I simply don't know for absolute hundred per cent certain. I haven't had sex with either sex, if you get my meaning,' complained Linda, in exasperation.

'Yes, I get your drift, Linda, but honestly I don't think it is anything at all to worry about. If people want to label you, then let them.'

'I understand that, Maggie, but it doesn't make it any easier, or any more pleasant to accept, particularly from people who don't even know you properly.'

'Why not? It's their problem, not yours, Linda.'

'Guess so. I just wish they said or wrote the truth about me for once.'

'I can empathise. It can't be pleasant reading lies about yourself in newspapers,' agreed Maggie. 'Have you ever had, what I would term, a real and proper boyfriend?'

'Not really. The rigours of the tennis tour and travelling don't make it that easy.'

'Only a suggestion, Linda, but why not try that first? Get yourself a boyfriend and work on the practical difficulties with you having to travel so much. I'm not saying you should rush out and get yourself a boyfriend tomorrow, but maybe it is something you might think is worth trying over the next few months. Is there any suitable boyfriend material that you know of?'

'None. Most of the guys I know are tennis pros on tour and are so not really my type, except perhaps for the odd one or two. There *is* a French guy I kinda like being around. Thanks anyway, Maggs. It's clearly food for thought. Whilst we're on the subject, who is that gorgeous looking hunk over there?' Linda asked, pointing over to someone wearing only the skimpiest pair of shorts and nothing else and who was digging a hole in the ground with a spade using his bare foot.

'He's one of the gardeners who lives with us and volunteers his services in return for food and accommodation. He's Aboriginal. He's a smashing fella, but he has a slight learning and mental health disorder. He was born with Downs Syndrome. Shall I introduce you to him?'

'No, no, that's all right, don't bother.'

'Oh, come on,' enthused Maggie, 'I'd really like you to meet him.'

Maggie grasped Linda's hand and, slightly against her will, physically marched her over to where the gardener was working.

'Linda, let me introduce Willy Gilhooley to you.'

'Hi, Willy,' said Linda, offering her hand out to which was joined by Willy's firm, but extremely moist handshake.

A polite, but instantly forgettable, conversation between the three of them ensued for a further couple of minutes before Sister Margaret remembered she was due in Church for a prayer service at three o'clock. As Maggie and Linda made tracks back to the Chapel, Sister Margaret walked backwards whilst shouting to Willy, 'Come and join us later for dinner.'

All three met up at the dinner table around seven o'clock that evening.

For Linda it was like a throwback in time, as if from some old, black and white movie she had watched on the television. Hundreds of years originally back in time probably, she thought to herself. The dinner table setting was one of five or six such tables, huge thick rustic tables sitting in an enormous empty vessel of an open courtyard.

How weird is this? What a quite surreal atmosphere.

There must have been sixty to eighty-odd nuns all dressed the exact same, with only a handful of others like Linda and Willy.

Linda took the time to look at all the faces individually around the various tables, without appearing intrusive. This inspection told her nothing specific, except allowed her to absorb the unique atmosphere created by the constant murmur generated by some quietly spoken conversations that were taking place, but always in a low, almost monotonous flat tone of voice.

The food served was simple and Linda was pleasantly surprised by how good it tasted, certainly better than it looked, but thought she had better not enquire as to what it actually was, just in case it made her change her opinion. The many diverse conversations she had over dinner with Maggie and

Willy had been a revelation especially with Willy who, as it turned out, had quite an engaging sense of humour, Linda thought, to somehow complement his well defined and toned body. Linda reasoned with herself that it was impolite to enquire about Willy's disability. Yes, Willy was a little slow on the uptake, Linda could detect that, but he more than made up for that deficiency in other ways. Willy was obviously an interesting character and Linda was most certainly enjoying his company.

Perhaps Sister Margaret could sense it also - confirmed, as if by design, when she asked to be excused early as she had duties to perform at four o'clock the following morning, and suggested it best if she called it a night and duly departed.

Linda and Willy continued chatting away effortlessly to each other, oblivious to what was going on round about them as they were still laughing and joking with each other long after all the other tables were deserted. Linda even felt comfortable raising the recent lesbian related issues, indeed it sparked amusing banter between the two of them. This then, probably wholly unintentionally, prompted Willy to boldly ask Linda the overly personal question, 'Do you enjoy having sex?'

'I don't know,' Linda finally volunteered after recovering from the initial shock of such a direct and personal interrogation, 'as I've never had sex with anyone before.'

'You're kidding me? Thought all sheilas had sex even before leaving school?'

There was, for the first time, a tangible awkward pause in the conversation.

Willy broke the silence by nearly shocking Linda off her seat with, 'Do you want to have sex with me then. Try it out? Find out if you're a lesbian or not?'

This remark-cum-offer completely dumbfounded Linda. Here she was in a Catholic convent being asked to have sex with a volunteer gardener and she found herself not dismissing the offer outright. *Why?* Linda suspected a partial answer to that near rhetorical question may well be that this sex dilemma had been slowly boiling up within her for several years now, and any time she thought about the matter it was as if her head was ready to explode with extreme levels of intrigue.

This was a truly bizarre situation; a real one-off set of unique circumstances, an opportunity even – one, not to be missed, perhaps? Then, she reasoned with herself that she had experienced virtually all the other recognised normal vices such as alcohol and drugs, so why not sex?

'Okay, I'm up for it. Let's just do it,' said Linda, 'quickly, before I change my mind or regain my senses.'

She felt surprisingly excited at how uncharacteristically daring she was being. For her, there was even a thrill attached to getting herself into Willy's room within the convent annexe building without being noticed. Willy's room was just about how Linda imagined it to be: it had a bed, a small bedside table and a single cupboard. That was it. Apart for a picture of the Virgin Mary on the wall; as soon as she stared at it, Willy quickly removed.

Willy was not slow in making the first amorous move. He kissed Linda as if the kiss really meant something special to him.

As for Linda, she was feeling exactly how she felt immediately before an important tennis match. She was trying hard to stay calm and in control and be confident, as well as being excited and full of nervous energy. Stacks of adrenaline rapidly flowed through her body.

Starting by slowly undressing Linda, Willy was soon fondling Linda's ripe nipples, which gave her a sensation that she had never experienced, let alone enjoyed before. Linda started to squirm with ecstasy, but this inevitably was only the beginning of the erotic contact.

Before Linda even realised it, she was naked on the bed and Willy's tongue was wandering lazily through the Scottish like heather of Linda's pubic hair in an attempt to find the cairn of her clitoris. He succeeded. His tongue then proceeded with darting movements in her wetness. Linda was now experiencing a pleasure, a sensation, that she had hitherto never imagined possible. Even simple things like Willy's grunts excited her.

Within no time, Willy's athletic lower body was pumping Linda like a power drill. About one per cent of Linda's subconscious was fighting with what little discipline and self-control she had left, particularly as she fleetingly reminded herself of the sheer absurdity of where she was and what she was doing. One per cent was nothing like enough, though, to be materially altering anything, let alone putting a stop to it.

It was all one-way traffic. The journey was a long one, too: four long hours as it so happened. For much of the ride Willy was just banging away relentlessly with a few pit-stops to engage in some of his more creative manoeuvres which had Linda reeling with absolute desire and pleasure and then ultimate satisfaction.

Willy might be handicapped by having the learning capacity of a ten-year-old, but thanks to practical habits and an encouraged culture from his aboriginal upbringing, he had evidently developed skills and techniques more expected from a James Bond type character, if only in the bedroom. Linda and Willy made passionate love on five separate occasions during what remained of the night.

In the early morning, over breakfast, Linda wondered why it was ever called casual sex as there was nothing casual about what she had experienced a mere few hours earlier as she daydreamed over a bowl of cold porridge and milk. Last night had certainly been a major highlight in her life so far. And equal to the feeling experienced when winning an important tennis match. The buzz was brilliant – no question. Her only minor disappointment was her compelling reluctance to share any of the detail of her excitement with anyone else.

Should I? Shouldn't I? It was a recurring inner thought and a difficult proposition to digest.

Sister Margaret had joined Willy and Linda for breakfast and whilst Maggie was her usual cheerful self, Linda could detect a different side to Willy. He appeared impassive, almost disinterested. *Is he nervous? Embarrassed? Maybe he's simply exhausted? Couldn't blame him if he was.* But Linda was detecting something other than tiredness, though she could not put her finger on it.

Linda, herself, was certainly feeling a little bit embarrassed being in Sister Margaret's presence, given what had happened between her and Willy. However, she soon forgot about that as Maggie had this alluring habit of making everyone relaxed and able to enjoy her warm and welcoming company.

The only important dilemma Linda had to decide seriously upon was whether or not to confess to Sister Margaret what had happened last night. She decided she was far too embarrassed to do so. For now, at any rate.

After breakfast, Linda walked alone and slowly round the glorious convent grounds and was admiring what a terrific gardener Willy must be as the whole area was extremely picturesque and colourful, with a variety of healthy plants and flowers. It was yet another typically cloudless summer's day in South Eastern Australia and Linda was feeling this peace and serenity was a million miles removed from the tennis lifestyle she had endured for so long.

Her mind soon turned to the fact that she would have to drive back to Melbourne later that day as she had a quarter-final match to prepare for tomorrow. What was she going to do about Willy, though?

The experience and the pleasure derived from the previous night's activities was still swimming around in Linda's mind as she drove back to Melbourne late that Sunday afternoon. As she drove, inevitably she was starting to feel tired having had virtually no sleep now for forty-eight hours. Sleep was now a priority. An absolute must.

Linda did not have her intended good night's sleep as it was interrupted by the noise she could hear coming from the adjacent hotel bedroom of what was clearly two other hotel guests enjoying a lengthy and high octane session of sex. The two things Linda wanted to avoid were noise and any reminder of sexual activity. As it happened she got both, and this resulted in her lying awake constantly thinking about Willy and on occasions getting irritated by the interruption at the sheer din coming from next door. And importantly, getting little-to-no sleep.

Over breakfast Frank was slow to start a stilted conversation until he eventually observed, 'You look anything but fresh and your usual enthusiastic self.'

'Anything special you want to discuss about this match against Teliana Pereira this afternoon?' asked Linda, sounding as if she only moderately cared.

Frank shook his head.

Linda was scheduled to play on the Margaret Court Arena. She was playing in a quarter-final match of a Grand Slam event and yet secretly wishing she was a hundred miles away down the coast in Warrnambool with Willy.

When Linda found herself losing the first four games and winning only two points in the process, she suddenly realised she had to start motivating herself considerably more otherwise there was a real danger the match would run away from her. However, she never really got the chance to exercise her self-motivational skills and she lost the match 6-0, 6-1 as she patently did not have the necessary energy in her body to respond to the pressure she was put under by the powerful and consistent stroke play of the Brazilian. It was true that Linda's thigh had improved slightly with the weekend's rest from tennis, but it was not a hundred per cent and had certainly restricted her movement around the court.

Linda almost felt relieved to have lost as this meant she could probably get back in the car and drive straight back to Warrnambool that evening. The scale of the defeat had scarcely registered. In actual fact, it had been over five years since Linda had ever lost by such an overwhelming score line in any competitive match.

Frank appeared at first extremely perplexed by her performance. Probably embarrassed as well. That embarrassment seemingly turned to annoyance when Linda made it known she was not particularly interested in any post-match analysis with him.

'I'm perplexed, pet. What went wrong out there?'

'Don't rightly know, coach.'

'And it don't sound as if you care either. Aren't you ashamed? That was dire out there. In fact, it don't get more embarrassing than a score line of 6-0, 6-1.'

'Thanks for reminding me. What the heck do you want me to say, Frank?' Linda could now gauge from Haffey's facial expression he was angry at her failure to alleviate the tension by only offering up a token explanation for her defeat.

'Look, Frank, I haven't slept properly in the past couple of evenings. I met up with this guy and we had fantastic all-night sex in a dormitory attached to a Catholic church. Anyway, you were right all along, my thigh injury could have benefited from further physio treatment. Happy now?' Linda sounded as mentally exasperated as she was physically tired.

This honest explanation, however patronisingly delivered, backfired on Linda, as it resulted in a heated verbal exchange - the first ever between them.

Linda stormed off to the car and just as she did so she bade Frank a farewell with a, 'Sod you, I've far got better things to be doing than arguing with you.'

And Frank's retort of, 'How selfish can you get, well you're on your own now, pet,' only emphasised just how severed their working relationship had abruptly become.

*   *   *   *   *

For Linda, driving her hired car considerably well over the legal speed limit on the journey out to Warrnambool, she was starting to feel, for the first time, incredibly frustrated. The realisation of just how badly the match with Pereira had gone and how with the benefit of hindsight she actually had, she conceded, badly let herself down. As for Frank, she still felt he had no right to react in the manner he had. He too had behaved unprofessionally, firstly as a paid coach and unsympathetically also as a friend, and Linda thought she could well do without that sort of support.

For Frank, he instantly decided that this was it for him. No more working with Linda. It was over. He too was deeply frustrated, even a tad bitter. He had, after all, travelled to the other side of the world to try to help her. He did not do so for any meaningful or substantial financial reward. Far from it. Frank's only slight regret was he still had much faith in Linda's tennis ability and potential to win one of the major tennis tournaments. He was confident much progress had been made under his guidance, although that would now be confined to the memory bank.

At Melbourne Airport, on his way back to England, Frank met a familiar sports journalist who he had in the past shared the odd beer or two with. His name was Ian Girot.

'I see Linda's out of the singles, Frank.'

'Aye.'

'Mind you, isn't she still in the mixed doubles with a very good friend of mine, Julien Bonneau? So, what went wrong in the singles, Frank?'

Girot caught Frank somewhat off guard and at a very low ebb and Frank volunteered what Linda had been up to. Why she was physically so unprepared for such an important match. Frank was, even if momentarily, feeling a bit hostile towards her and this led to him spontaneously mentioning the convent and the cousin nun and the sex without truly giving the matter a great deal of thought. And certainly Frank was not giving any real consideration to the implications of talking to a British journalist. No sooner was Frank on his flight out of Melbourne when he started to regret having had the conversation with Girot. He knew he had acted unprofessionally and, more importantly, even betrayed some confidences.

He also mulled over in his mind on the long trip back to the United Kingdom that working in Australia with Linda, without Drew and Gerry's presence and influence, had most definitely not been the success he somehow had originally hoped it would be.

*   *   *   *   *

Linda temporarily cheered herself up by fantasising about the prospect of meeting up with Willy again and eagerly anticipating that it would result in another wild night of passionate lovemaking. Then she thought of Sister Margaret and felt just a tiny bit self-conscious regarding her own selfish intentions. Maybe she should take Willy away from the convent to a nearby hotel room? Spare everyone potential embarrassment.

On arrival at the convent Linda could not initially track Willy down in the gardens. There seemed little choice left but to seek her cousin's assistance to establish Willy's whereabouts.

'I'm sorry, Linda, but Willy has left us.'

'What do you mean, *left*?' frowned Linda.

'He went yesterday,' added Maggie as if slightly bemused by Linda's reaction. 'Anyway, it's real nice to see you back again so soon. I hadn't expected you, though.'

Linda was momentarily panic stricken as she tried, as inconspicuously as possible, to find out more about where Willy was and, or even, why precisely he had departed. Eventually there seemed little alternative in her eagerness to establish these details other than to mention her true interest in Willy and the reasons why she actually had returned so soon and unexpectedly. It was a big mistake. Sister Margaret's attitude abruptly changed as she made it abundantly clear that she felt betrayed by Linda's behaviour whilst her guest.

'Disrespectful in the extreme,' Sister Margaret pronounced to Linda as she seemed to reluctantly explain that Willy had, in fact, gone back to his aboriginal and ancestral village and real home, but she had no idea where exactly that was nor how to contact him. Or, at least, was perhaps more likely not prepared to say so.

'I have to confess, Linda, I am bitterly disappointed in you. I befriended and trusted in you. I offered you counselling for any soul searching you felt you needed. I did not expect you to jump into bed with the first guy I introduced you to. Maybe some of those stories in the newspapers you told me about and how they were malicious and slanderous lies about you were in fact true?'

'With the greatest respect, that's hurtful and grossly unfair of you, Maggie, if you don't mind me saying so. It was *never* my original intention to sleep with anyone, let alone someone you introduced me to. In fact, it was the furthest thought from my mind when I first came here. I promise you,' pleaded Linda.

'Who is Ian Girot?' asked Sister Margaret.

'Doesn't ring any bells – why?'

'Oh, just someone by that name contacted Mother Superior this morning asking about you and your stay here and about an affair with one of the gardening staff happening on the premises.'

The atmosphere was, by now, extremely tense. Linda felt increasingly embarrassed and did not know what to do, nor say, for the best. She truly had valued Sister Margaret's company and friendship; however, there was no denying the fact that she had only returned to the convent in an act of lust to see Willy again, not Maggie.

'I think I had better go back to Melbourne then.'

'Yes, I think you should,' agreed Sister Margaret.

So, in a relatively short space of time Linda had quite literally lost an important tennis match, lost Willy, too, and suspected she had even lost the friendship with Maggie. Not to forget the bad blood now between her and Frank.

Maybe sex isn't all it's cracked up to be, after all? sighed Linda to herself, trying hard to find a mildly amusing slant to this saga. Though, much as she wanted to lighten the atmosphere, she could not find anything witty to share with Sister Margaret before leaving the convent.

On the drive back to Melbourne, Linda suddenly remembered she was still playing in the mixed doubles. Her participation in this event was more a sort of favour to, and at the insistence of Julien Bonneau, a promising young French player. Linda had got to know and like Julien after they first got talking at Aeroporto de Lisboa eighteen months ago whilst having to wait several hours at the airport due to a baggage handlers' strike. Julien was from Paris and was the spitting image of Thierry Henry, the world famous soccer player. Well, at least she thought he looked like Henry. Not the best looking Frenchman ever born, but Julien was physically as fit as any professional tennis player on the tour and had the same easy-going attitude to life that Thierry Henry portrayed. Linda enjoyed playing mixed doubles with him. It was always *va va voom* on court with him, she sometimes muttered to herself. Julien was a highly talented, if somewhat inconsistent, shot-maker. He did not take the mixed event too seriously and Linda found the relaxed atmosphere in marked contrast to playing singles, which was all about maximum mental and physical preparation at all times and often the only real enjoyment was usually derived from the satisfaction of winning. Whereas with mixed doubles it was invariably enjoyable, particularly with Julien as a partner, and the end result was not of particular importance to either of them.

Slightly against even their own expectations, Linda and Julien had managed to get through to the semi-final stage of the mixed and, despite all Linda's trials and tribulations over the past few days, she was now rather looking forward to this semi-final encounter. She had never won any Slam event of any description and had not even won any competition with Julien as her partner. Maybe that was all about to change?

Linda was somewhat surprised at just how excited and hyperactive Julien appeared before the match against the Spanish pair, Ruben Hidalgo and Conchita Martinez, the No.1 seeds in the competition. Julien confirmed this excitement by turning to Linda and saying in an assertive tone of voice, 'Let's make absolutely sure we win this one,' which was an ever so simple, yet pronounced, mark of determination that she had hitherto never seen from Julien, either before, during or after any of their previous competitive matches together.

Linda was more than happy to oblige him. Apart from the obvious reason that winning this match might just lift her own spirits, then certainly playing in a Grand Slam final, albeit in mixed doubles, seemed a reasonable worthy professional aspiration to have.

Julien arguably played the match as well as he had ever played with Linda as his partner. He was by far the best player on court that day. His range of shot, and correct choice of shot, made the two Spaniards look pedestrian and unimaginative and always on the defensive and appearing solely content to rely on mistakes from their opponents rather than being capable of pulling off winners of their own. Julien kept a high and consistent standard up throughout the match and he and Linda ran out convincing winners by the score line 6-4, 6-2 and were now through to the Australian Open final of the mixed doubles.

Because of Julien's impressive performance, Linda found herself automatically giving her playing partner an exaggerated hug of sheer gratitude at the end of the game, as opposed to the customary quick kiss on both cheeks. This hug, unbeknown to Linda and Julien, clearly became something of a slight embarrassment to Martinez and Hilgaldo who were waiting much longer than is customary at the net to offer their own polite congratulations to their opponents.

'Let's have a celebratory drink and meal tonight,' pleaded Julien.

'I'd love to Julien, but can I suggest we leave it until after the final and we'll do something special, eh? Crazy, special,' giggled Linda.

'Okay, I'll buy that.' Julien sounding giggly, too, at the prospect.

'Anyway, I am so desperately in need of a good night's sleep before the final,' protested Linda.

When she got back to the hotel there was a note left for her by Frank. It was not an overly friendly note. It told her that Frank would not work with her again and reminded her that there were considerable outstanding personal expenses that she must arrange to have settled and forwarded to him without any further delay. The scribbled note did however contain a postscript to wish Linda well for the future, but Linda simply did not recognise Frank from the content. She was fairly sure he had written it in a moment of haste and anger.

Linda and Julien's opponents in the final would be Linda's old foe Cathy Zerova who was partnered by her compatriot, Igor Andreev. They were the No.2 seeds in the event, overwhelming favourites to win the final.

If there was one person on the women's tour Linda did not like as a person, then it was Zerova. *No manners. No etiquette. Ill tempered. Ungracious. Lacking in any personality.*

* * * * *

Julien was not playing as well in the final as he had in the semi-final. This seemed to be a combination of sometimes trying to be just a bit too ambitious and creative, and thereby failing to replicate his success of audacious shot making from the previous match. In contrast to the older, slower, less aggressive Spaniards in the semi-final, the Russians Zerova and Andreev were more alert and responsive to Julien's creative, but unpredictable, style of play. Conversely, Linda was playing better in the opening set in the final than she had done at any time during the semi-final, probably because of her feeling physically sharper having had a good night sleep, at long last. Also, her thigh strain was no longer restricting her movement in the slightest.

Zerova and Andreev won the first set on a tie break and probably just about shaded it and deserved the one set advantage. Although Linda was playing fairly well, she was not making a substantial contribution towards point scoring. She was, especially, experiencing great difficulty with Andreev's angle of shot and disguise of shot as opposed to the traditional problem of sheer physical power created by a male opponent.

In some ways Linda and Julien also had difficulty getting in the zone as a cohesive partnership. Sure, they were committed to winning this trophy now that they had got to the final. But, they were also acting out a slightly artificial entertainment show for the near capacity crowd. For Linda and Julien it was a difficult transition to suddenly be serious and professional with each other. Whereas, in direct contrast, Zerova and Andreev gave themselves a high five acknowledgement each and every time they won a point. Something they were well used to doing from the very first point they won in their first round match of the tournament, and the many others they had played in together over several years.

Indeed, Zerova's exaggerated celebratory antics were starting to wind Linda up more than just a little. Her over-reaction to winning a point made it seem like it was a match point won. The time taken and performance given in celebrating a point sometimes bordered on the theatrical. Only it was not entertainment in the slightest, to Linda's mind.

She was not a bad loser in any shape or form, and rarely got involved in any show of gamesmanship and certainly had never done before in a relatively relaxed mixed doubles event. However, it was inescapable that Zerova, after about an hour's play, was irritating Linda enormously.

The score was now one set to the Zerova/Andreev partnership and at a crucial point in the second set at 5-4 to Linda and Julien, with it being love 30 on Zerova's service game. Zerova then served an ace to Linda to make it 15-30 to which Linda made exaggerated clapping gestures towards the umpire, at which Zerova immediately stormed over towards the umpire's chair, assuming Linda was querying her serve being somehow a disputed fault.

Linda then punched the air and shouted over to Zerova, 'Darling, I was only saying what a *magnificent* service that was of yours. Well played!'

Zerova won the next point with a serve and winning volley and again Linda reacted as if she, not Zerova, had just won Wimbledon instead of actually losing a point in a mixed doubles match in Melbourne. Linda's over-the-top reaction at having lost a point seemed to wholly perplex Zerova and it was perhaps no surprise that she served a double fault to Linda at 30-all which gave Linda and Julien a fortuitous set point. The unexpected followed and Zerova served a consecutive double fault and the match was now all square at one set apiece.

Everyone in the near capacity Rod Laver Arena could plainly see that Zerova was furious as she hurled her racket in the direction of the tennis bags beside her resting chair and shouted something in Russian towards Linda.

'She's well rattled now,' breezed Julien.

'Serves her right,' smirked Linda. 'Now, let's take advantage before she regains any sort of composure. She doesn't play nearly as well when she's in this frame of mind.'

'Cheat,' hissed Zerova out of the corner of her mouth as she walked past Linda at the change-over to start the third and deciding set.

The match continued to be an extremely close affair, with all four raising their game and playing confidently. It was great entertainment for the crowd and the rallies just got longer and longer and better and better. The deciding final set, perhaps inevitably, was a protracted one, with neither couple finding it possible to break serve.

At 8-8 Linda played three consecutive winners, but they were extremely lucky shots benefiting from net cords rendering the ball being unreturnable. It was *the* decisive final juncture in the match and the last major twist to the contest. These lucky breaks, by virtue of net cords, gave Linda and Julien a 9-8 lead with Julien's serve to follow. Julien proceeded to boom down two aces to Zerova and two huge first serves to Andreev to give them the initiative, sufficient enough to win those particular service points.

Linda and Julien were the new Australian Open Mixed Doubles Champions.

Zerova refused to shake Linda's hand at the end, which only made victory even sweeter for Linda. Linda and Julien hugged each other like they had never hugged anyone before, certainly not on a tennis court. They were both extremely pleased with themselves.

'Does this now mean you'll have a crazy session with me tonight? asked Julien.

'Try stopping me,' enthused Linda.

It was evident they were jointly experiencing a rare *joie de vivre* moment.

That evening a formal dinner and dance function was scheduled at the Sheraton Hotel in the middle of Melbourne. It was made clear by the tournament organisers to Linda and Julien that it would do themselves no favours if they opted out of this rather staid social event. In fact, they both suspected, they might face a fine imposed by the WTA if they tried to give it a body swerve.

As a compromise, Linda suggested to Julien that they put in an appearance, and then after any formal, predictably boring speeches or presentations they make some polite excuse about having a plane to catch. But instead actually take themselves off to some night club and celebrate privately together.

Julien's only response was unsurprisingly, 'Bring it on.'

The award ceremony and meal at the Sheraton Hotel was indeed uneventful and it seemed a few others had the same quick exit strategy that Linda and Julien were contemplating, so when they did eventually leave the Sheraton nobody seemed to be the slightest bit bothered by their premature departure.

Neither Linda nor Julien as a rule drank champagne, but with Julien's French upbringing he insisted on an expensive bottle of champagne and, of course, this was the perfect excuse for them to indulge themselves for once. Linda was only inclined to have an alcoholic beverage on the occasions she went out with Drew and/or Gerry, which over a period of twelve months was not that often – maybe two or three times maximum.

As it happened, Linda and Julien got through not one but two expensive bottles of *Dom Pérignon,* although they were hardly aware of that fact, so much were they intensely engaged in simply enjoying each other's company. The night absolutely flew by and before they realised it, it was three o'clock in the morning. No matter, they were both still buzzing with excitement from winning the mixed doubles and increasingly from being in each other's company. Not a tired eye in view. Indeed, they were both behaving as if they were teenagers mildly inebriated for the first time. Only they were not teenagers. They were mature adults, even if temporarily drunk ones, and they were being continually tactile towards each other.

It became increasingly inevitable where this would lead.

*   *   *   *   *

To say Linda thoroughly enjoyed the experience of making love with Julien would be, just as it was with Willy, an understatement. Although Julien was not as good a lover as Willy had been - that was for absolute certain, Linda conceded that fact to herself - however in Julien's defence he was handicapped through alcohol whilst Willy's stamina without having any alcohol in his bloodstream had surely been quite an advantage. That said, Julien's performance did not disappoint Linda and in fact might even have scored higher than Willy on artistic merit and verbal interaction, Linda laughed to herself.

Linda was definitely starting to get the hang of this casual sex business, her only modest regret now being not to have tried it out in earlier life.

What another eventful trip to a Grand Slam this had turned out to be, Linda thought, as she recollected events of the past couple of weeks whilst lying in bed with Julien fast asleep beside her. Preying on her mind were three outstanding issues that were still left sort of up in the air.

First, there was Willy. Well, she could not think of anything that she could practically now do about that situation. Perhaps it was simply best to put Willy down to a one-off experience in life.

Then there was Frank. Her thoughts on Frank were that he had over-reacted and could be persuaded to come and coach her for The French at Roland Garros. He was not a priority. Anyway, he was probably by now back in Devon.

What was more urgent was Sister Margaret. Linda wrestled with her conscience regarding Maggie. Should she simply leave it until next year when she was back down in this part of the world and re-visit and then try and mend fences, or should she go back today just to be seen to be at least making a really special final effort before leaving the country? Linda decided that a special effort was indeed called for as she truly had an affectionate disposition towards Sister Margaret. She wanted their friendship to blossom, even though she conceded that might be difficult, given Sister Margaret and Linda's complete opposite lifestyles - not to mention often living on different continents.

'What are you up to today then?' Linda smiled broadly as she gave Julien a quick but passionate and tender kiss on the lips as he showed signs of awakening.

'Gotta catch a flight to Bombay. Jeeeez – look at the time! I'd better get a move on. Last night was one of the best nights I've had for years.' Julien returned the compliment of a tender kiss on Linda's lips.

'Always a pleasure – never a chore,' laughed Linda. 'We must do it again some time. We really must.'

'Absolutely, mon chéri. Why not come and stay with me when you're in Paris for The French?'

'Okay. I might just take you up on that offer,' simpered Linda in quick acceptance, whilst screaming to herself - *try stopping me you great big hunk.*

Was this love then, she wondered.

Later that same day, Linda made her way back to Warrnambool, fervently hoping to find her newly beloved cousin in a wholly different frame of mind from that of their recent meeting.

However, Sister Margaret was to disappoint Linda by being clearly still very cool towards her.

The predictable but natural smile on Sister Margaret's face was still there, however noticeably suppressed. Any attempt at conversation seemed stilted and awkward.

Linda left the convent after barely a thirty minute stay, feeling dejected and clinging on to the hope that maybe if she somehow kept in touch with Maggie by sending her the odd card or letter, then come the following year Maggie might be in a more receptive and forgiving mood. As the days rolled by, Willy had become more and more of a distant memory. Nonetheless, Linda was fairly sure she could never, ever forget Willy, even if she lived to be a hundred years of age, and as long as she avoided Alzheimer's disease.

*   *   *   *   *

Linda managed to book a flight out of Melbourne that evening, bound for Rome.

At one of the airport reception areas a man approached her saying that Frank Haffey had suggested he introduce himself.

'Sorry, I didn't quite catch your name,' enquired Linda.

'My name is Girot. Ian Girot.'

French Open, Roland Garros, Paris

Drew and Gerry sat in silence whilst drinking their pints of *McEwans Export* in a public bar in Waterloo Street, Glasgow called The Alhambra. The Alhambra was a city centre establishment that held special, happy memories for both of them, from the days of their youth when they had spent a disproportionate amount of their lives in pubs. It had, however, been quite some time since either of them had set foot back inside The Alhambra, not least because Gerry now lived in England most of the year. It was early-to-mid May time and every year Gerry tried to make it back to Glasgow to play in the official West of Scotland Tennis Championship held annually at Newlands Tennis Club. Gerry always entered the doubles seniors event, usually with Drew as his partner, although Drew's depreciating physical condition in recent years did not always enable him to participate.

This pub rendezvous was the first opportunity since Linda's adventures down in Australia that Drew and Gerry had to communicate face-to-face. Drew was perhaps more philosophical than Gerry was about all the adverse publicity that Linda had attracted, especially once Ian Girot and his newspaper articles made much, and then some more, of Linda's exploits at a certain Catholic convent. That philosophical approach was easier for Drew as he knew exactly how the tabloid newspaper world worked. Consequently, Drew was pretty reasoned and calm about any negative publicity as being tomorrow's fish and chip wrapping paper and therefore quickly forgettable. In any event, his own newspaper-cum-employers over the past few months had periodically printed some positive articles about Linda, particularly her charity work assisting the Sports Relief charity organisation in Kenya, and on her tennis triumphs at the Australian Open mixed doubles, as well as a recent victory in the Estoril Open in Portugal.

One matter Drew and Gerry were equally perturbed about was Linda's finances, or to be precise how quickly their original injection of funds was dwindling. Cash flow was fast becoming a priority that they had discussed on numerous occasions from a distance over the telephone and the odd email exchange, but this was now a critical issue that needed constant monitoring and addressing.

Probably this helplessness - being unable to actually transform Linda into an instantly wealthy sportswoman - was the very reason why there was an awkward silence between them in The Alhambra bar. Neither Drew nor Gerry was over eager to raise the matter of finances, regardless of the fact that was the main reason they had arranged to meet up that particular day.

Eventually, Drew half-heartedly ended a long period of silence and raised the thorny issue of finances, indirectly at least, by commenting about Frank Haffey. He questioned whether or not he was an unaffordable luxury to have back on board coaching Linda for the forthcoming French Open at Roland Garros, or whether he was a necessity if Linda was to ever fulfil her true potential in the Grand Slam events.

'I'm not so sure Frankie's interested in working again with Linda. When I had a quick beer with him down in Dartmouth only three weeks or so ago he still sounded frigging pissed off about what went on down in Melbourne,' offered Gerry.

'Stop being so flipping negative, mate. I'm sure with a bit of forethought and encouragement Frank can be persuaded.'

'Okay, I'll leave that in your capable hands, you sanctimonious smart-arse,' hissed Gerry.

'Nay bother, pal. You just leave Frank and Linda's working relationship to me to sort out. Just like I sorted Summerfield.'

'Okay then, I will, pal. What about the ever-decreasing fund of money? That's a more important issue, surely to God? Linda's barely covering basic expenses from her winnings on the tour,' snapped Gerry, finally raising the all-important issue of finances.

'If it hadn't have been for her winning the mixed down in Melbourne and in Estoril, then the finances would be in the deep shit, mate. Mind you, the six weeks spent down under came with some hefty travel costs and expenses. And the trip to The States was financially a bit of a mare, too.'

'I ken. I ken. But she's generally showed pretty good form of late and if Linda hadn't apparently been so unprofessional in Melbourne, well, who knows?' shrugged Drew.

'I guess we've little choice but to review the finances again after Wimbledon,' moaned Gerry.

'Yeah, that's right mate, always look on the bright side. You negative arsehole. In case you've forgotten, traditionally that period of the year is quite a lucrative time for Linda after The French. She's got Eastbourne, Edgbaston and then Wimbledon all with low expenses and normally does fairly well prize-money wise. That period could just prove to be the catalyst. But I kinda agree with you, it is a bit of a worry if she doesn't make, say, at the very least fifty grand during June and July,' conceded Drew.

'As long as she remains fit,' muttered Gerry. 'Maybe she'll win the mixed at Wimbledon. Not bad prize money.'

'You knobhead - Linda wants to be setting her sights a lot higher than the effing mixed doubles. I haven't put my life savings on the line for that pitiable moment of glory,' thundered Drew. 'By the way, are you coming along to the fitba match on Saturday? I've reserved a ticket in the director's box for you.'

'Sure mate. I'll be there. Of course I will. Thanks for the ticket by the way,' Gerry responded, almost sounding genuinely grateful, for once. Until, that was, Drew mockingly queried Gerry's lack of any football heritage due to his Catholic upbringing.

Drew had been a non-executive director of Partick Thistle Football Club for just a little over five years. It was yet another passion of his in a generally rather hectic life. In fact, football had been Drew's very first passion in life. He had been going to watch his team play at their Firhill ground since his father used to take him to virtually all home games from when Drew was about six or seven years of age.

Drew's non-exec role was a strictly part-time one, expenses only, and was suitable reward for his boundless enthusiasm and commitment to the club's fund raising activities over a long period of time. As a newspaper journalist (or columnist as he preferred to be called), and as a loyal supporter of the club, he had got to know all the directors personally over the past twenty odd years. This eventually led to Drew being offered a non-exec position. He never got tired of the football banter that existed within the club. Whether that be with the chairman, his fellow directors, the players, the supporters, the grounds staff, even in the company of the dotty elderly tea lady. Drew found it easy and natural to exchange football-related banter with her.

Partick Thistle Football Club was considered, with every justification, by most Glaswegians to be very much the poor relations of a football mad city like

Glasgow, where football (or *fitba* as it is popularly referred to in Glasgow as) was more like a pseudo counter-religion to many in more ways than one. Whereas the two rather more illustrious Glasgow-based teams, Celtic and Rangers, had huge popular support, Partick Thistle's sole objective was to survive from one season to the next.

Survival was something The Thistle or The Jags were particularly struggling to achieve with operating debts spiralling out of control due to ever-increasing player wage demands and decreasing numbers of paying customers through the turnstiles.

From attending board meetings with fellow directors, Drew was only too well aware that the financial situation of *his* club was perilous. There had been countless rumours and speculation in the local newspapers that a property developer wanted to purchase the club and redevelop the whole ground area to incorporate a major new private housing scheme. The reality was that the board of directors had indeed convened to discuss an outline proposal put forward by the large property company by the name of Digby Construction plc. Essentially it was a proposal to fund a major redevelopment of the whole club - relocating the playing area, complete new facilities for the club, new shop, new restaurant facilities, with, in fact, Digby Construction offering to fulfil every Partick Thistle fan's wildest dream at no expense to them, or the club. The only stumbling block was that as the development costs required huge amounts of capital investment by Digby Construction, they were only prepared to offer a very modest sum for the actual purchase of the existing club to include the surrounding land. That offer was not a particularly financially attractive proposition to some of the board members who had originally invested not inconsiderable sums of money of their own over a number of years.

'It's a sick kind of blackmail,' fumed Angus Timlin, the chairman of Partick Thistle FC, during the hastily convened meeting of the board of directors.

After a moment's silence, whilst everyone tried to digest the chairman's remarks, someone almost apologetically then asked him to explain the rationale behind his statement.

'Well, it's obvious what the tactic is. Digby Construction must know from their own accountants, who will have completed at least partial due diligence on the club's financial and commercial affairs, that we are in dire difficulties and can't keep up the ongoing operational and basic repair and refurbishment expenditure necessary. John Digby fucking knows he has the majority support of the die-hard fans, who are greatly attracted by the conversion of a crappy dilapidated ground to a new ultra-modern stadium with all the contemporary facilities that go with it. Digby probably even believes he can name his own price, suspecting we are all desperate to complete *any* deal. Well, Digby can go and stuff his offer up his arse,' fumed Timlin again, in a bitter tirade that left everyone at the meeting speechless, including Drew.

The following day Drew received a wholly unexpected phone call from John Digby, the mogul spearheading the prestigious property plc. It was an invitation to have lunch together. Drew had never met Digby before, although he was vaguely aware of his reputation as being a bit of a ruthless business charlatan. On one hand, Drew was extremely uneasy regarding this proposed meeting – on the other, he was equally intrigued as to why this luncheon appointment was being suggested and with him alone. Digby maintained on the telephone that it was purely a social meeting and that suggestion rather annoyed Drew that it should be promoted by Digby as such, as Drew thought it would have been evident to even a ten-year-old that it simply *had* to be to discuss Digby Construction's business plans for Firhill.

Drew still wondered why him – why had he apparently been singled out by Digby?

This was just about his first question, after the initial exchange of courtesies and display of pleasantries when they met up at the Stanley Bistro in Glasgow's infamous Sauchiehall Street.

'So, why did you want to meet me – me in particular – John?'

'I think you are a true fan of the football club and have the interests of the true supporter at heart.'

'And the other directors don't? Is that what you're saying?'

'Look, I suspect all the supporters will want this deal of mine to go ahead. They get a brand new stadium with lots of modern and comfortable facilities. Are the board not aware how unpopular they are with the fans at the minute?' reasoned Digby.

'Aye, I guess so, but, come on now, my fair-minded colleagues on the board will only want to negotiate a sensible settlement or offer, John. What you have put on the table is derisory. The board individually get very little return on their original financial investment in the club. Not to forget their time given over the years and they all lose their executive position within the club.'

Digby quickly interjected with, 'That's what I wanted to talk to you about, Drew. You can keep your directorship position after the acquisition.'

'And the others?' asked Drew.

'No. They are a spent force. No deal.'

Drew was not happy with the direction this conversation was going. He was already regretting agreeing to meet, even if he had naïvely accepted it was only a social occasion over lunch. If the other directors had known the content of this discussion, then Drew was sure they would equally not be happy. An understatement if ever there was one, he reminded himself.

'Look, Drew, you have sway with the supporters,' continued Digby. 'They feel they know you from your newspaper articles, that you truly have the best interests of the football playing side of the club at heart. If you were to break ranks with the board and come out to publicly approve or support our plans, I believe it would make all the difference.'

'I simply can't and won't do that,' protested Drew.

'How's about if I made it worth your while. Say a hundred grand?'

After an excessive period of time without any further comment from either of them, the silence was eventually broken by Drew's considered suggestion that without being inhospitable or appearing rude to his host he thought it best if he left the table and the restaurant. Drew duly did leave, feeling totally bewildered and disturbed over what had just happened.

The next day there was reference made to the meeting between Drew and Digby in the *Glasgow Herald* with a journalist quoting 'unofficial' sources that said a meeting had taken place and Drew was trying to broker a deal between the club and an unnamed major property developer. Drew, naturally, was furious. But nothing like as furious as his fellow directors were, who called another emergency directors' meeting. Drew attended the meeting and acknowledged the fact that the lunch-cum-meeting had indeed taken place, but it was all innocent, albeit Drew did concede, that with the benefit of hindsight, he had acted naively. Drew vehemently denied to his co-directors that he accepted any bribe made, nor had he even offered to assist Digby in any shape or form. The unsubstantiated and malicious rumours that were circulating were highly embarrassing for Drew, not least as some had the amounts as stated in the newspapers as being on offer to him as being in excess of one million pounds.

Drew, with the approval of the board of directors, issued an immediate press statement, which confirmed he was in complete agreement with the board's policy of not actively seeking a new owner – unless it was advantageous to *all* parties. The statement also made it clear that he was confident that with the current successful run in the Scottish Cup there would be considerable spin-off financial benefits that would enable the board to invest in further refurbishment and upgrading of the stadium, solely for the fans benefit.

Partick Thistle Football Club had, in fact, reached the semi-finals of the Scottish Cup for only the second time in their 135 year history and that match was, as it so happened, scheduled to take place within the next ten days.

*　　*　　*　　*　　*

Once more, Drew and Gerry had entered the veterans doubles event in the annual West of Scotland Tennis Championships at Newlands Tennis Club, in South Glasgow. It was by far the most prestigious tennis tournament held in Scotland and attracted an impressively varied field from all round the world, albeit from very low ranking professional players. This tournament also offered Drew and Gerry the ideal once a year opportunity to keep in touch with auld acquaintances they had known, some for best part of forty years.

Although a prestigious event for Scottish tennis, it always clashed with a pre-French Open ranking tournament near Paris and, therefore, historically, made it virtually impossible for Linda to compete. As, yet again, was the case this particular year.

Drew and Gerry first entered the Newlands-based tournament when they were juniors many years ago and both made a conscious effort to annually meet up and continue to play in this event. These days, though, participation for Drew and Gerry was sensibly restricted to the seniors' event. However, it still served a purpose of giving them the discipline, or the excuse, at least to meet up once a year and play some competitive tennis together. Newlands Tennis Club was a mere five minute car drive away from Hillpark where Drew and Gerry were still country members, although their visits to Hillpark were now limited to once, perhaps twice, a year, usually only for a knock-up together and a few drinks afterwards in the clubhouse bar.

Hillpark Bowling & Lawn Tennis Club, to give it its full and official name, was formed not too long after World War I in 1924. When Drew and Gerry originally became junior members, in the early 1960s, the club then boasted seven clay courts and was a thriving and active club with healthy membership numbers in all categories, men's, ladies' and junior's sections, and was generally considered to be a premier league tennis club in the West of Scotland Region. But now it was restricted to just four courts, had an embarrassingly small membership, and was no longer a force in competitive tennis, even in the immediate South Glasgow area. Three courts had been sold off -

democratically or undemocratically - thanks largely to a voting system favouring the bowling section of the club and the same three courts were now three private nondescript residential bungalows. The elderly members of the bowling club, which always enjoyed a huge membership, probably three times the size of the tennis section, would no doubt have seen this asset disposal of the tennis courts as valuable real estate to raise club funds as being inevitable. Progress even. However, it only served to highlight that there was never a good relationship between the differing generations of the bowling and tennis sections. In fact, with some individuals, the animosity bordered on an unhealthy emotion of hate, all unaccountably sectarian and rather bigoted and flawed behaviour to be found in such a recreational and social environment. For Gerry and Drew, and many other Hillpark tennis members, this hatred was most certainly real and had become ingrained in them over the past few decades or so regarding those 'arrogant and pompous auld farts who once sold off our tennis courts'. Similar strong feelings were reciprocated by the bowling club members, only they had an entirely different tale to tell. Drew sometimes likened it to just how Rangers supporters viewed Celtic fans and vice-versa.

Drew and Gerry could, at best, be described as competent club players. No more, no less. The opinions they held on each other's respective tennis abilities conflicted somewhat.

Drew believed Gerry was now showing marked signs of growing old rather too quickly of late. It seemed to Drew that Gerry was playing tennis as if in slow motion. His reflexes and reactions were almost non-existent, notwithstanding, Drew conceded, that Gerry looked the part as he had impressive ground strokes, particularly off his backhand, and was a stylish stroke player. However, Drew found it hard to lose sight of Gerry's excess weight. He also sometimes worried that Gerry might be playing his last competitive tennis at Newlands, if not this year, then certainly it was not far away when Gerry would simply have to call it a day. It stood to reason. Well, it did to Drew.

Gerry, in turn, believed Drew, even when in a rare sober state, was one of the most irritating players to partner at tennis. Drew was clinically obese and sluggish around the court almost to the point of being stationary most of the time and would constantly and recklessly lash out at too many shots to try to play a flamboyant, almost absurd, outright winner at every given opportunity. The only problem was that winners were becoming a rarity for Drew – yet another issue that did not seem to resonate with him, just like his drinking way too much vodka. The only aspect that was predictable about Drew's tennis game was the fact he could be guaranteed to serve at least two double faults on his service game, mainly because his first serve, although undeniably fast, was ridiculously wild and inaccurate. His second service action resembled a lob shot from a ten-year-old learning the game for the very first time. Consequently, Drew was a liability on the tennis court. Again, it stood to reason. Well, it did to Gerry.

So, all in all, it was hardly a perfect partnership made in tennis heaven. And it was hardly any surprise to any neutral observer that Drew and Gerry had contributed virtually nothing technically to Linda - be it strategy, coaching, preparation or tactics. But as long as each believed they were covering up for the other's inadequacies, and the dogged loyalty to each other remained, it was still highly likely, health permitting, they would continue playing in the veterans' event at Newlands TC for many years to come, albeit, more often than not, for just one round only.

And so it was to be this particular year. Drew and Gerry predictably lost in the first round 6-2, 6-2. Naturally, Drew believed he had played the only positive tennis with his occasional winners, whilst it could be assumed that Gerry believed he kept the result more respectable than it probably deserved to be by constantly having to cover for his erratic partner. Both Drew and Gerry showered after the short match – quite why will remain a mystery as certainly neither of them had broken sweat whilst playing. They then proceeded to enjoy some customary banter and a few beers together in the clubhouse consoling themselves privately, and also publicly to anyone prepared or sufficiently interested to listen, that each had individually played considerably better than the other.

*　　*　　*　　*　　*

Linda was initially enjoying herself staying at Julien Bonneau's parents' impressive manor house about a two hours drive away from Paris on the outskirts of Montereau.

Not quite how Linda remembered the original invitation from Julien to stay with him in his Paris pad. However, once he explained it was only a rented two-bedroom flat (one that was shared between six people as they did not all live and work permanently in Paris due to the nature of their various occupations and work commitments) any romantic attraction that the flat might hold quickly wore off with Linda. Being a guest at the spacious, almost luxurious, manor house instantly became a more appealing and acceptable alternative.

The Montereau location meant some fairly lengthy car journeys to play firstly in the Internationaux de Strasbourg and then Auxerre - both clay court tournaments and ideal preparation for the main reason for being in France, the French Open at Roland Garros. The car travel and long journeys were not a hardship for Linda as they were done jointly with Julien, although she was certainly beginning to wonder if Julien's parents enjoyed having her around. Maybe it was the cultural differences, or perhaps simply Linda's limited command of the French language, which was admittedly pretty basic. Whatever, it was becoming increasingly hard work, particularly when it was expected of Linda to sit down to a formal and protracted six, or seven, course typically French evening meal, which in itself was hardly ideal preparation for any forthcoming competitive match. Julien's own constitution seemed well adapted to these late evening feasts, but Linda's battle with it was making her to look more and more as if she was being deliberately ungrateful towards her hosts by leaving much of the food on the many different plates served up.

'I don't think your parents take to me that much, you know,' protested Linda.

'Pay no attention to them.'

'So, you actually know they don't like me then?'

'Stop being so paranoid,' Julien replied, as if to pacify. 'They're throwing a big formal *balle* for my birthday on Saturday and once they see just how much all my friends like you, they'll start to warm to you, I'm sure.'

'How many are coming to the *balle* then?' enquired Linda.

'About two hundred.'

Oh joy of joys, thought Linda to herself, whilst at that precise moment in time she could think of little else that was further removed from her Ayrshire and Scottish roots. She was feeling decidedly uncomfortable with the prospect of this grandiose and formal social event, and a French one at that, but of course she would try and get herself motivated and show some enthusiasm, if only for Julien's sake.

'You know something that surprises me, Jules, darling? The fact that neither of your parents has mentioned to me anything even remotely connected to tennis, nor the fact that we won the mixed at Melbourne. Isn't that a bit weird? Are they not proud of your achievement?'

'Nonsense, I think they are.'

'Well, they've said sod all to me about it,' Linda grumbled. 'I get the distinct impression I'm not that welcome here.'

'Nonsense,' repeated Julien. 'You've said that before - I'll have a word with them. They can sometimes be a trifle anti the English.'

'But I ain't English!' screamed Linda in mock anger.

'Quoi?'

'No. I'm Scottish!'

'Er, but it's the same thing isn't it – being British?'

'You and your family have got a lot to learn about me,' warned Linda.

That evening Linda decided to put her foot down and state as politely but firmly as she could that she only wanted a bowl of a simple pasta dish followed by some fruit as she had an important match the following day. Julien's sister and husband arrived unexpectedly and unannounced to Linda, for the evening meal, together with five friends of theirs who, it was evident from the minute they all entered the house, were all made to feel like they were royalty by Monsieur et Madame Bonneau.

Linda even wondered if they had been invited in a conspiracy to undermine her, intimidate even, and found it even more très difficult now to try and socialise and make any meaningful conversation in French. It became clear to her, whether through another temporary bout of paranoia, that it likely would be a deeply embarrassing and unpleasant time over the next few, but seemingly long, long hours during the evening meal.

Yes, she did get presented with a simple pasta dish, but it seemed from Linda's limited understanding of the conversations that her requested limited menu requirements were quite often the butt of her fellow diners' humour and conversation.

Linda could not remember feeling so indirectly humiliated and downright frustrated and even rather angry, such were the emotions running through her mind. None of the Bonneaus' guests made the slightest attempt to converse with Linda in her native tongue, not one – not even Julien. To make matters ten times worse, it seemed to Linda that Julien was not the slightest bit aware of what was clearly going on. He appeared to be having a *balle* all to himself. Selfishly, he seemingly wallowed in being the unsubtle centre of attention; it was that obvious, even to Linda who could only understand a mere fraction of what was actually being spoken.

Determined not to stomp off in a transparent show of petulance to the others, particularly to Julien's parents, Linda instead opted to show the stiff upper lip in true British tradition. She privately resolved to *knee*

Julien in the nuts as soon as they both retired to her boudoir.

Somewhat predictably, Linda and Julien had a rather frosty post-supper conversation, which certainly resolved two matters for Linda. Firstly, that Julien's parents, as confirmed by Julien, held bigoted anti-English sentiment and were not at all keen on their precious son having one as a girlfriend. And secondly, their partnership, off court at least, was now at an end. Linda had seen such an unexpected and pronounced self-centred side to Julien's behaviour that evening that was impossible to ignore and not act upon.

Bigots. Arrogant French pigs. Not the whole nation. Perhaps not even Julien.

M & Mme Bonneau most definitely, though.

*　*　*　*　*

Drew felt he had to communicate something to John Digby in return for all the stress endured from snide comments made to him by his fellow directors at Partick Thistle FC, the supporters, and the players. Even the tea lady was giving him a bit of light-hearted grief over his alleged involvement with this unsavoury character, Digby, masquerading as a respectable property and business tycoon.

Consequently, Drew asked for a meeting with Digby at his plush riverside office complex by the River Clyde. The meeting was duly arranged. Digby probably readily agreeing to it expecting some positive late developments or change of stance from Drew. Nothing could have been further from reality. Drew had decided it was prudent to have his lawyer present as the actual purpose of the meeting was for Drew to put Digby on notice that any further unsolicited contact made with him, or any further financial offers or bribes, would be immediately reported to the Strathclyde Police.

'What fucking bribes, you lying cunt?' thundered Digby.

'You know only too well, and the fact that you deny all knowledge just shows what low-life scum you are,' spat Drew equally aggressively as if he were a gangster. Well, almost as aggressively.

As Drew and his solicitor began to make a dignified but hasty retreat out of Digby's office, Digby fired what could only be taken as a warning shot, 'You'll regret getting on the wrong side of me. You cunt.'

Drew half turned round, but still kept on walking, 'Was that a threat, pal? Well, I ain't the slightest bit scared. Some thugs tried to beat me senseless in New York recently and I recovered from that nay bother. Send your hired bully boys after me if you think that'll achieve anything.'

The next few hours Drew spent contacting every Glasgow reporter he knew, and sort of trusted, as he tried to call in a few personal favours to help improve his rating and persona with the general Scottish football fraternity.

The outcome from these journalistic contacts was that they delivered over the next few days, in all the Glasgow newspapers (and even some Edinburgh and Aberdeen ones) a staggering amount of positive story-lines in their respective papers. All were conveniently associated with the forthcoming big match that Saturday in the Scottish Cup semi-final match, Partick Thistle versus Aberdeen.

Gerry was Drew's personal guest that Saturday in one of the hospitality suites at Hampden Park and found himself mixing with various dignitaries or those Gerry would surely perceive to be important people. These seemed to range from directors of other Scottish football clubs, managers from other clubs both Scottish and further afield, retired players, and some fairly recognisable faces from public life, including the British Prime Minister and the Secretary of State for Scotland. Gerry seemed absolutely fascinated by the occasion and was clearly thoroughly enjoying every minute. Drew, on the other hand, was well used to meeting and dealing with such important people through his years as a journalist, having interviewed many at one time or another. Anyway, Drew's priority that day was not the dignitaries; his thought and commitment was solely Partick Thistle associated and allied to the outcome of the ensuing match against Aberdeen, the significance of which was all too apparent to Drew. A win would be the most momentous result and Scottish football achievement in the past fifty years, and a win would also do wonders for alleviating the current financial plight of the club.

Aberdeen, however, were favourites. Hot favourites. Indeed, Drew could place a bet at attractive odds of 33-1. So he did, £50 on The Jags to win.

Partick Thistle had recruited a young and highly motivated Dutch coach by the name of Ruud Vanderkaamp, who had been appointed only at the start of the season. His display of boundless enthusiasm helped camouflage a lack of practical coaching experience, not to mention any record of achievement as a professional coach/manager. But, at least, Ruud's lack of experience and achievement meant he came cheap to Partick Thistle FC.

The main action Vanderkaamp took was to recruit a couple of skilful midfield players (one a right-sided player, the other left-sided) and start to build a team and a unique system and a style of play around them.

Not surprisingly, the two players Ruud recruited were from the lower leagues in Holland, where he managed to secure their services cheaply on a twelve month free loan and trial period. It meant a radical change to the way the game would be played by Partick Thistle, which traditionally was a typical Scottish style that hitherto seemed to be restricted to vigour, determination and the will to win rather than planning, tactics and a high level of skill and fitness.

From the very kick-off, this cup-tie was loaded with action, drama and excitement. It was obvious that Aberdeen's initial prime tactic would be to target and stop The Thistle's midfield Dutch duo playing their normal stylish and creative passing game. Consequently, it was hardly any surprise to see a series of crunching, agricultural tackles made on both of them in the first ten minutes of the match, with the only seeming consolation being that the referee deemed several of them illegal tackles and showing three Aberdeen players the yellow card.

The game was played at a fast and unrelenting pace. Both teams were creating enough chances to score goals, but a mixture of bad finishing and bad luck prevented either team taking the advantage. The goal-less-match was heading for extra time as it entered the last five minutes or so. The game then unexpectedly took a dramatic turnabout. A foul was, yet again, given for a crude tackle on one of the Dutch midfielders and, much to the annoyance of the culprit from Aberdeen, he remonstrated his frustration by provocatively kicking the ball wildly into the crowd where the majority of The Jag's supporters were seated. The referee immediately took out his yellow card again, only to realise that he had already booked that same Aberdeen player earlier on in the game and consequently had no alternative but to issue a red card.

Aberdeen were now down to ten men. Within seconds, that became nine men when a remarkably stupid and inexperienced Aberdeen teenage player swore aloud to confirm his disgust at the referee's decision, and he, too, was sent off, having also already been booked for a prior offence. Almost unbelievably, Aberdeen were now having to see out the match with nine men, and, more importantly, would have to play out an additional thirty minutes of extra time if the score remained nil-nil. It did. With only nine players, it was all too much of a handicap for Aberdeen and The Thistle scored twice in extra time to win 2-0 and were now through to the Scottish cup final, a feat considered impossible by just about every knowledgeable Scottish football pundit. Only five months earlier at the start of the football season, that opinion would have been held too by the players, the directors and the longsuffering supporters of Partick Thistle FC.

It most definitely included Gerry.

It might even have included Drew, *Roll on the Final, pal.*

*   *   *   *   *

'What about the *balle* on Saturday then? enquired Julien.

'Enjoy it.'

After an awkward further few moments silence Linda continued, 'I'm catching a train around lunchtime for Paris and I've booked into a small B&B in the St Germain area. Can I hang about until lunchtime?'

'Of course you can,' said Julien, as if clearly resigned to the fact that he and Linda were no longer an item.

'Oh, and can I borrow your bicycle for the morning? I think I'd like to take a wee ride around the village to kill some time before my train is due.'

'Bien sur.'

'Ta. Yer say guid tay me,' acknowledged Linda sarcastically.

'De quoi parlez-vous?'

Although Linda was as physically fit as any woman her age, cycling was not one of her more proficient sporting-related talents. Showing a complete lack of concentration, aided and abetted by her mind still in overload from events the previous evening, and also temporarily forgetful of the fact that the French drove motor vehicles on the right and not left side of the road, Linda turned a sharp corner and had to take immediate evasive action to avoid a head-on collision with a vintage Citroën CV. Luckily for Linda, she did avoid any head-on collision, but in doing so went careering down a steep embankment by the side of the road. As she tried to get herself up from the awkward fall she immediately realised that she had done some damage to herself, at least to her leg, as it was absolute agony to bend the knee.

The doctor who later that morning examined Linda at the A&E Department of the Montereau General Hospital, by chance, did not speak any English whatsoever – or as Linda suspected in her current state of mind, the doctor perhaps did not want to speak any English. However, Linda consoled herself knowing that the WTA had first class doctors and physiotherapists on hand 24/7 and she was sure the extent of any damage would be quickly assessed as soon as she got herself up to Paris. And fortuitously she was at least mobile enough to travel by herself up to the French capital.

The damage was professionally assessed later the following day, after X-ray results were available, as being the slightest of slight tears to the knee ligaments. The physiotherapist ventured to say that it was extremely difficult to predict precisely as to how quickly it would heal. The obvious advice was to rest and not play for a few weeks. But that would mean she would have to miss the French Open, a Grand Slam event, and she occasionally reminded herself these major championships had a limited lifespan for her now. It was uncertain how many more she would be able to seriously compete in; to win.

Perhaps unwisely, Linda mentally started to prepare herself to compete in the tournament. And, if needs be, to spend extra time on the treatment table with physiotherapy treatment and exercises and have the odd pain-killing injection to get through any scheduled matches. She reminded herself, with Frank Haffey no longer on the scene, then practice sessions need not be so intensive, nor strenuous. In fact, Linda decided she would, once again, probably opt for the high-risk strategy and cancel any attempt at pre-match practice, or at least it would be restricted to the absolute bare essentials. Not having any coach in Paris with her provided this rather random, if somewhat perverse, beneficial consolation.

Or, so it seemed. If only to Linda.

*   *   *   *   *

Much to Drew's genuine surprise, but sheer delight, he had been offered the position of chairman of Partick Thistle Football Club.

There was only one practical drawback and that was the role would be full-time and Drew would have to manoeuvre some form of early retirement package from his employer, the *Daily Mail*. Did he really want to give up journalism, which still after all these years offered assignments that were usually interesting and challenging and sometimes even exciting? Certainly his journalistic exploits were varied and never dull and had brought him into direct contact with colourful characters who usually had all achieved something impressive or interesting within their own lives. Being a full-time journalist afforded Drew a working lifestyle that suited him down to the ground. But, did he have the balls to refuse the once-in-a-lifetime opportunity to become chairman of his beloved Partick Thistle Football Club? Naturally, he called upon Gerry for impartial advice. Gerry's view was that Drew should grab the opportunity with both hands without giving it any further consideration. Gerry boiled it down to yet more years as a newspaper hack as opposed to transforming his much treasured fitba club. There being surely only one decision to make?

In point of fact, everyone Drew spoke to was of a similar mind to that of Gerry. Even Drew's editor at the *Mail* reckoned Drew should accept, although he made strenuous efforts to convince Drew that his services at the newspaper would be genuinely missed. He reassured Drew that an attractive early retirement package would be the very least the *Mail* could offer after so many years of loyal service. Also, he predicted any severance package could be quickly negotiated and mutually agreed upon, and for Drew to dismiss that as an issue, or a concern, in his deliberations.

Just as Drew was about ready to make a final decision, he received a telephone call from a dispirited-sounding Linda in Paris. Spontaneously, Drew decided he needed a couple of days away from the pressure of making such an important life-changing decision regarding his career and he felt an immediate short-term visit to Paris might be just the ticket in helping deal with the decision making process regarding the job offer. In any event, Drew had not seen Linda in what seemed like ages, and he assessed on the telephone that she clearly was in need of some friendly and trusted company.

Any excuse for a trip to Gay Paree, Drew jokingly reasoned to himself, even if he had already planned to be in his favourite city in ten days time for the Slam event itself.

'Fantastic to see you, sunshine,' enthused Linda, as she flung her arms around Drew in a warm embrace.

'And you too, hen,' grinned Drew, and before Linda could say anything further Drew continued somewhat predictably, 'Let's find the nearest bar, shall we?'

'Okay, let's,' giggled Linda, instantly. She was so pleased to see a friendly face again and readily agreed to anything Drew suggested. 'But bear in mind I've got to do some serious physio training tomorrow morning.'

'Good show! Always the damn professional, eh!' laughed Drew.

Linda, half-conscious of the need for as booze-limited evening as was possible to have with Drew as a companion for the whole evening, proposed the upmarket L'Alsace brasserie. Her initial plan was that Drew would not be able to consume too many pints of beer there - if any at all - at what by her reckoning was a plush and posh essentially eating establishment. Although Linda should surely have known that Drew

177

had no problem drinking large quantities of *any* alcoholic beverage, whether it be beer or champagne or wine or spirits. So, really, the choice of a drinking venue should have had no relevance to her thought process.

As always, they thoroughly enjoyed being in each other's company, spiced on this occasion by the fact it had been a few months since Christmas in the UK, when they last met. Perhaps it was foremost in Drew's mind that there had been no previous face-to-face celebrations in acknowledging Linda's winning of the mixed doubles down in Melbourne. This prompted, or justified, champagne celebrations from the off – certainly something Linda had not planned for, nor expected, and Drew's persistence made it virtually impossible not to enjoy the quality champagne he had ordered and re-ordered. Before too long, Linda had let her hair down and had accepted that this was just going to be one of those nights she would have no option but to act unprofessionally. No amount of self-discipline would prevent the alcohol flowing amidst having an exceptionally enjoyable time in Drew's company, who made her cry quite therapeutically with laughter. This was just the tonic she thought she needed right now. It also went through Linda's mind that evening that she felt convinced she had matured more as a woman over the past six months than over the previous twenty-six year period of her life.

And that self-assessment, on her apparently newly acquired maturity off-court, in turn started Linda looking at Drew in a slightly different way to how she had previously regarded or judged him. Linda always suspected Drew had led a very colourful life and with it she presumed a colourful sex life, if for no other reason than the number of marriages he had gone through. She knew at least two had apparently fallen apart due to

178

extra marital affairs. In the past, Linda never felt the need to psychoanalyse Drew, nor felt any physical desire towards him. However, she could now see, suddenly and emphatically, even at his relatively mature age, a physical attraction in Drew that made him distinctly endearing. Linda detected a definite change in Drew's mood, almost as if, when she mentioned them, he was critical of those two affairs she had down in Australia with Willy and Julien.

Was Drew showing signs of envy and jealousy? Linda asked herself.

In the morning, they both regretted way beyond normal levels of embarrassment what had happened a few hours earlier. Not a single word was exchanged.

Drew departed the hotel room leaving a brief cowardly handwritten note. The almost illegible note said nothing of any significance, except that he had left to catch an early shuttle out of Paris bound for Glasgow.

Linda pretended to be asleep.

*   *   *   *   *

'You seem a bit subdued, mate,' remarked Gerry as he playfully punched his friend in the stomach.

'I'm okay. My mind's just a tad preoccupied, that's all,' responded Drew.

Preoccupied? Why? What with? thought Gerry to himself. *Not like our Drew.*

'Why, mate? Hey, you're now the bloody chairman of Partick Thistle Football Club, no less. Let's hope this isn't a mood swing associated with this demanding, but exciting new job of yours,' teased Gerry. 'And, by the way, I saw you on the telly last night being interviewed. You almost sounded as if you knew what you were talking about.'

'Eh? What the fuck are you goin' on about?' snapped back Drew.

Bloody hell. What is the matter with Drew today? Touchy or what? Has he been kicked out at home, again? More like, playing away from home...again! Sex maniac.

'Well, being a Jags supporter you can't know that much about entertaining fitba, can ye?' Gerry asked sarcastically whilst trying, again unsuccessfully, by the look on Drew's face, to amuse Drew and make him lighten up his mood with some of their usual brand of banter.

'And who is in the Scottish Cup final then – Celtic or The Jags?' mocked Drew in a dead pan tone of voice, 'I suppose you won't be there at Hampden on Saturday for the final to support me and the lads?'

'They're *your* lads now, eh?' sniffed Gerry, but with a wry smile on his face. 'Of course I'll be there mate – wouldn't miss it for the world. Might even want The Jags to win, more than I want The'Gers to lose.'

As Drew and Gerry were chauffeur-driven from their hotel in Pollokshaws through the main streets via Shawlands and Langside en-route to Hampden Stadium, all they could see were people wearing scarves and tammies and the like, as well as waving flags. All in the Rangers colours only. All singing what sounded remotely like the traditional Rangers' songs of support as some marched, whilst many others drunkenly staggered, towards Hampden Park. It was a genuine mystery to Gerry, from a young schoolboy age, why Rangers and Celtic commanded the football loyalty of the vast majority of this densely populated city. Sure, he fully understood the religious bigotry that was ingrained into youngsters when they first started playing the game at primary school, but it was always a major disappointment to Gerry that more did not show some initiative and independence, just like Drew had done by supporting the underdogs, The Jags. Or Clyde FC for that matter. Or Queens Park FC. Or any other Glasgow-based club. Gerry rather conveniently excluded himself as he felt he had no choice, what with being educated at a Catholic school. The logical, or illogical, thought being that there was only one truly Catholic-sponsored team in Scotland, and that was Glasgow Celtic.

As they approached Hampden Stadium, Drew and Gerry debated and agreed upon how it was a poor reflection of what it had been back in the late 1950s when they both first went there as very young lads. In those days Hampden Stadium was, without doubt, a national sporting arena to be proud of and where, for major matches, 147,000 spectators would be the expected capacity attendance. Needless to say, with that large number inside the ground it created its own special vibrant and intimidating atmosphere just by the sheer volume and number of spectators shouting and chanting in the uniquely belligerent and angry-sounding Glaswegian dialect.

Furthermore, Hampden Stadium was back then, in the 50s and 60s, a well-known stadium with a certain reputation all around the football world. Now, sadly, it was no more impressive than many a Sassenach First Division ground, and certainly had no special redeeming feature or uniqueness to it, be it architecturally or otherwise. Not even the 'Hampden Roar', as it was once notoriously known and feared decades back, could now be compared favourably to a full house at either Parkhead or Ibrox, the home grounds of Glasgow Celtic and Rangers respectively.

Gerry, now very much an anglofied Scot, having married a Sassenach and living in England, always thought it rather sad that Scotland did not have a national football stadium to match some of the other countries around the world. It was almost unthinkable that Wales, for instance, after many decades of playing at a dump of a ground like Ninian Park could boast of The Millennium Stadium to play their home matches - albeit there was the obvious consolation that the Welsh Football Association shared this venue with the Welsh Rugby Union. At least Scotland had not resorted to that dire situation, reasoned Gerry, although it was equally hard to accept that Murrayfield in Edinburgh, the home of Scotland's rugby union team, had an infinitely superior stadium to their football counterpart at Hampden in Glasgow.

All in all, there was still the not-so inconsiderable consolation that Hampden Stadium bore no resemblance to that corporate monstrosity called Wembley, where the Sassenachs played.

'By the way, mate, have you heard owt recently from Linda?' enquired Gerry.

'Naw.'

Gerry's enquiry was more prompted by his intrigue as to what the matter was with his unusually grumpy companion than he was about Linda. This should be a happy and proud day for Drew going to support his fitba team play in such an important match - The Scottish Cup Final - especially now as their chairman.

Drew's demeanour was a real mystery to Gerry. It was also starting to become a worry to him. Well, almost starting.

The Jags, playing in their proud and distinctive red 'n' yellow strip, was the team who looked more like they had previously played European Champions' League football, and not their illustrious opponents. Indeed Rangers were made to look rather ordinary by a young, eager, organised and skilful Thistle side. At half-time Drew's only concern, whilst having at least four large whiskies in a desperate but enjoyable effort to try and alleviate his nerves in the directors-cum-hospitality area, was whether The Thistle could sustain that level of performance for another forty-five minutes, whilst Rangers continue to underachieve in a fashion few could remember witnessing for many a Rangers' match.

Fortunately for Drew, and the estimated 7,000 or so Partick Thistle supporters in the 58,000 crowd, that is exactly what did happen in the second forty-five minutes. Against all the odds, Partick Thistle FC won the Scottish Cup for the first time in almost a hundred years by beating their local big-shots by the almost unbelievable score of 3-0.

It may have been unbelievable to most, but it was nonetheless a thoroughly merited victory even against a pathetically inept Rangers' eleven man team, which, on the day, was full of grossly overpaid and underachieving professionals. The fact that Rangers' fragile defence contrived to give away not one but two penalties under incessant pressure was testimony to just how one-sided the final had actually been.

What a fairy-tale beginning this was to Drew's chairmanship.

Partick Thistle would benefit financially by this Cup victory to the tune of about four million, Drew reckoned. By virtue of winning this tournament, it guaranteed automatic inclusion into European football next season - a first in the club's long history - with the incentive of further lucrative fixtures, especially if drawn against one of the top European teams. And if, somehow, The Thistle could sustain a decent run, then the club's financial difficulties would surely be confined to the history books.

Drew surpassed himself that evening as to the large quantity and variety of alcoholic beverages consumed as he planned with his drinking buddies an imaginary fixture next season with the legendary Real Madrid at The Bernabeu in Spain. A thoroughly enjoyable piece of hokum engineered by Drew's vivid imagination

For once, Drew had every reason to celebrate in such an inebriated fashion.

*   *   *   *   *

Linda was continuously cursing the fact that Drew's brief visit to Paris had proven to be counter-productive. Rather than be in an upbeat and positive frame of mind, she was feeling somewhat deflated and preoccupied, particularly with it being a mere couple of hours before the start of the first round match in the French Open at Roland Garros.

Linda deeply regretted having had sex with Drew. Moreover, she was actually angry and intensely disappointed with herself for allowing it to have happened. The queasiness she felt when she remembered *that* night – it was not as if she had, for once, even remotely enjoyed the sex. The detail remained a blur, although the evening in general was a bit of an ongoing recall of mental torture. The more she tried to dismiss the incident, then the memory of it just became more and more vivid and consequently the pangs of sheer guilt and embarrassment got greater too.

She also knew she was far from being physically well prepared to play an important tennis match and that, in part, was due to the fact that Frank Haffey was no longer there as a companion or mentor, let alone available to offer practical coaching support. Just to compound Linda's current woes, she had this suspicion that she was taking a huge risk continuing to play with the knee injury, which she was starting to question, was potentially worse than she had been led to believe by the medics.

It also seemed to her somewhat ironic that Drew had left Paris in such a rush to make his way back to Glasgow. The irony being that Linda did not particularly like Paris as a place and Roland Garros being red clay was not her preferred surface to play on, as her results from previous years testified. Drew, on the other hand, loved Paris so much he often stated that he could happily live there permanently and The French was by far his own favourite tournament of the year, perhaps surprisingly even more so than Wimbledon. Drew had once proudly proclaimed, in an article he wrote in the *Daily Mail*, that it was the only romantic international tournament on the entire tennis circuit. He loved to remind people that the first winner was a Brit back in 1891 (although he usually had to concede, when recounting this fact, that it was before it became the exact same tournament that it is today). In 1891, and subsequent years, it was played in a number of different venues until 1928, when it found its spiritual home and was thereafter housed on a three hectare site provided by the City of Paris and the area was named after France's heroic aviator Roland Garros.

Linda's first round match was to be against Nadia Likhovtseva from Russia who happened to be most likely nearing the end of her playing career. However, Likhovtseva was still an opponent to be taken seriously, if for no other reason than she had reached the Top 20 rankings a few years back and was always considered capable of an upset, as she certainly had the experience and guile needed to produce one.

It was a match that did little to get the small crowd even remotely enthusiastic as Linda was playing extremely erratic tennis and this resulted in few rallies. Certainly, the strong wind conditions were not helping either of them. Neither was Linda's lack of practice, resulting in poor timing of shots, as was her constant awareness of her lack of full mobility due to the knee being heavily bandaged. Although, in truth, that was probably a state of mind, rather than any debilitating physical handicap created by the knee itself. The first set went to Mrs Likhovtseva 6-2 and Linda was at that point even contemplating retiring early on the pretext that her knee was giving her far more pain than it actually was. At a changeover in the second set at 2-3 Linda reminded herself that she had never walked off court before a match had been concluded. *Never* – she was a professional after all, and, anyway, it was a pretty pathetic and fabricated excuse that was potentially on offer. Whilst she sat in the court-side chair, feeling sorry for herself, she could hardly believe her eyes, or her luck, as one of the tournament's medical team sprinted across the court and started to administer some form of treatment to Mrs Likhovtseva. It soon became apparent, during the next game or two, that Likhovtseva was also suffering from a knee injury, which was significantly restricting her movement about the court. The same could not truthfully be said of Linda.

This sudden change of events sparked a raising of Linda's own game and lifted her both mentally and physically. This promoted a resurgence of positive self-belief and Linda eventually won the match 2-6, 6-4, 6-1.

Although it was a relatively impressive recovery to win the match, an hour or so later it became obvious it was not to be without some cost. Linda could feel the knee start to stiffen up even after some physio treatment and an ice pack being permanently pressed against the joint.

It appeared to Linda there was at least one positive to take out of all this apart from the victory itself and that was the injured knee gave her the ideal opportunity to withdraw from the mixed doubles competition which she had originally entered quite some time ago with Julien Bonneau.

When told of Linda's withdrawal, Julien called Linda on her mobile and accused her of being unnecessarily vindictive towards him, as well as not acting in a professional manner. He tried to reason that this, after all, was the most important tournament for him as a French national and because of the late withdrawal it would not be possible to compete with someone else. Also, there was the consideration of the prize money.

So what? Mixed doubles is supposed to be a bit of fun. Right now, Linda could think of nothing she would want to do less than play tennis with someone she had no time for whilst handicapped by an injury.

Maybe the Bonneaus could organise another lavish balle for their precious son to remind everyone how very special he was?

Mischievously, Linda made it known to Julien that she was pleased rather than sympathetic over his prospective loss of earnings from not being able to participate in the mixed event. She felt relieved at the prospect of not having to be playing competitive tennis with him ever again. This not so little verbal spat between them would surely see to that.

Bonneau terminated the conversation with a short rant to Linda in French.

Linda felt it was game, set and match to her and brought back an appropriate broad smile across her face to register that fact. *Arrogant French pig.*

The following morning Linda's knee had swollen up considerably and her immediate reaction was she would now certainly have to withdraw from the singles event, as well as the doubles. However, later that same day, the swelling had decreased enough to offer Linda some belated hope. Nevertheless, the knee was still worryingly restricting her movement even to walk, and any substantial pressure put on the knee joint resulted in a sharp shot of pain.

Only sixteen hours before her second round match, she had the knee examined by a doctor and a known and trusted physiotherapist. The doctor was reasonably confident that the injury was not that severe and with a pain-killing injection and barring unforeseen twisting or jarring during the match itself, she would be able to physically perform to about 90% of her normal level. The physio did not dispute the doctor's prognosis and advice, but voiced concerns that any further aggravation to the injury could result in a possible lengthier optimum period to achieve full recovery from the injury – perhaps even the need for an operation on the knee.

The physio quietly reminded Linda of Wimbledon being only a few weeks away and that was her own favourite tournament throughout the entire tennis calendar.

It was an agonising decision in more ways than one. What made her ultimately decide was a throw-away comment from the physio, who she respected, that there might be a long shot chance that the injury might just respond positively to strenuous exercise as that can happen by way of working an injury off.

Would Gerry's imminent arrival in Paris be an added and unwanted distraction? *Does Gerry know what had recently gone on in Paris with Drew? Would Gerry insist Drew travel back to Roland Garros with him?* Linda shuddered with embarrassment at the very thought of Drew returning to Paris so soon. *Maybe Gerry will help me through this injury decision – should I play or not?*

Gerry was definitely no help. No help whatsoever. He said it was Linda's call whether to risk the injury and play, or not. *How friggin helpful and decisive was that? Does Gerry ever offer anything other than just encouragement? I suppose there was the investment in me* - but right then Linda had to dig that particular excuse for and on behalf of Gerry from the very depths of her subconscious.

Linda decided to play. And play she did. And play extremely well she did, too. So well, in fact, that she easily beat the American Betty Livingston 6-1, 6-3. And just as importantly, the knee felt fine all during the match. Amazingly, there was no pain whatsoever from the knee. That was until a few hours later when the effects and benefit of the anti-inflammatory injection had worn off, at which point in time one kneecap ballooned up to twice the size of the other.

The following day Linda hobbled around her hotel room more in an awkward stiff state rather than in any appreciable pain. Clearly, another visit to the doctor and phyiso would be required before her next match, this time against the highly-rated clay court player Maria Sanchez-Lorenzo from Spain. Linda knew this would be a particularly tough examination under normal circumstances, let alone with a gammy knee. Linda was more of a mind that this really was the right time to, at last, act sensibly and retire from The French. However, perhaps astonishingly, both the doctor and the physio were of the opinion that the medical condition of the knee ligament was actually improving slightly. Indeed, the doctor felt that with another pain-killing injection Linda would be able to play with the same numbness effect to the knee as she had against Miss Livingston. What seemed to Linda a pronounced swelling of the knee was nothing to be overly concerned about.

Certainly Linda found the diagnosis a tad difficult to believe as the knee did not look better to her eyes, nor to her mind. Although she conceded the fact that she had been playing no practice tennis in between her matches and perhaps that rest was resulting in minor hidden improvements to the ligament joints that she was unaware of. She also conceded that she had indeed been able to play the entire match against Betty Livingston virtually without awareness of her knee being a handicap. Not only that, she had managed to play well. And win.

The match against Sanchez-Lorenzo was exactly what Linda had expected, with extremely long rallies from both baselines. That was the Spaniard's natural game and one Linda felt she had little alternative but to adapt her own game plan around. After all, she was, even with the aid of pain-killing injections, not physically strong enough with her lack of full mobility, not to mention limited match practice and training, to play a varied all-court, all-action game. Linda's limited tactic was simply one of being patient and trying to keep her error count to an all-time low. And hope upon hope that her opponent had a 'bad day at the office'. To achieve this low error rate, Linda felt she was having to call upon all her powers of concentration. To a certain limited extent that took her mind away from the physical demands of the match which, due to the nature of the play, meant she was probably having to run twice the distance that she would normally be covering on court during long and sustained rallies. At one stage she was thinking that the last thing she wanted was for this match to go into a gruelling third and deciding set. Unfortunately for Linda, that is exactly what happened and it was to be a bridge too far for her.

At 2-2 in the final set Linda was crying with pain after being over-ambitious by stretching to try to return a blisteringly heavy top-spin forehand shot from Sanchez-Lorenzo. After an ungainly looking lengthy slide along the bone dry dusty clay, the ankle twisted after losing her poise and natural balance, and Linda immediately felt a sharp pain shoot up her whole leg. Even the pain killing injection in her knee was not sufficient to alleviate the excruciating pain. The match was over for Linda. A sporting death by a vicious top-spin forehand. She retired. She had no option. She could not walk properly without experiencing pain, let alone play tennis.

It was indeed an anticlimax in more ways than just losing. It had been a fact that Linda had never played before in the Phillipe Chartier Centre Court, the main court at Roland Garros, and had, until the injury, thoroughly enjoyed the unique atmosphere generated by the knowledgeable - if not always appreciative - French crowd, having a certain deserved and unparalleled reputation for a Gland Slam venue for booing the odd unpopular player, or two.

'I knew you shouldn't have played this match, Linda. It hurts me so, so much to see you in this state,' said Gerry as he stared at Linda's wooden crutch and, rather pathetically, seemed close to tears.

Not as much as it hurts me. What is Gerry on these days? Same drugs as Drew?

'I did ask you, Gerry, if you thought I should play with the injury. You never replied.'

'I love you too much to hurt your feelings.'

Eh? Oh, Gerry – you are starting to worry me. You really are, Linda thought to herself, as well as wondering if she ought to say it out loud to Gerry.

'If Drew was here, he'd say the same to you, Linda.'

'Yeah, right, of course he would,' replied Linda with as much sarcastic tone added to her voice as she could muster.

*   *   *   *   *

Drew was getting a mammoth buzz from his work at Firhill Stadium where he felt he was being treated like some sort of Messiah, particularly by those supporters easily influenced by some biased reporting in the newspapers that the Cup success was largely down to Drew. The reality was that he had no involvement in recruiting Ruud Vanderkaamp to Firhill and there was little doubt, even in Drew's mind, that any short-term success was a result of Vanderkaamp's coaching and football management skills.

The commercial activities and general interest in Partick Thistle Football Club had gone from it being restricted to one highly dubious offer from a probable corrupt property developer to loads of offers of sponsorship deals and interest in joint ventures. Indeed, Drew found he had to pinch himself when he received a telephone call from a senior executive representing the major supermarket group Morrisons plc, who were making initial approaches of a joint venture to purchase and leaseback Firhill with the guarantee of a fully-developed modern stadium.

Everyone would be a winner. The club would retain a 999 year leasehold interest at a peppercorn rent. In return, Morrisons would be the new freeholders and would pay for a complete redevelopment of the land to facilitate a supermarket for themselves and incorporate a compact, but fully modern, sports stadium at no expense to Partick Thistle FC. Perhaps it was surprising what some positive publicity in the newspapers and some success on the field of play could initiate. The board of Morrisons plc were rumoured to be impressed by the business ethics and acumen that Drew had displayed when he made public disclosure of the corrupt business activities and illicit approaches of Digby Construction. Although Drew jokingly conceded to his fellow directors that Nike had not, as yet, made any advances, it was with enormous satisfaction to him that Adidas had made a lucrative sponsorship offer, as had the brewing conglomerate Scottish & Newcastle Breweries plc. For Drew, he already had pleasurable visions of all the complimentary free booze *that* particular sponsorship would bring.

The future of Partick Thistle Football Club had arguably never looked more exciting and promising since it was originally formed way back in the year 1876. And Drew was going to personally revel in the prospect of the continuing success in the future with his beloved football club – surely that would now be the case?

*   *   *   *   *

Even if Linda had experienced bouts of professional depression before, then surely this was as low as it got? As she sat, once again, in yet another departure lounge of yet another international airport waiting for yet another delayed flight, she was thinking about the severity of the knee injury and how long she would be out of tournament play. She also was not relishing the next inevitable meeting with Drew, the memory still all too vivid of that fateful night spent in bed with him returning as instant nightmarish flash-backs. If it were at all possible, Linda was feeling as time went by even more, not less, guilty and deeply ashamed about that sexual encounter.

Would Drew have mentioned it to Gerry? She sincerely hoped not.

Out of the corner of her eye, Linda noticed someone remotely familiar making rapid strides over in her general direction. It soon dawned on her that it was in fact Ian Girot, the reporter who was responsible for the very damning, and largely inaccurate, almost slanderous feature on Linda in a national newspaper a couple of months back.

Linda immediately picked up her hand luggage and started to walk briskly towards the nearest ladies' toilet facility at the Charles de Gaulle Airport.

*   *   *   *   *

It was a questionable accolade that had been bestowed upon Drew that he now - on the plus side - was the centre of much adulation from a tiny minority of Glaswegian football supporters. On the negative side, he had gained an extremely low popularity rating with many of the bigoted majority of so-called fans of Celtic and Rangers. The pluses and negatives resulted from having been the subject of much media attention, particularly in the sports sections of newspapers, but also after being seen interviewed on local television networks.

As he lay in a hospital bed, in a relatively plush private wing area annexed to the NHS Victoria Infirmary in Battlefield, South Glasgow recovering from emergency surgery, he was trying to discuss with a young policewoman by his bedside the incident and the detail behind the brutal and unprovoked attack on him, and who conceivably might have been responsible for it.

Was it a vindictive and bitter football thug?

Was it the revenge threatened by John Digby?

Was he simply the victim of an unprovoked attack whilst in a drunken state?

Drew tortured his mind trying to remember what had precisely happened. Maybe he would remember once he was no longer suffering from concussion? There again, maybe not.

The All England Championships, Wimbledon

Drew had decided to move from the Gleneagles area in the Highlands to another picturesque part of his homeland at Drymen, by the banks of Loch Lomond - an area primarily populated by professional and wealthy business people working in Glasgow. This relocation enabled Drew to drive to his new workplace at Firhill Stadium in the north centre of the City comfortably in just over an hour door-to-door, whereas Gleneagles was just a bit too remote for such a regular commute. Drew could no longer enjoy the comfort of working from home as he had done as a journalist. Only the motorway between Perth and Edinburgh, and its airport links to London City Airport, had previously made it a relatively stress-free journey for him to the *Daily Mail* offices once a week.

As Drew and his sixth wife Enid had only just moved into their new home in Drymen and had hardly had the time to make themselves acquainted with the neighbours, they were most definitely not expecting any visitors at around 11.30 at night just as they were preparing for bed. The front doorbell sounded, followed almost immediately by a noisy banging of what Drew assumed to be emanating also from the front door.

'Who the fuck is that at this time of night?' he demanded.

'Only one way to find out, darling,' retorted his wife in a sarcastic tone.

'Mr Taggart?'

'Yes. Why?'

'I'm Detective Chief Inspector Renwick and this is my colleague DC Bryans. We would like to ask you some questions please about a John Digby.'

'What – at this friggin' time of night?'

'Sorry, sir, it's important. Please accompany us to the station, sir. '

'Christ Almighty, surely this can wait until the morning? What's Digby been saying about me then? He's such a shark that man, ye know?'

'Mr Digby is dead, sir. It looks like he was murdered earlier today. We're endeavouring to speak to people we suspect have had confrontations with him recently. And your name has already been mentioned to us, sir.'

As Drew was trying to digest the ramifications of this news as quickly as his tired brain cells would allow, he noticed out of the corner of his eye several cars with people standing directly by them. They were positioned further down the street as well as at the foot of his front garden, and it became immediately obvious that this was no routine questioning.

'Aye, sure, I'll come down to your gaff, Inspector, and answer anything you want. I've got absolutely nowt to hide. Not from you, at any rate.'

Drew had to concede that he felt more than a bit intimidated by the considerable posse of accompanying vehicles that drove into Stirling Police Station. And also the number of what he assumed were plain-clothes policemen and women followed in procession through the main entrance of the station. Although the duty sergeant and his small team of colleagues were courteous, the feeling of intimidation continued and he felt decidedly uneasy about having his photograph taken, together with fingerprints and DNA tests. This was all before he could find out exactly what was going on and what he was being accused of exactly, if anything, in connection with Digby's apparent murder. Quite possibly, the intimidation that he felt was not helped by the amount of alcohol he had consumed earlier that evening. He certainly now regretted having that extra large malt whisky just before he started getting ready for bed. Drew soon progressed from feeling intimidated to being somewhat disorientated, not helped by being a mixture of semi-sober and semi-awake, much as he tried hard to persuade himself how vital it was to remain fully alert, even as an innocent man.

Christ, why did I have those large whiskies? Must stay focussed and not say anything to the bizzies that I'll regret.

'Would you like to make a phone call, sir? Perhaps call your solicitor?' suggested DCI Renwick.

'No need. I keep telling you I've got absolutely nowt to hide – anyway, it's now friggin' two o'clock in the morning. My brief's not going to thank me for calling him at this hour. Do what you have to do. Ask whatever you want. Just get on with it. Please. Thank you.'

Trying to pre-empt any possible detailed and lengthy interrogation, Drew soon volunteered to DCI Renwick that he had indeed been recently involved with John Digby and that Digby had tried to bribe him with substantial offers of money. Furthermore, he suggested to DCI Renwick, in a slightly patronising tone of voice, that he should get one of his officers to check the background of the bribe allegations out with local newspapers, where well-publicised articles existed. He then emphasized that the bribe was exposed by him, and nobody else, insofar as he warned Digby that any further bribes would be reported to the police.

'But sir, why didn't you formally report this particular bribe incident to the police when it actually happened, and before it, according to you, sir, became high profile through the media?'

'Take yer point, but I was more concerned about the damage it was doing to my own reputation and credibility with my fellow directors at the fitba club.'

'All the more reason why you should have reported it to the regulatory authorities then, sir, surely? Did you even report it the Scottish Football Association?'

'Er, no, it simply never crossed my mind.'

'Really, sir?

'Yes, *really*,' said Drew, starting to get irritated with the way the questioning was going. 'So what are you trying to suggest by this line of inquiry then?'

'Well, Mr Digby apparently told a couple of his closest business colleagues that you wanted £500,000 for your role in the acquisition of Firhill Stadium. And when he refused, you weren't best pleased. Is that true, sir?'

'No – it friggin well isn't true,' responded Drew indignantly. 'I asked for nowt. Absolutely nowt from Digby. And that's exactly what I received – nowt.'

'It seems you had a meeting with Mr Digby at which time you had an acrimonious row with him and you actually physically threatened him,' suggested DCI Renwick, a comment Drew took to be delivered accusingly.

'That's complete bollocks. Who told you that load of garbage?' snarled Drew. 'In point of fact, I had my solicitor present and he can verify what was said.'

'When was that meeting, sir?'

'Oh, I can't remember the exact date until I can check my diary, but it was a couple of months back.'

'But we've been told that you met John Digby only last Friday.'

'Who told you that load of auld fanny then?'

'The club steward at Pollok Golf Club.'

'Eh? Ye what? Come again, who did? retorted Drew, now becoming highly agitated.

'I guess I should explain, sir, that Mr Digby was found stabbed to death in the locker rooms at Pollok Golf Club. The steward said he remembered you having a heated argument with Mr Digby in the bar only last Friday.

Drew tried to gather his thoughts as quickly as his now extremely tired and laboured brain would function, and after a few moments pause for reflection responded, 'Ah hah, yes. I remember now. Yeah, I was there having lunch with some members I know at the Club. I go there a few times a year. My best pal, Gerry King, is a country member at Pollok Golf Club and I've been there countless times over the years – they do a brill lunch.'

'And?' provoked DCI Renwick, giving Drew a full-on, eyeball-to-eyeball exaggerated stare.

'Yeah, sorry. I did momentarily bump into Digby at the bar and exchanged a few words – not very pleasant ones as I recall.'

'So, what did you actually say to Mr Digby then, sir?'

'Oh, I just said that I was surprised that such a prestigious and reputable establishment like Pollok Golf Club would allow low life like Digby in through the front door.'

'And his reply?' interjected DC Bryans.

'Oh, something along the lines of wasn't £100,000 enough for a greedy bastard like you? And,' stuttered Drew, 'and, and, at that I just then walked away, but okay, in doing so I may have said something along the lines of, "you'll get your comeuppance one day, pal," admitted Drew. His feeling of agitation was now replaced with nervous worry.

'And a few days later Mr Digby just happened to be found murdered at the very same place, sir?'

'Can I call Alan Liddell, my lawyer, please?' pleaded Drew, before sinking his exhausted head into his outstretched hands.

*   *   *   *   *

Linda was surprised at how well her knee injury was responding to treatment, much better than she had expected, and she was starting to wonder if some of this speedy recovery was solely down to a Dr Shiels, who had only very recently been recommended to her by someone at a social function by sheer chance. Dr Shiels just happened to be Glaswegian and a keen tennis player and seemed to take an instant and remarkably upbeat interest and liking to Linda as a patient. Early days; however, nothing seemed like too much trouble and Dr Shiels always made himself available and even went out of his way that week to make several unscheduled visits to see Linda in Troon, where she was going through some self-supervised light fitness training routines.

On returning early from Paris, Linda had assumed that the traditional pre-Wimbledon tournaments at Eastbourne and Edgbaston would have been non-starters for her due to the severity of her injury and, therefore, could only try and be optimistic that she would be fit and ready for Wimbledon itself. However, after six or seven days recuperation and acupuncture treatment and intense massages by Dr Shiels in Troon, she now found herself down on the south coast of England playing in one of the biggest grass court tournaments of the year, sporting a field almost as strong as Wimbledon.

Eastbourne, as a tournament venue, irritated and frustrated Linda in equal measure. All the top players entered the event, with the notable exception of the high ranking Williams sisters from America. The other competitors would enter the event, but constantly complain about the weather – the rain, the cold, the strong prevailing winds, as if it all provided a suitable excuse to complement the poor condition of the grass courts themselves, usually derided for only allowing 'lotto' tennis, such was the unpredictable bounce of the ball during rallies. That said, Linda rather liked Eastbourne as a place, being a refined old-fashioned seaside town and saw it as one of few towns retaining many of the characteristics that Linda thought a throwback to what many provincial towns would have been like in England from decades and generations ago - relatively crime free, locals behaved as if they respected each other and generally the place was well preserved with no graffiti or ram-shackle drug-ridden council housing estates or ghettos. But, there again, Linda wondered what the average age of Eastbourne residents was; it must be at least eighty! She also wondered if once she and her fellow tennis competitors had left town, would there be any black people remaining?

Linda was sitting, on her own, on a bench by the café next to the tennis courts simply killing some time with her computer laptop when Fred Shiels appeared unexpectedly and sat down beside her.

'What a pleasant surprise,' beamed Linda. 'And, what the devil brings you all the way down here?'

'Oh, I just thought I'd check up on my favourite patient.'

'What, you've come all the way down here just to see me? Come on now,' laughed Linda playfully.

'No, you're sort of right. I happened to be in London giving a lecture at the BMA. I had some free time, so I thought, Eastbourne isn't that far away and I wanted to see how my favourite patient was doing, and, talking of which, how is the knee?'

'It's not bad at all, thanks. There's virtually no discomfort during the matches and only a little bit of stiffness the following morning. By the way, what are those tablets you ask me to take just before playing?'

'Oh, they're just anti-inflammatory tablets. Nothing special about them. Why do you ask, Linda, out of interest?'

'Just that the only time I can guarantee absolutely no pain or discomfort is during a match, that's all.'

'Don't forget – during actual playing you are warming the muscles and joints and that helps loosen them up. Now, let me have a look at the knee.'

'What, right here?'

'Why not?'

'Goodness, you're one keen and attentive doc.'

Just as Dr Shiels was tentatively feeling Linda's knee, a middle-aged couple stopped alongside them. The large balding man in front of Linda said in an unnecessarily loud voice, 'Aye-aye, what do I see here,' followed by what was pronounced and irritating public schoolboy-like laughter.

Linda pretended to ignore the man. But neither he, nor his lady companion, moved on.

'Are you going to win Wimbledon then?' continued the man, snorting again with obvious exaggerated laughter after asking the question.

Linda deliberately continued to ignore the man by not looking in his direction, nor acknowledging his presence.

Then the smartly dressed lady companion by his side added, 'Sorry for my husband's lack of grace and manners. I'm Sandra Summerfield and this unfortunately is my husband.'

Summerfield? ...Summerfield? That name rings a distant bell. Is he the guy Gerry knows?

'How's the knee?' continued Sandra Summerfield, clearly showing genuine interest by the tone of her voice.

'It's a lot better now, thanks to the brilliance of this man here,' acknowledged Linda, winking directly towards to Dr Shiels.

'You don't know who I am, do you?' interrupted Hugo Summerfield.

'Should I?' Linda continued to studiously avoid even glancing in his general direction.

'How's Drew Taggart?' interjected Mrs Summerfield.

'He's okay. You know Drew then?' responded Linda approvingly.

'I'm Hugo Summerfield,' interrupted Summerfield yet again.

'Sorry – *who*?' asked Linda, implying she did not give a jot who he was.

'Come on, my love, I'm the guy who offered to be your private banker and sponsor,' retorted Hugo blatantly leering unashamedly at Linda's chest, and starting to perspire like a paedophile in a primary school playground.

The penny, at last, dropped with Linda.

'You evidently don't play tennis, being so obese?' Linda spat in Dr Shiel's direction, but it was nevertheless obvious her comment was directed at Summerfield.

As Linda got up from the bench she gestured to Fred Shiels that it was time to carry on the knee inspection elsewhere. She concluded the conversation by looking at Hugo Summerfield, for the first time, with as much displeasure showing on her face as she could manage, 'And for sure I ain't your love. Got it?'

Later that afternoon, Linda noticed Sandra Summerfield sitting on her own in the clubhouse staring at a cup of coffee and looking a little forlorn and decided to wander over and join her.

'Look, I'm really sorry if I came across as being rather rude earlier,' offered Linda, projecting a radiant smile to complement the verbal apology.

'Not in the slightest. It was obvious you were just showing, as best you could without actually acknowledging him, what a twisted arrogant pain in the arse my husband actually is, yes?'

'I guess so,' sniggered Linda. 'Sorry.'

'Please, don't be. As it so happens we're both keen tennis fans and have been coming to Eastbourne for several years. We live less than an hour's drive away in south Kent.'

'Look,' said Linda, 'why don't you give me your address and mobile number and if you fancy it I'll send you a ticket for Wimbledon in a few weeks time and you can come up as my guest? We can do afternoon tea, or lunch, or something similar, eh? With Drew if you like. I'll mention it to him.'

'What, no ticket for Hugo then?' laughed Sandra.

'Absolutely no way, José,' giggled Linda again. 'Anyway Drew needs cheering up. He's been questioned about some ludicrous and fabricated murder charge, you know, and currently is out on bail. Like I say - I think he badly needs cheering up.'

'Count me in,' confirmed Sandra as if genuinely excited by the prospect.

The knee injury was less troublesome, almost to the point when Linda believed it was just ever so slightly short of being completely recovered. However, she was now suffering from an irksome stomach sickness. As a precautionary measure, she had tests run and a blood sample taken at the WTA temporary medical centre at Eastbourne.

On reaching Edgbaston in the West Midlands, there was absolutely devastating news awaiting Linda from those very tests. She was confirmed as being in the early stages of pregnancy.

Linda was in immediate shock. Like in complete, deep, profound shock. Like in shock she had only experienced once before in her entire life - on being told of her parents' sudden death in the car accident over fifteen years ago.

What a moral dilemma for Linda this now was, the likes of which she never remotely had to face before. Should she discuss the pregnancy with anyone? If so, who? It was a shuddering reality check for Linda that she did not know or trust anyone or felt sufficiently comfortable enough with whom to share this powerful emotional dilemma. Up until this news, she had always believed that she could trust either, or both, Drew and Gerry implicitly on just about anything. But, somehow, this type of predicament had never even figured in any of Linda's wildest nightmares.

Although Linda did agonise on her lonesome for a measured short period of time over whether to terminate the pregnancy or not, it was a relatively straightforward decision insofar as she kept coming up with the same outcome - she had little choice other than to have an abortion. The alternative of having the baby would certainly signal the end of what little time remained of her career as far as fulfilling any of the major burning tennis playing ambitions.

Then, there was the money that Drew and Gerry had invested, only nine months ago, in her future. What,

Linda felt, was maybe of greater significance was whether or not she wanted to know who the father was – and, if she knew, what did she intend to do with that information? Her thoughts strayed to wondering what either Drew or Julien Bonneau or perhaps even Willy Gilhooley might want, or expect, or demand. Not that Drew or Julien or Willy's views, per se, would be a deciding or even major influencing factor in her decision over any abortion, but it was nonetheless one Linda debated with herself. Should she tell them? Establish who the father actually was? Linda was becoming more and more of the alternate opinion that she did not want to even go there for a whole load of differing reasons, particularly as now she had all but finally decided to terminate the pregnancy at the earliest opportunity.

Linda wrestled with her own conscience, and somewhat reluctantly and on balance, decided that it was such a deeply personal and controversial issue that it was probably best she should live with it in private and take it, and all the resultant emotional baggage, to her grave.

Making decisions had never previously been a problem for Linda. Indecision was not one of her traits. Now was altogether different though. Some reassurance would surely be a comfort. Consequently, she enlisted the professional assistance of Dr Keegan again. Keegan offered no specific opinion, other than to encourage Linda to make a decision quickly and decisively. Then, stubbornly stick rigidly by her own decision and never, ever, to torture herself at any point in the future with regrets or doubts over it and subsequent action taken.

Later that evening Linda broke down and cried like she never believed it was possible to do. Not crying through pain or crying due to any conventional grieving process, or through self-pity, but simply the emotional turmoil of her decision to end someone's life before it ever began. *It's all very well for Keegan to tell me what is for the best for me. What about what is best for my unborn baby? Do I really have **any** moral right to make that decision? Is abortion tantamount to murder?*

Edgbaston, the tournament that traditionally immediately precedes Wimbledon, was not in any event one of Linda's favourite grass court venues. She had in the past been scathingly critical of the grass conditions there, which she felt were not a patch on Eastbourne, nor anything like as good as the near perfect conditions of Wimbledon. For Linda, the best grass courts in the world were at Queen's Club in West London as she could testify to having practised there on many occasions, although never in any official ranking competition.

Edgbaston would now, and forever more, be synonymous to Linda for being the place where she received the devastating news of the pregnancy.

Gerry had spent the previous three weeks at his small cottage in Santo de Serra on the island of Madeira. He arrived back in the United Kingdom at Birmingham via an overnight stop in Glasgow to visit Drew, the purpose of which was to see if there was anything practical he could contribute towards the investigation-cum-possible murder trial. Subsequent to declaring himself surplus to Drew's requirements, he headed south for Birmingham to be with Linda.

Linda was kind of pleased to see Gerry's friendly face turn up at Edgbaston as he, at least, represented some much needed normality in her life just at this precise moment.

If only Gerry could have known what was going on in Linda's head - not to mention her body - right then.

Linda felt semi-embarrassed and half-annoyed at Gerry raising the issue of finances again with her. *Did Gerry not realise I am trying as hard as I can playing with a gammy knee? Did he not know of all my recent trials and tribulations and being pregnant?*

But, of course, Gerry was not to know. He had absolutely no idea. Linda quickly reminded herself just how unfair she was being towards him, especially with him having invested so much of his own money in her future. And here he was, as always, being totally genuine and expressing commitment to her professional well-being.

Gerry enquired if Linda was missing Frank Haffey.

'Not sure one way or the other. Haven't really given matter much thought. Why do you ask?'

'I'm back home in Dartmouth for the weekend. Maybe I could pop over and see Frank in Torquay and see what the lie of the land is like? Maybe I can persuade him to work with you during Wimbledon. Then take it from there, eh? Drew thinks it'd be good for you to team up again with Frank.'

'Okay, Gerry – go for it. I think I'd like to patch things up with Frankie.'

Linda withdrew from the Edgbaston tournament and made immediate arrangements to visit a Harley Street clinic in Central London.

Whilst playing in the annual Wimbledon event over the past decade or so, Linda had always stayed with an elderly couple who lived in a substantial and charming Victorian house in Putney, being well appointed by the River Thames. This arrangement dated back to when Linda first started playing in junior events not that many years after her parents' death.

Perhaps because Linda was an only child it seemed close friends of her parents felt an obligation, out of respect for the memory of Linda's mother and father, that the least they could do was whenever possible offer any practical help and assistance to her. The difficulty was for a young teenager to fully understand that emotional need in others. Nonetheless, Linda soon enjoyed staying with Mr & Mrs Dale in Putney and that was all that was wholly relevant then, as indeed it was now.

Putney had been Linda's first experience of life outside Scotland. At the age of thirteen she was fascinated particularly with London's seemingly never-ending catalogue of tourist attractions to visit when her daily tennis activities were finished with. And, of course, Wimbledon from a strictly tennis perspective was something else. It took two or three years for Linda to stop being in awe of the whole place. Even The Bank of England courts and the plush facilities and surrounds a few miles away at Roehampton, where she was able to practice courtesy of a business contact of Mr Dale, was something that Linda remembered and valued with great fondness from Day One.

Linda was having a light salad lunch at the Bank of England Sport Centre's cafeteria when she was told that her first round match at Wimbledon was to be against Ann Selbie, an up-and-coming junior from Staffordshire. And, who was Ms Selbie's current coach? Well, none other than Emilio Fazzi. Although Linda still regarded Emilio as a friend and held no grudge whatsoever against him, she nevertheless suspected those feelings were not altogether reciprocated as she knew from others that Emilio was still bitter about the way he had been dumped so unceremoniously by Drew and Gerry.

Quite possibly, this bitterness was not helped by the fact that Linda had made no apparent attempt to dissuade Gerry or Drew from their conduct. Anyway, Linda felt this issue of Fazzi's remembered pain added yet more spice to what was already an intriguing draw. Another Scotland-versus-England encounter, Linda thought, as her mind started to wander. Within minutes, she was already starting to gee herself up for this one.

Wimbledon was always special.

*   *   *   *   *

Gerry arranged to meet up with Frank for lunch at the Torquay Lawn Tennis Club around one o'clock, although Frank had forewarned Gerry to bear in mind that he had a large group of youngsters from the local Churston Grammar School booked in for a coaching session that morning.

Having taken the car ferry over from Dartmouth and made the short fifteen minute journey down to Torquay, Gerry was slightly taken aback when he arrived courtside by the fact that none other than Sue Barker was working with Frank on court.

Frank, a short while afterwards, on joining Gerry in the clubhouse bar, asked if he minded Sue Barker joining them for lunch.

'Sure thing. I'll organise a table.'

Frank then departed to return again about five minutes later declaring that Ms Barker would not, after all, be joining them for lunch.

'I did invite her but, when I said I had pre-arranged company and told her exactly who with, she made

211

excuses and implied she had last minute alternative plans for lunch, after all. Did you know she was born and lived just down the road in Paignton? In fact, played quite a bit of tennis here at this club. She's Paignton's best known celebrity, you know,' proclaimed Frank.

Probably because she's the only one, thought Gerry.

'So, you know why I'm here, big boy. What d'ya say, Frankie boy? Let's have one last throw of the dice. Shall we? You, me, Drew and Linda for two weeks max and then let's review after that, eh? Let's forget about what went on in the past.'

'And Linda? How's her head these days?'

'It's a damn sight better than her knee,' laughed Gerry, ruefully trying to be light-hearted about it. 'Seriously mate – Linda's well up for it. She's fully committed. No question. She realises she was bang out of order down in Melbourne. She accepts her behaviour was unprofessional, but don't forget, she did win the mixed doubles, so you and her must have done something right down in Oz, eh?' Gerry was pleased with himself for sounding so genuine and sincere even though he was embellishing matters somewhat, if not actually lying about them to Frank. He continued, 'If it's any incentive we'll pay ten per cent of anything Linda wins as prize money plus reimbursement of all of your personal expenses, of course. Generous or what, huh?'

'Okay, count me in for old time's sake. I like you guys, I really do admire what you've done for Linda - and you deserve some success for all the risks you've taken. I'll give Linda a call and we'll bury the hatchet and start again,' Frank smiled in agreement.

'Great stuff, Frank. I'm so pleased. Drew and I will be there for Wimbledon as usual, but there's been some unfortunate developments I must tell you about, involving the boys in blue from a certain constabulary and my dear auld pal.'

* * * * *

'I've got some really guid news for you, pal,' blurted out Gerry.

'If you said that under oath I'd sue you for perjury,' moaned Drew.

'You know those friggin' shares in Think Kids Entertainment that bombed?'

'How could I forget? I lost most of my life's savings in a blink of an eye.'

'Well, I've been working behind the scenes with an accountant with Power of Attorney granted by the courts for Think's assets. His name is Neil Harding-Deans and between us we've managed to successfully lodge an application with the courts over some serious wrongdoing. The hearing is scheduled for next week.'

'Serious wrongdoing – like what exactly?'

'Like fraud, like forgery, like embezzlement, like misappropriation of funds, like theft, like misrepresentation, like....'

'Aren't they all the same thing?' interjected Drew.

'Stop trying to be the smart arse. They're all crimes in their own right, mate.'

'Wow, does this mean I'll get all me dosh back?'

'Not yet, but *if* we win the court case, then *yes* it's highly probable.'

Gerry found himself, once again, being temporarily back in his element as he reminded and updated Drew on the background regarding the Think Kids Entertainment Company. How 43,000 shareholders were indirectly duped when making their original share investment, as the Company was being managed by a board of directors who, it subsequently showed, only knew how to do two things successfully:-

One, being how to raise large sums of money on a flawed prospectus based on misleading accounting and commercial activities from prospective institutional and private retail investors, and *Two,* how to spend that same money raised by paying themselves extravagant and disproportionate salaries and expenses, in return for doing precious little.

It arguably even made some City bankers who regularly received millions in unearned bonus payments look like charity workers.

It was a major scandal. It was a scandal that shocked even City Watchdogs who thought they had seen every conceivable scam over the years.

Gerry had offered his services on a voluntary basis to Neil Harding-Deans, shortly after Neil had his appointment ratified by the law courts. The primary aim of Harding-Dean's appointment was to investigate matters on behalf of shareholders and creditors and then to bring to book the guilty individuals in respect of any established illegal activity.

What Gerry and Neil were soon able to establish, on having direct access to all the company's records and accounts and bank statements, was incredibly that debts had mounted to £8 million, with gross income being less than £500,000 per annum. Yet, only a few months earlier, the company had issued a formal statement to the London Stock Exchange declaring that it was "trading ahead of expectations", hence thousands of private investors bought shares either for the first time or to top-up their existing stockholding.

Furthermore, Gerry and Neil uncovered an even bigger confidence trick being promoted and executed by a so-called Shareholder Action Group. This group (aptly nicknamed SHAG) was formed to raise further funds to protect their original investments by preventing the company legally folding and thereby rendering their shareholding and investment as worthless. The Shareholder Action Group, too, was a complete sham, being a committee of six individuals and so formed, supposedly, to act solely for and on behalf of shareholders to raise funds and submit a rescue proposal to the liquidator.

A wholly flawed and misleading prospectus had been submitted to the 43,000 shareholders and it spectacularly raised a further £7.2 million.

Within months all the £7.2 million money raised by shareholders to save the Company had been spent. And, it had been spent largely on fees for professional assistance from the likes of bankers and lawyers and accountants and liquidators and a select short list of individuals who were masquerading as shareholders, but were in fact little short of being crooks. Virtually nothing had been invested into core commercial activities to build the company back to operating profitably, thereby to enable the shares eventually to be traded once again on the stock market. It almost defied belief, as the same shareholders had in fact been very cleverly duped for a second time. The same small group of six individuals, claiming to rescue the company and acting for and on behalf of the 43,000 shareholders, simply seized upon the opportunity by benefitting financially to satisfy their own greed. It was a sting that Paul Newman and Robert Redford would have been proud to have played out, such was it a highly ingenuous and devious plot. Not only was it a sting, but it was tantamount to corporate theft.

'So, it's payback time for those thieving bastards who stole our money?' smirked Drew. 'You've got all the legal evidence, then?'

'Aye, indeed. All the culprits are running around like headless chickens before the court trial, all blaming everyone else but themselves. Any judge half awake will find them as guilty as hell, I'm sure of it, and the DTI and the FSA have been put on notice, too.'

'Who?'

'The Department for Trade and Industry and the Financial Services Authority, both of whom have a duty to stop this kind of fraudulent activity. The police and the CPS are already carrying out an investigation.'

'Where's me £30,000 cheque then?'

'Patience, dear boy, patience.'

*   *   *   *   *

'Hi Emilio – it's really nice to see you again,' breezed Linda as she warmly embraced Emilio Fazzi with a hug and a kiss on both his cheeks.

'How's the knee?'

'Oh, it's been great since I started seeing this new doctor.'

'Who is that then?'

'Fred Shiels – he's a marvel, you know.'

'Never heard of him,' said Fazzi, sounding positively dismissive. 'Are you looking forward to playing against our Annie today, then?'

'Absolutely. I see we're on Court No.1. Due to both being home girls, I guess?'

'Ah, shhhhhit. Is that Drew and Gerry over there? I'm off. Catch ya later. Hope it's a good game, Linda.'

Linda was really pleased that Frank Haffey had decided to come back and work with her, even if it was only for a couple of weeks. He was such an upbeat kind of guy, exactly what she suspected she needed right now. And because Frank was so disciplined and professionally demanding, it ensured Linda did not have much spare time to let her mind wander to more distracting and negative thoughts, particularly about the recent abortion.

Frank and Linda had a long and profitable workout on the practice court and Linda was feeling no twinges at all from her knee. Her spirits being generally uplifted with Frank being around and with no injury to worry too much about, she was sensing for the first time in ages that this could be the start of a decent run in a tournament. 'Fresh, hungry for success and raring to go', Linda had told Sue Barker when they briefly exchanged a few casual words just outside the ladies' changing-rooms.

Gary Richards, the roving television reporter from the BBC, was patiently waiting for Linda to finish her practice session to film and record an interview with her.

As per usual with Richards, he would try and make out he was his interviewee's best buddy whilst still managing to slip in a deliberately embarrassing or controversial question or two. Well, he certainly had more than enough ammunition to fire at Linda. However, it was limited to why she thought she had so spectacularly underachieved at Wimbledon and if any lessons had been learnt from the on-court and off-court shenanigans at the previous Grand Slams in New York, Melbourne and Paris.

Charming, Linda thought. Here was a British reporter at his best, only wanting to discuss negative or critical or controversial matters. But she exerted all her own charm throughout the interview and gave non-committal answers to the probing questions. She let Richards know when the filming stopped just how disappointed she was and told him not to rush back for another interview.

Somewhat perversely, Linda was reassured that she was feeling distinctly nervous before this match with Selbie. In fact, she was as tense as she had been for a long time and, as Frank reminded her, all she needed to do was channel that nervous energy in a positive manner.

Ann Selbie was a bit of an unknown quantity to Linda. Even though Selbie was British, Linda had never played against her in a competitive match. Her only experience of Ann was having practiced some with her in training sessions. Selbie, for seventeen years of age, was a powerfully-built girl in the mould of a younger Mauresmo, and Linda suspected from what little she did know about Selbie's game, it was probably well suited to a grass surface.

1st Round

As the players knocked up on Court No.1, Drew and Gerry swapped their seats in the area designated for players' guests so that they were as near as possible to where Emilio Fazzi was sitting. There clearly was no forgive nor forget on either side as there had been no acknowledging each other's presence, let alone any courteous greeting or handshake.

Just as Linda went back to her chair beside the umpire to remove her track suit top, Drew stood up and looked over in Fazzi's direction to gesticulate with his thumb and forefinger two zeros, to try to signal a 6-0,

6-0 score line message to Fazzi. This signal was then followed by a shaking of the hand and wrist in the commonly acknowledged fashion to show he thought Fazzi was a wanker.

It would have been impossible for Fazzi not to have figured out exactly what message Drew was trying to convey, but nevertheless, in return, somewhat pathetically he presented a puzzled expression on his face as if to respond that he had no idea what Drew's point was. Drew's momentary feeling of guilt for behaving like a ten-year-old naughty schoolboy was quickly forgotten on seeing the huge smirk on Gerry's face as he sat beside him. Even Frank chipped in jovially with, 'I hope the TV cameras didn't pick up on that.'

Oh bollocks, Drew chuckled to himself. *I'll get more looks of disapproval from Ms Barker next time I see her.*

In some ways the match was a bit of an anti-climax, as Linda showed far too much class and variety of shot, whilst keeping the error count down to a pretty acceptable rate.

Selbie, as Linda expected, did possess a powerful and penetrating serve but, when not being executed erratically, it was a rather predictable shot, and once Linda was able to judge the pace of it she had little difficulty returning the ball with interest. It was almost as if the serve was Selbie's only dangerous weapon. She certainly did not appear to have a game plan, not one that Linda could judge at any rate, or perhaps Selbie had simply not played anything like to her potential on grass.

The straight-set score line of 6-1, 6-2 adequately reflected how straightforward a victory it had been for Linda, particularly as the match only lasted thirty-four minutes. After the previous year's narrow and hugely disappointing defeat at this stage of the competition to Shilpa Mirza, this was a welcome and positive start to Linda's Wimbledon campaign.

Whilst everyone was standing applauding Linda and Selbie politely and sportingly off the court, it seemed Drew could not resist moving that bit closer to Fazzi so as to impart a few presumably not very polite comments about what he thought of Fazzi's coaching skills. And his lack of match play strategy and tactics, and how it was all too evident during the contest they had just watched.

Although Linda had not felt stretched in the slightest during the match against Selbie, she did feel unusually tired that evening and the knee for the first time in ten days started to feel distinctly stiff again and a very slight but nonetheless noticeable swelling had reappeared. Maybe it was just a consequence of playing on a pristine and lush, but slippery, grass court. As a precautionary measure she telephoned Dr Shiels, who said he would have a prescription sent to her as soon as he could practically arrange it – and would be more or less the same tablets she was currently taking, but a slightly more potent version.

'Let me know how they go,' requested Dr Shiels.

'Sure will. And thanks again. Sorry to have disturbed your evening. Are you planning to come down to Wimbledon?'

'There's the small matter of a ticket. Otherwise I'd love to come as often as possible. You give me the tickets and I'll give you the tablets. Sounds a fair deal, eh?'

'Definitely. Maybe.'

There was now a tangible strained atmosphere between Drew and Linda. Since Paris, any meetings or verbal exchanges between them had always been whilst in the company of others. Drew clearly was suffering from his own particular serious problems at the minute. Linda found it hard to imagine what it would be like to be out on bail on a murder charge. *Absolutely impossible Drew could kill anyone.* With the word 'kill', Linda's mind sharply deviated to the abortion. Again.

It had been six months or so since all three of them - Drew, Gerry and Linda - had been together as a threesome. Linda far, far preferred having their company any day of the week compared to lonely days in some far-flung place that consisted, to her, basically of tennis courts, a hotel, and an airport.

Frank had, it seemed, forgotten all about the disagreement and/or misunderstanding down in Melbourne. Linda got the distinct impression that everyone was of one mind, Drew, Gerry, Frank and herself included, that this was a pivotal short period of time in her career. Another complete failure might well signal the beginning of the end, regardless of much money still remained from Drew and Gerry's original investment.

Linda was not seeded for Wimbledon, having an official world ranking of No.35 after poor performances in France, then Eastbourne and Edgbaston, and because of her disappointing showing over the past three or four years at Wimbledon, she was not considered good enough for a seeded place.

I'll show 'em. Linda never felt more determined than she did right now. Now was a real opportunity to make the belated breakthrough into the big time. Linda momentarily thought of Dr Keegan and then reached for one of her tapes to instruct and develop her mental strength and deter any negative thoughts.

2ⁿᵈ *Round*

Linda was waiting patiently by the umpire's chair for her next opponent to turn up - a little known qualifier from Venezuela called Clarisa Brandi.

Quite bizarrely, Ms Brandi simply did not make an appearance and, perhaps more surprisingly, absolutely none of the Tournament Officials could offer any explanation as to why. It was later established that Ms Brandi had checked out of her hotel room the previous evening and all the indications were that she was heading back to South America.

Linda had been the beneficiary of a walk-over before; however, they could always be explained away by some injury or personal circumstance. Never, ever, a complete no-show with no explanation nor advance apology. Whatever the reason, Linda was now through to the next round, where and when she suspected it was inevitable a seeded player would lie in wait.

3ʳᵈ *Round*

The Argentinean player Clarisa Garrigues, who was seeded No.23 in the tournament with a World Ranking of No.7, was to be Linda's next opponent. If Linda was to have to face a seeded player, she was obviously happier that it was one who did not have an impressive track record at Wimbledon. Garrigues fitted the profile perfectly, indeed hard-fought first and second round victories were her first ever at Wimbledon. Garrigues, like most Argentinean players, did not feel comfortable playing on grass.

The tablets that Dr Shiels had prescribed arrived by the Thursday morning at Linda's Putney base and she was able to take a couple before her match with Garrigues on Court No.2.

Linda had expected, or at least hoped, to be going back on to one of the show courts. She felt sure that Tim Henman or Andy Murray would not be playing on Court No.2 for obligatory security reasons, which Linda sometimes thought was a tad lame excuse offered on Messrs Henman and Murray's behalf, although she fully accepted the fact that she did not command the huge interest level or the support they did. Notwithstanding that, she still could not help but feel slightly disappointed at having to play on Court No.2 for such an important match.

The cramped, almost claustrophobic, feel to Court No.2 - famous for its history as being the graveyard court of champions, and soon to be relocated elsewhere within the grounds - at least helped create a raucous atmosphere and the crowd predictably showed biased support for Linda over her Argentinean opponent. Maybe also, there was a high degree of sheer sympathy from a predominantly genuine tennis audience given the mixed coverage Linda had received over the past six months in the British press. Certainly, she was benefiting from a lot more vocal support than in previous years when she was almost an anonymous player, or maybe that was simply due to her non-performances.

There was no doubting the fact that the unique and lively atmosphere of Court 2 did something to inspire Linda, who gave as focused and as impressive a performance as she had done in quite a long time. Garrigues, as it so happened, was no push-over and, as she herself admitted later in the Press Room, that she too probably played as well as she had ever done on a grass surface. The games were blessed with entertaining rallies, sprinkled with some outrageous winners on both sides of the net. But, Linda won by the score line 6-3, 6-4 which may have flattered Linda somewhat, however as Frank reminded Linda afterwards, it was all about playing the key points well and winning as many as was possible. That was the main difference between the two players – Linda took her few chances when presented with them. Otherwise the match was deceptively close.

Linda knew prior to leaving Wimbledon that evening her next round opponent would be the German Martina Muller, the 9th seed, and a player Linda had played four times in the past and never beaten, albeit all matches had been three-set affairs and all extremely close encounters.

Linda had spoken earlier in the day to Sandra Summerfield, and they had arranged to meet up the following day for lunch at the Chelsea Kitchen restaurant down the still trendy King's Road in Central London.

Probably not exactly what Frank Haffey wanted to hear, but Linda stubbornly over-ruled his counter itinerary, citing the fact she felt her knee needed a rest, yet again, from playing. So, after a light work-out in the morning, she could then go off and have lunch with Sandra Summerfield in Chelsea and then enjoy some retail therapy at Harrods or Harvey Nicholls or wherever took their fancy. The look on Frank's face suggested he very reluctantly agreed, perhaps trying to transmit a more tolerant attitude than he had shown in Australia. 'Guess you know your body far better than me, pet.'

Linda had taken an instant liking to Sandra Summerfield from the time they met down at Eastbourne and somehow she suspected this extremely elegant middle-aged woman was talkative and interesting, without being overbearing and self-opinionated. Of equal importance, Sandra seemed enthusiastic to reciprocate and develop a friendship with Linda.

Without doubt, Linda had found it nigh impossible to build up a lasting and meaningful rapport with any of her tennis companions on tour. Most seemed obsessed with their fitness and their tennis as well as themselves, and few projected much depth to their character or personality. *There's always 'bitch slapping'. Always.* Although Linda conceded she might be exaggerating the situation a touch, however, the way she saw it, put a bunch of female tennis players together and they always bitched about everything and anything and everyone. Tennis, tennis, tennis. Success, success, success. Anything else, and everyone else, was a by-product.

A strange tingling sensation shuddered down Linda's spine when Sandra told her that the best sex she had ever had was with someone that Linda knew very well.

'You know, Drew, Drew, was the most incredible lover I've ever had,' confessed Sandra unabashed.

'No? Never?' Drew Taggart? I had honestly *no* idea,' she continued, 'when, when was this then?' Linda stuttered, trying to regain her composure.

'Oh, only about nine months ago. Actually it was when Drew came looking for that sod of a husband of mine, you remember, to sort him out regarding him trying to stitch you up with some sort of business deal.'

'Well, well, well. Three holes in the ground. Well, I never. You and our Drew, eh?' said Linda, trying to sound as unfazed as possible.

'You're so lucky to have such a loyal friend to rely upon,' insisted Sandra.

'Well, ain't I just. Well, ain't I just,' repeated Linda in an ever so slightly, if not altogether obvious, sarcastic tone of voice.

4th Round

That morning, Linda and Frank, began with having a strenuous work out on the practice court in preparation for the match against Martina Muller. A win would put Linda into the last eight of the competition.

On completion of the on-court training session, Linda sauntered over to where Drew and Gerry were sitting, both engrossed in reading newspapers.

'Hey, you two – I spent most of yesterday with someone you know.'

'Who was that then?' enquired Gerry.

'Sandra Summerfield.'

'Oh, yeah? She's a grand lass is Sandra – salt of the earth. Pity about that dickhead of a husband of hers,' muttered Gerry from behind his newspaper.

'She was asking after you both – particularly you, Drew.'

'I need a drink. Are you coming for one, mate?' Drew whispered as he sharply glanced in Gerry's direction.

'Bloody hell, Drew, it's only just gone eleven in the morning, pal.'

Linda bent down, rummaging through her large sports bag and on finding a bottle of hi-energy glucose drink said, 'Drew, here's a drink for you. And, it's far better for you, too.'

She looked up to where Drew had been, but he was no longer there.

Muller possessed a pretty similar type of versatile game to Linda and was having a successful season thus far, hence her low seeding at Wimbledon. Both Frank and Linda knew only too well that Linda could afford no off day against Muller and had to produce her 'A' game. Frank also reminded her that realistically there was nothing to choose between her and Muller, but there had to be a premium for Linda having such a staunchly patriotic crowd willing her on, particularly against a German sports person. And, to make sure she used that atmosphere in a positive manner, as hopefully it might just emotionally intimidate her opponent.

Linda wondered if Frank had deliberately overlooked the fact that her appearances over the years on the show courts were acutely limited because of her past non-performances.

Muller had unsurprisingly moulded her game along the lines of her childhood heroine, Steffi Graff, unquestionably the greatest German women player that ever lived. And Muller, too, had developed a similar fearsome forehand that Linda knew she had to avoid, or at least limit hitting shots to that side, and instead concentrate on her opponent's weaker backhand.

The match was played on a near perfect No.1 court surface and of course in front of a capacity crowd, most of whom, it appeared, wanted Linda to win. Linda's failures and under achievements from the past, it seemed, were all forgotten and the positive and enthusiastic coverage in the press and television had been greater over the past forty-eight hours than it had in the previous five years in aggregate.

Linda was playing as well as she could realistically have wished, but was finding it impossible to even get close to breaking Muller's impressive serve. Muller had one of the fastest serves on the woman's tour, with 125mph being registered not uncommon, and the rate of first serves counting was statistically particularly high at 87%. At 6-6 in the first set Linda had come nowhere close to even getting a game point on Muller's serve, yet had been a bit fortunate herself on her own service games, surviving seven individual break points in total. Linda reckoned by the law of averages alone it would surely not be too long before Muller did break serve. Tie breaks, by their very nature, are always critical junctures, but Linda knew only too well the significance of this particular one. To lose it would leave her most certainly a mountain to climb to win the match.

The crowd could not be faulted, as they lifted the atmosphere at the start of the tie-break to a level that would have inspired even a passive and grossly overpaid foreign Premier League professional soccer player. Linda was conscious of the fact that Muller had hitherto shown no emotion or reaction whatsoever to the occasion, or the atmosphere, and Linda wondered if that was a deliberate camouflage or just her natural conduct at such tense moments.

All Muller's actions, during and outside of actual play, were done at a brisk pace. With that very much in mind, Linda decided to take a small gamble and try to slow proceedings right down, justifying it on the over-excited and a hardly typical disciplined tennis crowd. When Linda was about to serve, or indeed when she was about to receive serve, she would deliberately pull back and ask for a few additional moments to allow the crowd to settle. So protracted were the delays they were desperately close to invoking a potentially disastrous penalty point against Linda. All of a sudden Muller's first serve was not nearly as accurate as it had been, and was having to rely upon her second serve during the tie break. *Pure coincidence? Were Muller's nerves starting to show*? Linda asked herself. This apparent break in the pattern of play may well have led to a minor break in concentration levels. It may even have been enough to give Linda the narrowest of narrow advantages, as Linda won a long tie break 12-10. Linda's own immediate analysis was that her uncharacteristic minor display of gamesmanship indeed had some effect. Certainly Muller's serve was suddenly and inexplicably less potent or productive. In fact, Muller's reliance on her weaker second serve, Linda believed, made the subtle difference and, therefore, was instrumental and quite possibly a major contributory factor that enabled her to win that vital tie break.

Linda also strongly suspected that winning this first set was absolutely crucial to gaining an extra boost to her own self-belief and confidence. It was fairly obvious that Muller was playing almost to her maximum and Linda certainly knew she, herself, could hardly play much better than she actually was. Linda was probably right, and Muller did not maintain the extremely high level of consistency in the second set that she had shown in the first. It was still mighty tight.

However, Linda deservedly won the second set, yet again, on a nerve-racking tie-break. With this second tie-break there truly only looked like one winner as Linda was, even to the few neutrals in the crowd, the player seemingly in control when it mattered most. Confidence had been a key factor. Linda was also being inspired by the patriotic crowd's show of enthusiasm. The adrenaline was pumping furiously through her whole body. No question. There had been no need for any gamesmanship either. Not in the second set tie-breaker at any rate.

It was the best performance Linda had given at Wimbledon, ever, beyond any shadow of a doubt in her mind. Nor was it in Frank's mind, as he effusively demonstrated later over a protracted post-match analysis and discussion.

After a victorious match Linda, as always, made a point of seeing and talking to whoever had been her guests and supporters in the visitors' box.

'Great win, Linda – touch and go though – you don't help me auld ticker you know. I absolutely *love* you,' crowed a clearly delighted Gerry.

'Sorry about creating too much excitement for you,' laughed Linda. 'Where's Drew then?'

'Think he's just this minute shot off to the bar – the match was too much excitement for him,' pleaded Gerry, as if speaking defensively on his friend's behalf.

'Or, too long going without alcohol, eh?' added Linda with a rare chill to her voice. 'Surprised he didn't have anything to say about me meeting up with Sandra Summerfield yesterday?'

'Och ye know Drew, he's probably only being a tad reticent – he's probably shagged her. Ye know Drew. He's had more lassies than I've had hot dinners.'

'That'll come back to haunt him one day,' Linda icily predicted, before adding, 'Right, I'm off to have a shower and then I promised to do another interview with Sue Barker. I'm trying hard to make amends for my silly behaviour on the TV with her at the BBC's *Sports Personality* thingy.'

'Ah yes, I do remember that,' remarked Gerry, seemingly, somehow, appreciating Linda's embarrassment. 'Was Drew leading you astray that night then?'

*Drew did nothing **that** night*........countered Linda indignantly to herself as she marched away from Gerry.........*not **that** particular night, at any rate.*

Linda's mind was vibrating furiously after her interview with Sue Barker, during which it fully registered that she had reached the quarter-final stage of Wimbledon for the first time in eight long years. When viewed objectively, a quarter final appearance, in itself, was no mean feat given Linda's historical lack of achievement at Wimbledon. Her current frenzied state of mind was no doubt helped by the amount of interest and excitement that was being generated by the general public, as evidenced also in the advertorial pieces that the BBC were presenting and hyping to increase their own viewer ratings.

Linda wondered if her being in such a relatively happy mental frame of mind with all the recent tennis success, that this might be an opportune moment to address and resolve the outstanding matter with Drew about the pregnancy and abortion. It just did not seem right, Linda considered, to sweep the entire issue under the carpet, not for ever and ever. Although she found it relatively easy to heed Dr Keegan's advice of not regretting any decision made, the same did not apply to being able to forget completely about the actual abortion itself. It was a psychological burden, which, after due consideration, she decided was not one that she wanted to take alone to her grave. She could not entirely pretend that sleeping with Drew was one of those things that simply happened. In any event, Linda was intrigued to know what Drew's own thoughts and feelings were. Was he equally embarrassed and angry? Drew had still never acknowledged what had happened in Paris, let alone discussed it.

It was an increasingly uneasy relationship festering between them, and the carefree and fun friendship and banter was not what it had been, that was for sure. It disturbed Linda to see a dilution of this treasured friendship. But, on the other hand, if she did discuss the whole matter of them having intercourse, was she not being deceitful by not mentioning the pregnancy?

Slightly reluctantly, Linda decided to postpone any immediate plans to discuss the matter with Drew, and perhaps subconsciously still hoped that instead he would be the one to take the initiative and raise it with her first. If not, she felt the best option was to slowly, ever so slowly, work on getting their relationship back to what it once was. Then, from a re-established position of friendship and strength, she would raise these highly delicate personal issues frankly and openly with Drew. But, not until then.

Well, that's a plan. For now. Isn't it? Linda's mind clearly needed some convincing if she had to even ask that question of herself.

Quarter-Final

'Hell's bells, Frank – my knee has really stiffened up. Wonder why?' complained Linda immediately after he insisted upon a ten mile road run round Putney Heath and then over to Wimbledon Common. *Jogging. Running. So boring. I hate it. No wonder my sodding knee is so damn sore!*

She had already taken the precaution of telephoning Fred Shiels, whose suggestion was perhaps fairly predictable, to double-up on the dosage of the existing prescription. 'I know how much this quarter-final match means to you tomorrow. I'll be there myself. I'll bring more tablets with me.'

Drew had returned back down to Wimbledon from Drymen after the weekend, giving everyone the impression that his solicitor was entirely confident that the Crown Prosecution Service may be dropping their case and with it any murder charge against him. Drew seemed heartened by all the support and encouragement he had received from the staff at the football club, as well as from Enid, his wife. So much so, Drew confided in Gerry, that a part of him actually wanted to stay at home in acknowledgement of that support. However, a far greater consideration was that he had come this far with Linda, and he was not about to miss out on what everyone was optimistically hoping, with potentially only three matches remaining, that this

233

might be 'it'. What they had all dreamed about for so, so long.

So, it was to be yet another showdown for Linda with her arch-rival Zerova. There were so many incentives for Linda to win this particular match, but none eclipsed the prospect of being through to the semi-final of Wimbledon. Not even the warped, deeply personal, satisfaction of thrashing Zerova.

Linda had hoped the match would be played on No.1 Court which she was starting to superstitiously feel might be a lucky venue for her. Instead, the match was scheduled for Centre Court, the first time Linda had played there in four long years; she had never previously won on that court.

This is no time for superstition. No time for negative thoughts. This is the ultimate place to aspire to as a tennis player. All the 'greats' have played on Centre Court. And are all the greater for playing here and winning, not through losing here, Linda reminded herself.

Zerova was seeded largely on the strength that she had reached the quarter-final last year. Zerova's current form on grass was difficult to assess as she had struggled in the first round against a qualifier, and indeed had to save a match point in a close three-set encounter. Conversely, she would be playing Linda on the back of her greatest win in her career to date by eliminating the current Wimbledon champion, Ingrid Corbourgh, last Friday afternoon in the last sixteen of the competition.

Linda was not suffering from any lack of confidence, especially as she knew she had the game to beat Zerova, evidenced from some previous meetings between the two. Just how the obvious bad blood between them would manifest itself - especially after

Melbourne when Zerova even childishly refused to shake Linda's hand at the end of that mixed doubles match - presented yet another interesting facet to this encounter.

The match was perhaps predictably played in a tense atmosphere both on and off the court and, in truth, both competitors were showing more than a few signs of nervous tension through their respective performances. There was absolutely nothing to choose between them in the first set except when, decisively, at 5-all, Linda strung together three consecutive winners that broke Zerova's serve. And, although the next game on Linda's serve was one of the most exciting and close games imaginable, vitally Linda managed to win the all important critical points, and thereby be one set to the good.

The second set mirrored the first. It was error-strewn and again there was absolutely nothing to separate the player's performances. It could have gone either way except for, again, Linda having a short purple patch for a few consecutive points on Zerova's service and that was enough to enable Linda to win the second set also.

7-5, 7-5 was the match result, leaving the crowd to breathe an audible sigh of relief, perhaps to conceal the fact that the match itself had not been a great spectacle. The all-important fact, for them as well as Linda, was that Linda would now be playing in the Wimbledon semi-finals for the first time ever.

* * * * *

Gerry and Drew were at Gerry's studio flat in Pimlico having a drink, or three, whilst they watched the BBC's *Wimbledon Match of the Day* presented by John

Inverdale on the television before preparing to go up to Soho for a meal they had pre-arranged with some of Drew's old journalist colleagues and friends.

There was a knock on Gerry's studio flat's internal front door, which was in itself unusual as there was an external intercom entry phone system linked to various individual flats located street-side beside the building's main front door.

'Shit, who the hell is that?' Gerry started walking to the door. 'Must be one of my neighbours.'

'Where's that fuckwit mate of yours?' shouted a clearly angered Hugo Summerfield shoving the door fully ajar as soon as Gerry had partially opened it.

Summerfield, then immediately barged his way past Gerry and made straight for Drew, whilst allowing his bulky frame to do damage to some decanters on Gerry's free standing drinks cabinet as he stormed by.

'What the *fuuuuuuuuuuuck!*' screamed Drew as he was thumped unceremoniously on his face by Summerfield's large clenched fist. Drew fell to the floor and landed awkwardly, banging his head against the coffee table in front of him.

'Why the fuck did you do that, arsehole?' yelled Gerry.

'He shagged *my* wife, in *my* bed, in *my* house,' screeched Summerfield as he staggered back out of the tiny studio flat, leaving Gerry looking at his friend lying on the floor. As he recovered from the shock, he soon realised that Drew was unconscious. He hastily telephoned the emergency services.

Drew was taken by ambulance, still in an unconscious state, to Guys and St Thomas' Hospital, only a short drive away, immediately opposite the Houses of Parliament in Westminster.

Gerry was, almost pathetically, wishing he had not gone in the ambulance, so as to avoid the ordeal first-hand. As the minutes went by without Drew regaining consciousness, he became decidedly panic-stricken about Drew's true state.

After a wait that seemed to drag on for several hours, a doctor eventually came to see Gerry in the private reception area. To Gerry's immense relief, the doctor confirmed that Drew had regained consciousness and was in a stable condition. There was a concern regarding any possible internal bleeding or blood clots and after tests and scans it would not be until at least the next day before there could be proper clarification of his condition.

'He's been given a mild sedative just to relax him and he's still suffering from some minor concussion, I suspect, so it might be advisable to come back tomorrow to see your friend,' suggested the doctor.

Fuck me, thought Gerry to himself as he sat in the back of a taxi on his short return journey to his flat in Pimlico. *What is it with Drew and him always ending up in hospital with his face all battered and bruised? Fuck me.*

The following morning Gerry could not wait to get back over to the other side of the River Thames to the hospital.

'Well, mate, I have to say I've seen you look far worse,' joked Gerry, trying to make light of the situation as he suspected that would be the way Drew would want it.

'Aye, I'm sure you have, pal,' acknowledged Drew, clearly pleased to see his dear old friend.

'Have you been told the results of the tests and things, mate?'

'Yes, it appears there's no nasty fractures or blood clots, thank Christ – except for a tiny wee fracture to ma cheekbone.'

'Jesus, that eye looks bad. Can you see out of it?'

'No, not really, it's pretty blurred vision.'

'Are you going to sue Summerfield?'

'What for? What's the point? He only did what I would have done if the roles were reversed. Anyway, I'd like to try and keep this all from the missus if I can.'

'What, tell Enid you walked into a lamp-post drunk?'

'Yeah, somefink like that. Now, don't make me laugh, it hurts ma face, man. And, oh, please tell Linz not to come up here to the hospital to visit. I hope to be discharged later this afternoon with a bit of luck.'

'You gonna be able to make Wimbledon tomorrow though?'

'Probably not, mate, but if Linda makes the final, then wild horses wouldn't keep me away.'

Semi-Final

It was Thursday morning and both the semi-finals were scheduled to be played that day. However, it was pouring with rain and the weather forecast was not promising at all, with further showers more likely than not. Frustratingly for all concerned, the newish electronic roof system over Centre Court had been operationally prone to be, on occasions, fairly unreliable. It would open and shut perfectly fine, but the sophisticated automatic humidity and temperature control system was not functioning properly. Not sufficiently to satisfy health and safety regulations.

Consequently it rendered the show court likely to be out of action for the day.

Linda had the option of a work-out in the indoor courts, but decided against that as she was still, as ever, not overconfident about the condition of her knee. No need to aggravate it, she reasoned. Although she did not admit it to Frank, she knew full well that it was far stiffer and less supple and flexible than it ought to be, even after lengthy daily physiotherapy sessions.

The semi-final draw saw Linda paired against the fourth seed Samantha Pratt from Australia, whilst the fifth seed Jie Zheng was to play the No.2 seed Shuai Peng, both from China in the other match. Linda was moderately content with the fact that she had avoided playing either of the Chinese girls and would have chosen Pratt as her preferred opponent.

There were short, almost awkward and stilted conversations in the plush competitors' lounge area where Frank and Gerry and Linda tried to pass away some time whilst it still continued to rain heavily outside. Linda was beginning to be more than a little suspicious that Gerry had not appeared to come up with a wholly convincing story about why Drew had spent yet another night in hospital, and why she apparently was not permitted to visit him. Her suspicious mind worked overtime as Drew had not even telephoned her to wish her success for the forthcoming match, although Gerry had explained, more than once, that Drew was likely to be still suffering from concussion. And, when Linda casually mentioned, amongst many things whilst just making idle conversation to pass the time of day, that if she won her semi she was planning to invite Sandra Summerfield as a special guest to the final, her suspicions were again aroused and amplified by the speed of Gerry's comment that there would not be enough space in the VIP allocated area to accommodate Sandra Summerfield. To which Linda tartly replied, 'I'll invite who I want to invite. Drew will want Sandra there, won't he?'

'Eh?' Gerry looked genuinely bewildered by Linda's comment and question, which noticeably had done little to clear the air or lighten a uniquely odd atmosphere between them. If only Gerry knew that Linda knew that Drew had had sex with her and Sandra Summerfield, then the atmosphere might have been a somewhat different one. Not better, just different.

The rain delay meant the semi-final match did not start until six o'clock in the evening which, in turn, meant that Linda had by that time unwisely spent a disproportionate part of the day in various radio and television and press areas being interviewed. Come six o'clock she was beginning to question the wisdom of that. Although not feeling physically tired, she was a tiny bit weary of how much the day had psychologically appeared to drag on and mentally taken out of her. Not forgetting the hidden pressure of a Grand Slam semi-final on home soil to a hugely expectant crowd and nation.

In some ways it was, weather wise, the type of evening that Wimbledon always traditionally seemed to get, or suffer from – thick, greyish overcast skies above and an appreciable sharp drop in the temperature. At least, the rain had, at long last, stopped.

The Centre Court was only at half capacity when Linda and Sam Pratt entered the arena, the subdued crowd being a perfect match for the gloomy looking skies above.

This is not how it ought to be on a semi-final at Wimbledon, muttered Linda as she walked out on to court. She even found the need to wear her tracksuit trousers during the knock-up; initially simply as a precaution to prevent the knee becoming cold and stiff. But, so cold was it, for July at any rate, that Linda almost seriously considered playing with her track-suit on before jokingly and self-mockingly reminding herself that would only make her look a bit of a wuss in Gerry and Drew's eyes, and decided against it.

Linda found it peculiarly problematic to get any sort of consistent rhythm into her shots and, more worryingly, a real effort to get fired up in a way she thought would happen automatically. Linda's play in the opening set was certainly lack-lust and uninspired. It had most definitely not inspired the biased home crowd and this lack of any mutual inspiration possibly resulted in no small measure in Linda losing the first set 6-3.

Pratt, still the bookmakers' favourite to win, being fourth seed, had played competently enough without seemingly having to significantly extend herself to any degree. At 2-4 in the second set, just as it was starting to look like Linda's Wimbledon adventure was soon to be at an end for this year, it began to rain again, and much to Linda's relief, the umpire suspended play. Shortly afterwards, Linda got an extended reprieve when told that play had in fact been suspended for the day as the forecast for the remaining hour or so of natural daylight left was for prolonged heavy rain.

For the first time since their reunification after Melbourne, Frank absolutely lost his temper with Linda, and in no short measure either, when they eventually sat down later that evening.

'You looked like a zombie out there, girl. For goodness sake, what the hell was the matter with you on court?' demanded Frank.

'I just couldn't get into the match. Sorry.'

'Sorry? Sorry? What's there to be sorry about? Saying sorry to me is pathetic. What about Gerry and all the money he has invested in you? Same with Drew. Some way to repay them when the *real* moment of truth arrives in your career.'

'I'm not playing poorly deliberately, you know, Frank.'

'Of course you're not. I realise that. Of course I do. But where is the hunger in your eyes that was there in the first round match or against Zerova or against Muller, eh? Where is it? I simply don't see it. You looked to me as if you were simply going through the motions.'

It was a wake up call that fortunately was allowed to be made just before it was all too late.

The weather the following day was back to brilliant summer blue sky, if not altogether warm sunshine, and Linda had somehow managed to psyche herself up to go for glory right from the very first point, or "shit or bust" as Gerry had not so eloquently, nor technically, contributed.

For the first fifteen minutes after the re-start against Pratt, Linda played what was arguably the best tennis she had ever played in her whole life. As a result, she managed to get spectacularly and against all the odds back into the game and level the match score at one set all. By doing so, this transparently completely rattled her opponent. So much so that Sam Pratt never truly fully recovered from the scale of Linda's entirely unexpected fight-back and with the momentum now dramatically shifted in Linda's favour, she continued to perform to a very high standard indeed, no doubt helped by unparalleled quantities of adrenalin rushes. In a thrilling and high quality third and deciding set Linda managed to win 9-7, much to the absolute delight of the packed and jubilant Centre Court crowd, and most probably a huge television audience, too.

So exciting and nerve-racking were the final few games, this resulted in the by now uncontrollable crowd giving Linda a rapturous standing ovation which seemingly went on and on. It was indisputably one of the most memorable ladies semi-finals ever played on Centre Court and for it to involve a home grown player – well, it was the least this fervent and patriotic crowd could do to frenziedly expose their appreciation.

Afterwards, in the changing room, Linda slumped down into a chair. She was absolutely physically and mentally drained. She knew she had played as well as she ever could have dreamed of. She had extended herself to the maximum and she was quietly feeling extremely proud of herself for doing it when it mattered most. She knew that previous night she had been perhaps less than ten minutes away from going out of the competition. Now, here she was in her first-ever Grand Slam singles final.

The physical feeling of exhaustion was compounded by the sheer exhilaration being shown by nearly everyone Linda bumped into, whether it be friends or television commentators or just members of the public. It quickly was becoming emotionally tiring, too. She had never experienced such an out-pouring of affection towards her by so many people, all within such a short space of time.

Linda's mobile phone, she thought, would self-destruct if she received any more text messages – the most important one being from Drew who made the comment – '*See you tomorrow sunshine*'. It was the only text Linda had the time to reply to – '*c u 2moro not b same witout u luv L xx.*'

With the semi-final match being rain-delayed overnight there was not long to wait for the Final – it would, in actual fact, be as soon as tomorrow.

Frank and Linda eventually found time together and Linda thanked Frank for his harsh words spoken to her the previous night.

'No worries, pet. You know it's nowt personal. Whatever I say to you I do with your best interests in mind, absolutely nothing else. No hidden agenda with me.'

'But you can't be right all the time, Frank, can you?' teased Linda.

'Okay, fair point,' laughed Frank. 'How's the knee behaving itself, by the way?'

'During the match it was absolutely fine, but right at this minute it feels flipping stiff and worryingly sore, I don't mind admitting. Might take a double dose of those wonder pills of Dr Shiels before the match tomorrow.'

*   *   *   *   *

'Hey mate – I take it you watched the match on TV?' gushed an excited Gerry on his mobile to Drew. 'Will you be able to make it tomorrow, pal?'

'I'll be there, don't ye worry about that, pal.'

'Would you like me to organise some security cover for you?'

'Eh? What are you going on about now, you complete and utter fuckwit?'

'Just trying to help a dear old friend from getting yet another senseless battering,' mocked Gerry.

'Fuck off……..pal.'

It had indeed been a truly exhilarating if ultimately exhausting day for Linda and she was almost relieved finally to be able to sit down over supper with Frank and Gerry and reflect on what had almost certainly been the most memorable day of her sporting career so far.

All three of them broadly discussed what the next day might bring and how best to try to plan the day so as to minimise any distraction or disruption to the main, and the all important, event, the tennis match itself.

Linda jokingly questioned if she was going to have the energy left to endure another day like today so soon, without any proper rest and recuperation either physically or mentally. Frank reminded Linda of the dangers of any anti-climax and how it was vital to stay in the right frame of mind and in the zone.

It was unanimously agreed that Linda would limit herself to just one interview only with the BBC, with perhaps one token one for the American network NBC and that would be absolutely it until after the match was completed. All the other media, particularly the newspaper journalists, could take the same hike as all the photographers wanting, or more like demanding, Linda's time and attention.

'Will Drew definitely be able to make tomorrow then?' Linda asked Gerry.

Gerry made some comment about having organised a chauffeur for Drew for the day who was SAS trained. His cryptic comment could only have been yet another feeble attempt to appear humorous. His timing and delivery of such witticisms was so often poorly executed. Anyway, he had overlooked the fact that both Frank and Linda knew little of the circumstances behind Drew's recent hospitalisation.

'I've invited Sandra Summerfield along,' added Linda, opening her eyes as wide as they would spread as if to appear to be making some grandiose gesture with the invite.

'Is that altogether wise?' enquired Gerry.

'Why ever not?'

'Just that it might be a tad embarrassing for Drew, that's all,' said Gerry, clearly having another memory lapse by forgetting that Linda knew nothing of the fact that Sandra Summerfield's husband was the very person who just a few days previously had landed Drew unconscious in a hospital bed. There again, Gerry was still not to know that Linda was only too well aware that Sandra and Drew had fairly recently slept together.

'Oh, really, Gerry - embarrassing? Why's that then? Embarrassing for whom?' asked Linda, whilst staring directly at Gerry full-on hopefully to see some visual reaction from his facial expression. *What did Gerry really know?* wondered Linda. *He surely must know something?*

'Embarrassing? No, not at all, sunshine. I was just thinking about that balls-ache of a husband of Sandra's, that's all. I just don't want that geezer anywhere near the VIP enclosure. Don't like the arse one bit. Never have done. Neither does Drew.'

After supper had finished, Linda took a taxi back to Putney. All she could now think of was her overwhelming desire to go straight to sleep in her bed. The only other prominent thought in her head was that knee of hers was distractingly uncomfortable. Consequently, she decided to take yet another one of Dr Shiels's prescribed magic pills before she went to bed, just to be on the safe side and to ensure she did not have disrupted sleep due to any potential throbbing physical pain. She was certain a good night's sleep was an absolute prerequisite for her body to recover in time for the final from all the physical as well as the mental strain of that particular day.

*   *   *   *   *

'**No! No! No**! Never!'

'Say yes and Mr, Mrs won't be harmed.'

'Where are they? What have you done with them? I want to know they are safe. You haven't harmed them? Have you?'

'Throw the match tomorrow. Then they will be okay. Yes? Otherwise……..'

'**No**, please, **no**. I beg you.'

'We pay you well. You throw match tomorrow with Shuai Peng. Yes?'

Linda was in a perspiring, trembling state as she faced a brace of extremely intimidating Chinese thugs.

The Final

Linda's journey on a bright sunny Saturday morning between Putney and the Wimbledon complex somehow managed to highlight the fact that many authentic sporting enthusiasts within the capital city were gripped by what seemed genuine excitable anticipation. The long queue of spectators waiting patiently out on the main streets of Wimbledon greeted her drive past like a unique Mexican wave. It sent continual tingles down

Linda's spine. This, unfortunately, did little to alleviate her throbbing headache.

Bloody hell, that was one helluva restless sleep last night. One scary nightmare. Those Chinese hoodlums. It was all a dream? Wasn't it?

Everywhere Linda went in the next hour or so, everyone, but everyone, was recognising and acknowledging her presence, either smiling at her, shouting words of encouragement to her with a tiny minority getting carried away with inappropriate and inconsiderate attempts to get her to sign this or that tacky souvenir. An early feature of the day was the constant camera clicks from every conceivable angle – front, back, side, even up above from various other vantage points. It was all soon enough to become particularly irksome, especially when people Linda did not even know approached her, or as close as security attendants would permit, howling and shouting over others to try to start up a meaningless one-sided conversation. The few people Linda did actually know were, of course, different, but she still, nonetheless, found it difficult always to sound as if she were being completely relaxed and genuine whilst being forced to make banal replies to equally banal questions like, 'How are you feeling?'

Conversely, on the positive side, Linda felt she was gaining some inspiration from the continual volley of words of encouragement and advice to enjoy the moment, which was by far the most common phrase or advice on offer by so many pseudo sports' psychologists.

It, therefore, was a refreshing relief to get out on to the practice court and hit some balls and not have to make conversation with anyone except Frank. He had been exceptional, not only as a coach, but also as a solid companion and friend over the past couple of weeks and the relationship had proven to be pivotal to getting this far at Wimbledon, and had been nothing like what it had deteriorated to in Australia.

*   *   *   *   *

'Linda, there's something I have to say to you and I think now is as good a time as any to say it,' pronounced Frank mysteriously. He continued, 'I've decided this is definitely *it* for me. Last match as a professional coach. The travelling, being away from my family, the lovely Devon countryside, it's too much of a wrench. I'm getting too long in the tooth. Of course, I will miss the excitement and adrenaline rush of it all, but you're at last a huge sporting success, win or lose today. The prize money alone will now make you financially secure for the rest of your life. You'll attract fantastic sponsorship deals and that will guarantee you'll attract the services of a replacement top professional coach. Someone full-time, too. Nowt short of what you truly deserve, pet.'

Linda stared at him. Frank stared back, and with a broad smile slowly developing on his face, he finished his pep talk with, 'I've said all this to inspire you, Linda – not to clog up your mind with any distraction. Go out there and win it – you're the best there is.'

'Wow! Frankie. I know Gerry mentioned something about this just being a two week trial, but things have gone so well though. This is still one heck of a shock. You're a top-drawer coach, Frank - the best, in fact.'

'Well, thanks, pet. But I've made up my mind. I'm retiring. Now, you want to think of my decision only as being a positive. The sole reason I say all this, right here, right now is this is effectively the last chance you have to make an old coach a happy old man. Send me into semi-retirement content in the knowledge that I have contributed something tangible to the professional game I love so much. As coach to *the* Wimbledon champion – let that be my legacy, eh? Let a part of you desperately want to win this title for me, if you so like. Go on, do it for me, pet. Present me with a highly personal and prized retirement present from you, eh? Something truly special and unique just between me and you. Something money can't buy.'

Frank concluded his final words of encouragement as best he could with, 'Have the desire to win today and crave that desire like you crave fresh air.'

They spontaneously engaged in a lengthy embrace which must have been an unexpected activity to many of the 300 or so court-side onlookers, which by now included Drew and Gerry as well as Dr Shiels and Sandra Summerfield.

'How's the injury?' enquired Fred Shiels anxiously when Linda took another short rest and liquid intake from hitting some balls with Frank.

'It's plainly not right, Fred. I'm convinced I'll need that cartilage operation you mentioned to sort out, once and for all, what I assume is obvious permanent ligament damage, but there's no doubting whenever I take those magic tablets of yours the pain almost immediately disappears.'

'Don't forget what I said to you, Linda – they are strong pain killers, so don't go taking too many.'

Linda could not quite recall Dr Shiels ever previously mentioning this advice and asked if it was still permissible to take two tablets before the match that day.

'Yes – I guess it won't do any harm now,' came the reply, which only left Linda for the first time wondering if she needed to mention to Fred the quantity she had actually been taking of late. Linda decided that after the final she would re-assess the injury with a clinical specialist and it would be done as a priority. Whatever happened, Linda consoled herself that these would be the last two tablets to be taken, ever.

Linda started walking back from the practice courts to the main dressing room area when she was somewhat startled to have Ian Girot slither in front of her from nowhere and try to start a conversation with her.

'I heard you had a pregnancy terminated recently. Is that true?' smirked Girot, as if, said knowingly.

'No comment,' rebuked Linda.

'So, it is true then?'

'Look, watch my lips, I said no comment. Got it?'

'Was the father Monsieur Bonneau? Does the father know?' continued Girot, undeterred.

'Look, I said I had no comment. What don't you understand about that? Hey, Gerry, help me out here and get rid of this toe-rag for me.'

This was precisely the aggravation and distraction that Linda wanted to avoid a couple of hours before stepping out on to Centre Court on Wimbledon final's day.

God, I could swing for that Girot guy. Has he got it in for me, or what? muttered Linda just out of hearing distance of Gerry.

Fortunately there was much preparation to attend to in the relative privacy of the locker room in the last hour or so leading up to the start of the match. Consequently, Linda found it moderately easy to forget about the encounter and verbal exchange with Girot - for the present time at any rate - if only because, the game with

Shuai Peng was the last remaining obstacle to securing ultimate tennis glory.

Peng was a typical Chinese tennis player who had a good all-round game with no outstanding asset, but importantly no recognisable weakness either. What was probably Peng's renowned attribute was her ability to play all the critical and important points well and make them productive and ultimately successful, such was her exemplary positive mental attitude and conditioned and unfazed state of mind. She enjoyed a reputation for being emotion free and her error count was consistently by far the lowest on the tour. Peng had won the Australian Open, was a finalist at the French Open and was now clear favourite to win the Wimbledon championship with the bookmakers and the many retired professional tennis pundits working at Wimbledon for various media and broadcasting companies. Although there would be only one clear favourite with the predominantly partisan paying audience that day.

If there was one tennis nationality that Linda did not particularly like, it was the Chinese. She had misgivings about the American academy system, but at least it occasionally produced players with an individualistic personality to match their tennis ability, with Roddick and Sharapova being prime recent examples. China had an academy set-up similar to the American one, only their students had to work twice as long as their American counterparts, and were treated in many ways similarly to Army conscripts. The tennis camp scene in China, Linda had been led to believe, was an Army style boot-camp operated by the Chinese State. Just swap would-be tennis professionals for would-be soldiers. Everyone looked the same, dressed the same, had similar discipline and behaviour and principles, and were so precise and consistent in everything they all did it was almost impossible to tell them apart.

From Linda's viewpoint, this background helped polarise the differences, as tennis professionals, between her and Peng. Linda was not a bigot; anything but. She thought she knew lots about the distasteful subject, having had no option but to share her whole life with so many bigots because of the colour of her skin. The reality with the Chinese players was that she simply could not be impressed by how the system worked and the tennis clones or robots that it ultimately produced.

Linda had played Peng before, about two years ago and on a hard-court surface. Therefore that previous encounter in itself would not really provide any indication as to how this match was likely to be contested. Linda had watched with Frank video recordings of Peng's play at Wimbledon, which disappointingly did not provide any hints at to how best to play her. The tapes simply reaffirmed that there were no obvious weaknesses that neither Frank nor Linda could detect in Peng's game. Although not exactly a weakness, it was noticeable that it was never Peng's strategy to play the unexpected or heavily disguised shot or take any undue risks with overly adventurous shots. It was always, but always, percentage tennis – albeit played to a highly consistent and exacting standard.

Voicing his opinion and concern, Frank warned Linda that if she tried to play Peng at her own games then she might as well concede defeat, and the coveted Wimbledon shield, to Peng before the game even started. Frank's alternate more constructive and positive advice to Linda was to play as many varieties of strokes to try to orchestrate as many different types of rallies as was possible and not to get embroiled in the pace of game that Peng felt comfortable with, or felt she was controlling or dictating.

Frank reminded Linda that, although she might not outwardly show it, Peng would be nervous and would probably believe that she was representing the largest populated nation in the world and there was an inevitable burden of responsibility that went with that privilege. Frank, more than the once, stressed that Peng had never won a Wimbledon title, and again to take all the positives from that particular important fact.

'And, also, Peng will sure know that she is favourite,' reasoned Frank, continuing with, 'a positive start is an absolute must. Get the crowd to participate in creating tumultuous noise levels of support. Just for you, pet. Just like they did in the Muller match. That in itself might just unnerve Peng. You never know. Remember Linda, it will mean you will have to play an unusually expansive game and take more calculated risks than you'd normally do. Go for broke, pet,' continued Frank earnestly, if only repeating himself. 'If you don't, then you'll probably have to rely on Peng having an off day and that is such a rare event it would be an exceptionally high risk strategy for you to adopt,' he warned. 'And yeah,' his voice rattled on, scarcely penetrating the edge of his thoughts, 'be ultra-positive and feel really good about yourself and actually demonstrate to everyone just how confident you are with your body language. First couple of games, Peng will not ordinarily make any mistakes whatsoever if you simply stick to your typical game plan. So, surprise her if it's your serve first, produce a couple of really big, unexpected second serves. Bring her into the net with some of your cleverly disguised drop shots. Try some bizarre unorthodox shots on her return of serve. Above all, take risks, pet. Go for the edge of the lines. They all want you to win out there. You and I know full well you *can* win. You most certainly *can* win. It's one against one. Get the crowd hyped up from the very first point. It will unnerve her. I'm convinced of it. This is your moment – seize it, Linda. You *will* win.'

*   *   *   *   *

Drew and Gerry sat beside each other and wallowed in what was happening. They reminded each other that this had decidedly been worth all the financial risk-taking, headaches and heartaches, the fulfilment of a joint ambition that had all too often seemed like an unrealistic visionary aspiration and fantasy. The moment truly was sheer undiluted pride and joy for both of them. Way beyond words of expression.

A few seconds before Linda appeared on Centre Court, they shared a manly hug in typical rugby-land style in an open display to seal their extreme emotions of gratification towards each other.

'Just look at her. Isn't she the best, ever?'

'Aye, stoating.'

'Black Tartan Slammer.'

'Aye. Black Tartan Slammer.'

'Aye.'

This was indeed a long way down the line from when they had first met Linda as a youngster at Hillpark Tennis Club. A very long way.

*   *   *   *   *

Resplendent in her predominantly white tennis dress, tinged with her favourite tartan, Linda walked out on to

255

Centre Court to a real cauldron of noise. Then she paused for a split second or two to look up at the players' guest enclosure area to witness the evident sheer joy, most especially on the faces of Drew and Gerry. She wished she could freeze the moment, so she could enjoy it for a bit longer. But before she knew it, Linda was concentrating and reacting to the umpire's call of, "Play".

She got off to the absolute perfect start by winning her opening service game to love. Starting off as she meant to carry on with two high risk second serves at over 115 mph speed, she executed comfortable volley winners earning two easy points whilst the other two points were won on equally daring and high risk shots.

The following game, on Peng's serve, was perhaps inevitably not quite so successful, with Linda continuing to play bold but unpredictable shots which entailed the odd error or two. Nevertheless, although Peng won her own opening service game, it went to deuce three times and that particular game could just as easily have been won by Linda. It was a highly encouraging start made by Linda and one that the crowd showed its appreciation for in no uncertain terms.

No matter how hard she tried, Linda found it difficult to achieve total concentration levels, especially during end changes as she sat in the seat by the umpire's chair. Emotional thoughts and flashbacks were all too prevalent. Fortunately, any negative thoughts entering her head were easy to dispel just as soon as she looked over and got the attention of Drew or Gerry or Frank or on several occasions 'framed' all three of them. She had never seen them so animated; all three were highly charged and nervous wrecks by the look of them, but in a way that only sent positive signals to Linda.

The electric atmosphere in the arena was almost superfluous, so unsporting was it with every and any remotely crucial point that Peng won in the early stages of the set being acknowledged only by a bizarre silence. The only exception appeared to be from the Royal Box and some other limited areas clearly occupied by corporate guests on their best behaviour, and suitably attired as if they were hoping to be presented to the Queen.

Linda established a 6-5 lead in the first set and suddenly thought to herself what if she tried to play Peng at her own game, which would be for the first time in the match? *Just the next game only?* Linda decided on a dramatic change of tactic. Try not to make any errors, be ultra conservative in her whole approach. After all, Peng simply had to win the next game, otherwise she would lose the set. There surely was no better timing than this to test the resolve and the most impressive aspect of Peng's character – her mental aptitude – giving her a practical examination in a very tight situation.

This all resulted in unusually protracted rallies with lots of *ohs and ahs* and other nervous noises from the enthralled crowd. Every single point in this critical service game was the same, long and uncompromising, but for Linda encouragingly, marginally successful as it went to deuce and it seemed this surprise change of tactic had indeed unnerved Shuai Peng as Peng seemed to be concentrating on expecting or trying to anticipate Linda's attempts to do the unexpected or the unorthodox. Instead, Linda just stayed on or around the baseline and played conservatively to simply put the ball back in court, nothing more, nothing less. It was a war of attrition which Linda suspected Peng would ordinarily have won nine times out of ten had it not been for the fact it was Peng serving in a final of a Grand Slam to stay in the set.

Whereas Peng outwardly still looked her usual cool, calm and collected self to everyone, Linda strongly suspected she was not feeling that way internally, otherwise the game would have been over five to ten minutes previously. The fact that it was yet another deuce point and the fact that Peng had lost all her points in that critical game from unforced errors, as opposed to winners from Linda's racket, said it all to Linda.

It perhaps hardly seemed fair that the high quality set hinged on a dubious line call at deuce which was given in Linda's favour (television and technology confirmed Peng's shot to be 'in') when the lineswoman called it 'out' and the umpire chose not to overrule the call. Peng had the right to ask the umpire to clarify or overrule the call via Hawkeye. Hawkeye was a system loathed by some of the top ranking professional players, mainly because it was bizarrely and conveniently considered by a select few to be inconsistent and therefore inaccurate. With the Chinese mentality, they saw Hawkeye as being in conflict with their inbred discipline to accept all forms of officialdom.

This lucky break, through a dubious line call, inspired Linda to try to continue with her lucky streak and, as the next point was on the advantage point, she suddenly decided to change tactic yet again and went for a quick outright winner off a tentative and slow paced second serve from Peng. Linda's booming return of serve smacked the top of the net and landed fortuitously inches over. It was impossible for Peng to return. Linda's good luck had indeed continued.

More importantly, Linda had won the first set 7-5.

Although enjoying absurdly premature celebrations, Drew and Gerry could not resist triumphantly hugging each other yet again. Then they, presumably, quickly realised how immature that must have looked before continuing instead applauding as loudly and as proudly as they thought they could get away with within the traditional etiquette they were expected to observe as privileged temporary guests of the Royal Wimbledon Club. However, they still managed to look like a couple of smug but demented seals as they clapped hands. By contrast, Peng's guests in the players' VIP area sat glum-faced which had been their demeanour for much of the prior forty-five minutes or so, only punctured by the odd meek smile and short session of polite and controlled hand clapping whenever Peng won a point, regardless of whether it be the first point in any game or a more crucial 'game' point.

Much as Linda tried to maintain the same sort of game plan in the second set, she was not to be quite as successful. Probably a combination of the fact that the effect, or benefit, of any surprise tactics had worn off and Linda's failure to reach the same exceptionally high standards of execution especially with the more high risk shots.

As a consequence, Peng won the second set 6-3. Not quite as comfortable as the score line might suggest, though. More relevantly, the match was now all square and evenly poised, with all to play for in the deciding set.

The tension everywhere was palpable.

As Linda sat on her chair between ends and towelled down her arms and legs, she could definitely feel some pain when her hand went over her knee - *sugar*, she quietly muttered to herself - grimaced again, and then decided to take another pain-killing tablet. Just to be on the safe side.

The match was fast developing into a classic. There was an unparalleled atmosphere, even for a Wimbledon match involving a Brit. Linda, needless to say, was today a Brit and not a Scot. Not today at any rate. Not by popular demand.

The match continued to be an ultra tense, close affair that was being played with variety of shot and was a fascinating contest between two players of completely opposite styles of play and personalities and complemented by tennis of an extremely consistent high standard throughout, with frequent hypnotic long rallies.

Even Linda was beginning to wonder if the charged atmosphere created by the partisan crowd was affecting or influencing the officials as she benefited from yet another extremely close line call. That must have been the fourth or fifth in the match and they had all been called in Linda's favour. For the first time certainly in this match, probably in this tournament and maybe even all season, Peng actually challenged the latest controversial-cum-questionable call, which even to the many biased viewers did seem to clip the backend of the line but was called 'out' by the lines-official. In truth, Linda was unsure, one way or the other, so had little to contribute to the situation except to signal with an automatic shrug of her shoulders to Peng that she was uncertain. Peng, in turn, seemed to take that to mean that Linda was signalling the ball was in fact good, and this prompted Peng uncharacteristically to take issue with the umpire. An almost half-hearted, apologetic attempt at a protest by Peng over this dubious line call lasted no more than a few seconds and bizarrely she never officially requested a Hawkeye ruling and seemingly graciously accepted the umpire's decision. But then, amazingly, proceeded to serve her very first double fault of the match. It was to be a major turning point as Linda took that service game from Peng and it gave her the slightest of possible edges, score line wise, and a distinct advantage to be in a position to serve out herself for the match - and the championship.

Linda tried to rush through a quickly constructed strategy in her own mind as she waited for the ball boys to produce a changeover of new balls. *Big first serves? Just make sure the first serves go in, regardless of speed? Prioritise the error count down to zero? Be brave and positive and go for some winners? Let Peng make the errors?*

Attack? Defend? Play conservatively? Play aggressively?

Linda need not have formulated any last minute strategy for that particular game. Shuai Peng simply went to pieces, for all to see.

It almost defied belief the fundamental errors that came from Peng's racket. It was almost as if she could not hit a cow's backside with a banjo. She never hit one single ball back into court that game, that very last game.

Why?

Who cared?

Certainly not Linda.

Neither did Gerry. Nor Drew. Nor Frank.

*   *   *   *   *

'Speaking for myself, and I'm sure the whole crowd here, and those watching on TV at home, how did you manage to cope with the atmosphere and emotion of the last few points? I almost couldn't bear to watch it, it was that tense,' giggled Sue Barker in an excitable schoolgirl-type voice at the side of the court on a live

BBC interview just prior to the official presentation of the famous and coveted Wimbledon Plate.

'I don't know, Sue. It's all a bit of a blur, you know. Before I forget, Sue, can I just say a special huge thanks to those three guys over there? Without them this would not have been possible. Frank my coach, of course, and Gerry and Drew who I owe so, so, *so* much to. I absolutely love them both to bits. And also, sorry, I almost forgot, Dr Fred Shiels who has worked wonders with my recent injury problems.'

*   *   *   *   *

'See here, hen – appreciate you've got loads on your mind and tons of pressing commitments, but I really do need five wee minutes of yer time. It's kinda important, ye know, otherwise wouldnae ask,' begged Drew.

'Sure, of course, Drew. I don't know precisely what's gonna happen over the next few hours, but I suspect it'll be bedlam. Look, why don't you let me go have a shower and change and we'll slip off somewhere private on the complex for half-an-hour or so. That okay? Is that enough time for you?'

'Perfect. It's important,' thanked Drew.

Linda could somehow tell it must be important just from the expression on his face.

As she showered and got herself all glammed-up for the ensuing barrage of photo shoots and press and television interviews, she was still in a complete trance with excitement as to what had happened over the past couple of hours. It was the ultimate feeling of pure self-satisfaction, she thought – except when her mind momentarily wandered and started to question what Drew might conceivably want to talk about that was so important all of a sudden. *Why'd he not mention anything earlier on in the day? Was it about **that** night in Paris? It must be, surely? At long last. Has he been waiting until Wimbledon was over? Did he not want to disturb my concentration away from tennis? Was that it?*

Linda and Drew met up again in the main foyer and greeted each other with the briefest hug and a kiss on the cheeks, but with long-lasting beaming smiles on each other's faces. It was almost as if they had never seen each other for years instead of just under an hour or so ago. It was also in marked contrast to the tense atmosphere that had existed between them over the past month.

'You know what – this has got to be the happiest day of my life,' announced Linda triumphantly.

'I know, ma dear. Mine, too, probably. You don't know how proud I was today, especially when you held up the famous auld plate. Ye know, for once I was pissed silly but this time only with sheer pride and joy. Nowt else. Not alcohol. Not drugs.'

'Oh, come on now, Drew, put me out of my suspense: what's this you want to talk to me about that's *so* damn important. Why'd you not mention anything this morning if it was *that* urgent and important? Is it bad news? Come on, let's go into this First Aid room over here, there's nobody in there for now,' ushered Linda almost as if in a motherly fashion.

'Sure thing, hen.' As they walked, Drew turned to her to add, 'The only reason I didn't mention anything sooner was I didnae want to spoil your preparation and concentration levels for the biggest moment of your life.'

'Look, if this is all about what went down in Paris, can't it wait until another day? I'm fast starting to feel emotionally drained right now,' said Linda in a strange

263

mix of being half-earnest and half-hearted. Earnest to satisfy her curiosity, her heart did not want to hear bad or sad news – not so as to spoil today of all days.

'No, Linz. Not about Paris. Well, not exactly. To be honest with you, I'm being told by my lawyer that the police fully intend to charge me formally with murder any day now as they are under increasing pressure to be seen to be doing something proactive. I'm apparently still the only real suspect, not helped by the fact that I do not have an acceptable alibi for the time that Digby geezer was murdered.'

'Why is that, Drew?' quizzed Linda.

'Because I was with you at the time he was murdered!'

'Can't you simply say you were with me in Paris then?'

'Yeah. I could. But the alibi has to intrinsically involve you to a significant extent to make my alibi watertight as acceptable evidence, and prove that there was no conceivable way I could *ever* have been at Pollok Golf Club at the time Digby was murdered.'

'Surely that's no problem, Drew? Just say you had a meal with me and then we went back to our respective hotel rooms,' offered Linda.

'I could try that, but sod's law, the pathologist is putting Digby's death at sometime between midnight and two in the morning. I should explain there was apparently a dinner/dance function on at the golf club that evening. You know what the Polis are like, they might wear it that I was sleeping peacefully in some Paris Hotel or alternatively they will say it was all a conspiracy theory or convenient ploy as a cover story, like I booked into Paris, and then travelled back immediately. Could do it in three to four hours door-to-door, I guess, at a push.'

Drew momentarily seemed to be trying to compose himself and almost as if for effect put both his hands over his face before continuing. 'Also, stupidly, *very* stupidly, when I first made my signed written statement to the polis, for some silly reason I said I was in London that night, simply to not involve you by ever mentioning Paris. You'll appreciate when I originally made that statement to the screws it never crossed my effing mind I was later going to be up on some goddamn murder rap. Now, can ye no see? I have the *real* problem if I go back to those CID geeks and say I wasn't in London after all, but in fact was in Paris. It'll just open a can of worms. As well as me being charged with trying to pervert the course of justice, my credibility will be shot to pieces and it counts for very little right now, especially with the Strathclyde CID.'

Again Drew paused for thought, coupled with aggressively forking his fingers through his thick-set greyish-black peppered hair. 'I know this is a huge ask, a *huge* ask, Linda, but would you be prepared to make a statement confirming that we slept all that night in the same bed? Honestly, I'm convinced it's the *only* sure-fire way I'm going to get myself out of ending up in a court room on a murder rap and reliant on the good sense of a jury, which frankly doesn't exactly fill me with confidence. With your evidence, I can then say that I only lied about where I was to protect your good name. Hardly a hanging offence, eh?'

'Hell's bloody teeth, Drew. I do take your point, but what about Enid?' questioned Linda.

'What about her?'

'Well, does she know?'

Drew hummed and hawed for a few moments before saying, 'Look, Enid knows I've had overactive interest in other woman. Jesus, I've been divorced enough times because of my acts of infidelity. What she doesn't know more than simply that, doesn't harm her. The *only* matter that's important to me is getting out of this absurd murder rap.'

'Charming,' replied Linda. *Little wonder Drew's been married so many times. The ever popular adulterer.*

'Sorry, I didn't mean it to sound that way.' Drew seemed to realise he was digging a hole for himself and some damage limitation was urgently required. 'Look Linda, us sleeping together was one big, big mistake by both of us. Something, I suspect, we will both regret for the rest of our lives. But I've always held you in such high esteem and with such complete and utter genuine fondness. You are such a gorgeously attractive woman. What I guess I am trying to say, is that night in Paris, it was *all* my fault that it happened, or my stupidity in the first place that created the atmosphere and circumstances that in turn allowed it to happen,' he confessed. 'I feel *so* ashamed I couldn't contain my lust for you. I truly feel I have compromised our wonderful, our absolutely wonderful friendship.'

So, at long last Linda had received an explanation - of sorts. It was, seemingly, all about lust, coupled with a guilt trip. Well, that was Drew's version of events at any rate.

What about me? My feelings? Linda sighed to herself.

Linda wondered, for a split second or so, whether or not this was the opportune moment to tell Drew she had been briefly pregnant. Once again, her instincts told her it was not. She was still in such high spirits from the thrilling tennis victory. She did not want to spoil this day in any way whatsoever. When all said and done, she did feel extremely sorry for Drew's undeniably serious predicament, and quickly reasoned with herself that it would not alleviate his troubles over the murder charge if she mentioned the abortion. Furthermore, there was no certainty Drew was the father. Drew had, after all, sacrificed so much for her benefit over the years. Maybe this was payback time from her to Drew? She knew mentioning the pregnancy today would only serve to get something off her own chest but would do little for improving Drew's current state of mind or troubles.

'Okay, Drew – I'll do it. Can't say I'm at all happy about it, though. But I guess all you are doing is asking me to tell the police the truth. Eh, what a colourful life you lead,' said Linda with a smile starting to slowly illuminate her face and immediately lightening the whole atmosphere. 'Come here and give me a cuddle and remind me how brilliant I am at being Wimbledon champion.'

'With pleasure, ma dear, with the greatest of pleasure.'

Drew then walked out of the First Aid room shouting *'yes'* to himself in the loudest most exaggerated, but silent manner, before departing through the main entrance. He sent a text to Emilio Fazzi with *"u r a dikhed tenis coch told u so r s ho"* and then called Gerry to see if he was up for a few beers that evening.

'Yip, fine by me. Bring Linda with you?'

'No, pal. After all the photo shoots and interviews, she apparently just wants to enjoy the whole experience in the relative peace and quiet of Putney with Mr & Mrs Dale. She's invited us tomorrow night to the big civic gala for the winners. You'll be up for that, pal?'

'Sure will, pal.'

*   *   *   *   *

Gerry and Drew met up at Gerry's favourite watering hole in Pimlico, The Slug & Lettuce, a stereotypical 1980s yuppie establishment. They invited as many friends of theirs and of Linda's as they knew who might want to come and join them to celebrate her victory. There was also the promise of a free curry when the pub closed at eleven o'clock at the local curry house, where Gerry was a well-known regular customer, usually eating on his own.

'Mighty generous of you throwing in the offer of a free curry. Will the restaurant be able to accommodate everyone?' joked Drew, already sounding and acting half drunk.

'Maybe, maybe not - but you and I are on a roll, buddy. Not only with Linda, but I have a fantastic bit of financial news that I only heard about yesterday. So, I'm feeling extra generous tonight.'

'Oh yeah, like the sound of this before you've even told me owt,' slurred Drew, 'but please don't insult ma intelligence or these guid folks here tonight - as nobody, but nobody, will believe any bullshit about you being generous all of a sudden.'

'Remember those Think Kids Entertainment shares we both lost a fortune on?'

'Yeah,' slurred Drew again, 'remember? You yanking ma chain? Of course I sodding well remember, ye fucking dopey eejit.'

'Well, you'll be pleased to hear that a couple of the ex-directors have now been formally prosecuted by the ECU.'

'Who the fuck are the ECU when they're at home?' Drew staggered backwards slightly, only because of his inebriated state, and not from the news Gerry was imparting. 'You keep on throwing these bloody organisation names at me – what was it before? The FSA or the DTI, or whatever it was?'

'The ECU, mate - they are part of the police force who specialise in business fraud. They are called The Economic Crime Unit. It gets even better, when I tell you that one of the ex-directors is actually worth a whole heap of money. Multi-millionaire,' blurted out Gerry excitedly.

'People with big deep pockets, huh?'

'Exactly,' bellowed Gerry. 'The judge has found them guilty of fraud and deception on a grand scale and they will have to pay back to shareholders of the company almost twenty million. All those lying, thieving two-faced directors have been barred for life from holding any directorship position within any company. And two of them will be spending the next few years locked up courtesy of Her Majesty's Pleasure, giving them plenty of time to consider their misdeeds.'

'Blimey Charlie, Gerry – and what exactly does that mean for the likes of us?' squeaked Drew in one of his many high pitched drunken voices which would manifest itself when he was over-excited after consuming loads of alcohol.

'It means, me auld mucker, that we'll get paid a one-off dividend virtually equivalent to what we lost in the share value before the shares were suspended from being traded on the London Stock Exchange.'

'Well, fuck me! Another drink, mon ami?'

'Aye, stoating idea, pal.'

*   *   *   *   *

The traditional Wimbledon Ball on the Sunday evening was the formal end of tournament celebration for the winners. That said, it primarily provided an opportunity for all the many high-ranking officials connected to the tournament to be rewarded for their contribution towards the fortnight's organising of events with a lavish, but free, night out. It was always a glitzy occasion for the paparazzi to indulge in taking photographs of some rich, but not so famous guests, not to mention the Wimbledon winners dressed in unusually formal attire.

Drew and Gerry had occasionally discussed how they looked forward to the event if only to savour the honour and prestige of entry as official guests of the Wimbledon champion. And, if only for once in their lifetime, just to sample and gain first-hand experience for themselves of what the Wimbledon Ball was actually like.

The recovery time-span after a lengthy night out for Drew and Gerry was getting longer and longer as the years rolled by. The actual amount of alcohol drunk at The Slug & Lettuce in Pimlico, together with the copious quantities of wine and champagne drunk in the curry house, followed by a visit to a night club in Chelsea until about 4am, all proved to be a serious handicap for them, even come mid-afternoon the following day. It was a wonder neither was suffering from alcoholic poisoning. Or liver failure.

So hung over were they both, they debated by text exchange, considering if they did not turn up to the Wimbledon Ball would it cause any embarrassment for Linda? Tempting as it was to say that it would not, they both reluctantly agreed they had to put in an appearance – if only, now, for Linda's sake.

Even wearing his absurdly thick-framed Dolce & Gabbana dark tinted glasses, Drew's face was still prominently showing the scars from the injury that Summerfield, or a coffee table, had inflicted upon him earlier that week. This attracted much sympathy from everyone with whom Drew came into contact, and it was an obligatory conversation starter. However, the facial injury offered more than that for Fazzi, who was a surprise guest, courtesy of the Lawn Tennis Association.

Fazzi clearly took some delight in coming over to Drew. He stared at Drew's injury, and then simply laughed straight into his face, never uttering a single word. Drew was furious and wanted to swing for Fazzi there and then, but given the circumstances this was hardly an appropriate time, nor the place for that. Instead, as Fazzi walked away, Drew shouted to him in a heavy sarcastic tone, 'Hey Faz – Linda will need a new coach when she defends her Wimbledon title next year. Can ye recommend anyone suitable?'

On witnessing this verbal fracas develop, Gerry made his way without delay over to Drew and reminded him that there were only so many inflicted blows his body could recover from.

'You're right, mate. I'm going to have a quick word with Linz and call it a night. See you on Tuesday at ISI's office in Chiswick?'

'Yeah, I'll be there, mate. Can't wait to hear what financial deals they're prepared to offer.'

*   *   *   *   *

On Tuesday at 10.30 am prompt, Drew, Gerry and Linda walked together into ISI's impressive, if not prestigious, office complex in Chiswick, West London to join a small group of hyper-energetic young marketing and legal people transparently intent on making a polished and impressive series of formal presentations - so slick and professional that much as Drew and Gerry were perhaps tempted to appear smart-arsed by asking a few questions, it all seemed to have been catered for. There was only a danger of them looking stupid or ignorant by asking a question that the answer had already been provided for.

International Sportsman Inc, being pretty much the biggest organisation of its kind with affiliations all over the world, could almost guarantee initial financial returns as well as long-term financial security. They even had the luxury of deciding which clients they wished to work with and represent, not the other way around.

Their client list – particularly sporting categories – would impress anyone, let alone Linda, Drew and Gerry, even though they probably already suspected it would have been nothing short of being the crème de la crème.

ISI were offering a deal to manage Linda's on-court and off-court activities and were putting a conservatively projected income in year one, as being current Wimbledon champion, circa twelve million. Drew asked for that figure to be repeated – perhaps he had misheard it the first time around? A few vacant-looking faces (three faces to be precise) around the executive conference table might have explained some likely elementary mental arithmetic going on. It certainly did seem evident that all the financial worries regarding Linda were dramatically and excitingly and abruptly at an end. There was as much relief on all three of their faces as there had been sheer joy a few days earlier on Centre Court.

'Now, how's about some *real* celebration? Just the three of us this time,' demanded Linda in an enthusiastic tone of voice on entering the lift after leaving the meeting room with the ISI personnel.

'Nothing I'd like better, believe me. Not today for me, though. Sorry. I've some unfinished business at the cop shop back in Glasgow tomorrow. I want to catch the earliest shuttle from Heathrow back home, then have a good night's sleep so as I'm bright eyed and bushy tailed to finally get these effing murder charges formally dropped. Plus, I have a really important AGM to attend to at the fitba club on Friday. What are you guys doing over the weekend? Why not come up to Glasgow for a weekend break and we can go back to where it all began and celebrate properly – just the three of us. What d'ya say?' suggested Drew with what he evidently thought was an inspired idea of his.

'What a night back at the tennis club at Hillpark for auld times sake – is that what you're suggesting?' queried Gerry.

'Blimey – I can think of more exotic places to have a good night out – but under the circumstances, nothing more appropriate, eh?' giggled Linda. 'Sounds a *great* idea to me guys. No way I'm playing again until I have the results on whether or not I need a cartilage operation, which hopefully will be later on next week when a decision will be taken.'

'So, let's do it!'

'The three tennis musketeers will drink the Hillpark bar dry on Saturday,' yelled Gerry ecstatically, almost pathetically in danger of sounding hysterical. But, still not being the slightest bit humorous.

*　　*　　*　　*　　*

273

Drew was extremely apprehensive about this planned meeting with his lawyer, Alan Liddell, and the Strathclyde Constabulary. Effectively, he was asking them to agree to a major alteration to his original sworn statement so as to provide a conveniently acceptable and reliable alibi. Drew's prior concern centred around the fact that he knew this was not what the CID would want to hear as it would almost certainly put their murder investigations right back to square one.

And Drew was right. The DCI leading the murder inquiry was not happy at all, but realised the alibi of a signed witness statement from someone like Linda McKean would be a difficult one to break down. However, DCI Renwick seemed, at least, determined to give it a final try. The next four to five hours were spent trying to pick holes and contradictions in Drew's account of his trip to Paris, *why* he went to Paris, *how* he went to Paris, *what* he did when he arrived there, and all his movements in-between times, including having sex with Linda. All revisited, for Drew, in graphic detail. It was an extremely uncomfortable few hours for Drew with this aggressive and desperate-sounding Detective Chief Inspector, particularly as Drew's lawyer had pre-advised him to always try to answer as fully and as precisely as his memory recall would allow. The evidence thus far against Drew was flimsy in the extreme, hence the standard bail conditions, with the prosecution's case being restricted to one or two verbal arguments or disagreements with Digby and the fact that hitherto Drew had not provided a wholly satisfactory alibi as to where he was at the time Digby was murdered. There was no other material evidence, nor DNA that could link Drew to the crime scene.

After over four hours of interrogation, DCI Renwick appeared to somewhat reluctantly agree to release Drew and formally drop any charge over John Digby's murder.

Yet another close to a chapter in Drew's less than dull life.

After such an anxious and uncomfortable time spent at the Stirling Police Station, Drew was really looking forward to the AGM of Partick Thistle Football Club the next day at The Albany Hotel in Central Glasgow. He was also excited to be chairing his first AGM and to be reporting on, arguably, the most successful period of the club's modern era. Drew had prepared his speech to the invited audience and he was rather pleased with the draft material he had to present as it was all impressively positive and uplifting stuff. He also confidently expected it was bound to be considerably less stressful than his lengthy meeting with the police.

'Drew, can we get together over breakfast at The Albany?' requested Angus Timlin, getting straight to the point of his phone call.

'Sure. You're sounding very serious Angus. What do you want to talk about?'

'Better we talk in the morning, Drew, face-to-face.'

The following morning Drew met Timlin.

'Well, what's all this about then, Angus?'

'There's only one way to tell you this, Drew – and that is to be forthright with you.'

'But you always are, Angus.'

'Aye, well that's my way. See here – all the other directors want you to resign over this Digby murder allegation.'

'But I'm innocent. Completely innocent. The police finally cleared me yesterday of any involvement in anything to do with Digby's death.'

'I understand that, Drew. I read the press release yesterday. But mud sticks, you know. And there's a lot of mud being thrown in your direction at the moment. Murder, illicit affairs, physical attacks, bribery and corruption allegations,' countered Timlin.

Drew could not believe what he was hearing, 'But I'm completely innocent,' he continued to protest.

'Like I say, Drew – you are preaching to the converted. Still, it doesn't look good for the club from a public relations angle. Morrisons are already starting to make less than discreet noises that they may well pull out of the property deal. They are citing planning issues and difficulties and such likes as the reason. But, it could well just be camouflage. They cannot be seen to be doing business with a committee that are perceived by some within their own board of directors and shareholders as being corrupt or involved in murder investigations.'

'Well, *fuck me*! What a shock to the system,' responded Drew somewhat embarrassed by what was being said to him. He almost felt now he was actually guilty of something or other.

'I know. I know,' repeated Timlin as if trying to sound faintly sympathetic, 'and it may not be of any comfort or consolation to you, but all the board members, and I've spoken to every single one of them over the past twenty-four hours, are all extremely understanding of your personal plight. They are all, to a man, extremely grateful for all you've done for the football club. But, there is a common view that you are damaged goods right at this moment in time and you remaining on as full-time chairman will only damage the chances of concluding this vital deal with Morrisons. Can you not see that?'

'Well *no*, I *effing* can't, actually.'

'I'm afraid you only have two choices, Drew. You can resign your full-time position on the official excuse that other commitments prevent you carrying on, but you will continue to be a non-salaried, non-executive director. That may be enough to appease Morrisons. I'm sure I can convince them over time of your complete innocence of all the allegations against you. But it'll take time to allow a healing process as well as for memories to fade. The other option is for us to terminate your contract with the club and for you to then legally contest that action through the courts. But, I really don't want to be forced to take that option with you, Drew.'

'I need time to think here,' protested Drew.

'Frankly, there is no time. The board will be placing a vote of no confidence in you today if you don't resign before the AGM meeting takes place in the next couple of hours. They will not be able to get that motion passed today, but it will trigger an Extraordinary General Meeting in three weeks time with inevitable consequences, as no one will be voting for you. Plus, I should warn you that I took a telephone call from Ian Girot late yesterday afternoon wanting some quote from me. It appears he will very soon be publishing some article or other, and from what I could gauge it will not be particularly flattering to you - nor for Partick Thistle Football Club for that matter. Did you have a sordid liaison with Linda McKean? Good God, man, you're old enough to be her father,' sneered Timlin. 'And, and, I'm afraid there's yet more bad news, Drew.'

'Let me just lie down on the floor first on me back why don't you, and I'll open me legs apart so you can give me nuts a right good kicking. *What* more bad news?' growled Drew.

'I was given Rudd's letter of resignation yesterday. He's off to manage Heart of Midlothian.'

'What, he's been seduced by the Jam Tarts' money. How ironic, eh?'

'Yeah, but to be fair to him, they have offered double what we've currently paying him, even with bonus payments,' confirmed Timlin.

'Can't we match what he's been offered at Hearts?'

'No way, not with so much financial uncertainty over the club's future.'

'Why didn't Rudd come and see me then? Why did he resign to you, not me?' moaned Drew, starting to feel extremely sorry for himself.

'Think he was aware that you were in hospital and you were also out on bail on a murder rap; that may have had something to do with it,' replied Timlin with a heavy dose of sarcasm in his voice and a stern look on his face.

*   *   *   *   *

It was Friday and almost one whole week on from her Wimbledon victory and, almost as relevant, a few days after signing the contract with ISI, since when Linda had been working harder off court than she had imagined possible. She was thoroughly enjoying all the attention and variety of work that ISI had lined up. Although the work schedule was demanding, the change was indeed just like the equivalent of a rest period for Linda.

There had been numerous promotional activities and mini business projects to places like Harvey Nichols, where Linda was endorsing the launch of a brand new cologne. If that was not enough, there was already a tennis racket produced that had her name engraved on it and was being marketed by Lillywhites, the huge sports retailer in Piccadilly. Linda was staggered by how quickly these matters had been put in place. Staggered but suitably impressed.

Then there was an important photo shoot with *Cosmopolitan* magazine promoting a relatively new range of Nike sportswear. Not forgetting a lucrative deal with the jeweller Cartier, who wanted Linda to promote an extravagantly expensive new watch, which would be the main feature of their winter advertising activity across a whole variety of marketing campaigns right up until Christmas time.

Although Linda, come the end of each of the recent past few days, was feeling fairly tired with all this commercial activity, she nonetheless thoroughly enjoyed it. Being chauffeur-driven in top of the range limousines, and with every little organisational detail clearly all sorted out beforehand, the whole process was stress-free. All she had to do was meet fairly interesting senior executives from the various ISI contacts and just do whatever she was told. Linda had even been allocated her own Personal Assistant by ISI, a Toni Darton, who Linda found to be pleasant company, but ruthlessly efficient and extremely demanding of others to be equally efficient – except Linda, of course, who could do no wrong, seemingly no matter what.

Notwithstanding all the constant excitement and pampering, Linda was still very much looking forward to a weekend retreat up in her native Scotland and those very private celebratory drinks with Gerry and Drew they had promised themselves.

* * * * *

'So what's the plan of action for tomorrow then?' asked Gerry of Drew on his mobile phone.

'Why don't you and I meet up for a knock-up on court say at four o'clock, for an hour or so, then we'll use the antiquated cold shower facilities on site, get changed and get ourselves into the clubhouse bar for the next two or three hours. It'll be deathly quiet at that time of day. Nobody will be there to annoy us or telling Linda how proud they are of her or pestering her for sodding autographs. Then, later, when the bar starts to get a bit busy, we'll phone for a taxi and take ourselves up-town for a meal at Gordon Ramsey's new restaurant in Gibson Street.'

'Bring it on, pal.'

After the briefest of brief visits to Troon for a lunch appointment, Linda was back in Glasgow staying at the Tinto Firs Hotel preparing herself for a night out with 'the lads'.

The Tinto Firs was not much of an establishment to speak of, and more like a 2 star rating rather than the 5 star accommodation Linda had started to get used to within the past week courtesy of ISI. However, the Tinto Firs did have one distinct attraction in that it was within three minutes walking distance from Hillpark Tennis Club. As that was the main reason Linda was back home in Glasgow, then the Tinto Firs would do quite nicely as a base for a day or two maximum.

Meanwhile, Drew and Gerry were on court, each trying to make the other seem as old and as slow as was possible without it being too obvious and without resorting to pathetically juvenile behaviour. It was clearly fun for them both, in equal measure.

It was a gloriously hot and sunny summer's afternoon at Hillpark and both Gerry and Drew's towels were in constant use, such was the incessant flow of perspiration coming from their respective grossly overweight bodies.

Although they were not playing, as such, a conventional game of tennis, there was still much banter between the two and a stubborn element of determination within them both trying to show off to each other by chasing around the court as quickly as their unfit bodies would allow.

Suddenly, Drew tripped and fell awkwardly as he ran to get to a ball that there was never any danger he could remotely hope to reach. The extremely clumsy fall was not whilst actually trying to make a swing at the tennis ball, nor slipping on the poorly maintained, dry, dusty clay surface, nor did it even appear to be as a consequence of tripping over his own two feet.

Gerry at first suspected Drew was playacting, as he was occasionally prone to do between the regular bouts of light-hearted verbal abuse. But it looked such an ungainly fall, even by Drew's standards.

Drew, very gingerly and deliberately, got himself up almost as if he was in a daze. Gerry immediately saw some worrying signals, but tried hard as usual to keep up with the mickey-take with his far funnier and wittier friend.

'Gee, mate, I thought you were having a wee heart attack on me there.'

Drew didn't seem to see the funny side of Gerry's remark as he slowly dusted the red clay sand off his shirt.

'Sorry, mate, that was in poor taste. Are you okay?' continued Gerry.

'Yeah, I think so. Let's call it a day, shall we?'

Whilst Drew and Gerry were recovering from this incident and then the freezing cold water shower facilities, Gerry could not help but notice that Drew's mood had been noticeably subdued over the past ten minutes or so since the fall on court.

'Are you absolutely sure you're okay, matey?' asked Gerry again, sounding considerably more sincere and genuinely anxious than before.

'I wasn't going to say owt, but when I was in the St Thomas Hospital in Westminster recently they told me I might have to have a growth removed from my brain.'

'What a tumour!' screamed Gerry as if in disbelief, although he was surely not doubting his friend for one single second.

'Yeah, they're still carrying out tests to see if it's benign or not, and whether it is safe or sensible to operate.'

'Fuck me, mate,' was all Gerry seemed capable of shouting in reply.

'Look, Gerry, no way, but no way, do I want this to spoil tonight, especially for Linda. I honestly would never have mentioned anything to you either had it not been for that fall out there. It scared the shit out of me, I don't mind to admit. My poor sense of balance, I think, has to be a sign of a major problem. But, hey, conversation over. Let's not even think about it, let alone talk about it again. Certainly not tonight. Deal, pal?'

'Deal,' replied Gerry, still visibly in some shock over this traumatic and sobering news of his friend's possible serious health issue.

"Game, Set & Match"

Drew did the honours by opening the first bottle of champagne as the three of them sat in the small, but homely, clubhouse bar at Hillpark, which sits elevated on a hillside with panoramic views from huge windows on three sides. Just a pity the vistas had nothing to commend them, mainly consisting of row after row of fairly smart, but unexceptional private dwellings. There were two prominent bowling greens, always in immaculate condition, with the shabby-looking tennis courts conveniently hidden away behind the clubhouse and well out of view from the main lounge bar.

Drew, Gerry and Linda were all now behaving almost like immature, drunken *Big Brother* television contestants playing up to an imaginary audience.

Repetitive toasting – *"Linda McKean, **the** Wimbledon Champion"*.

A feat they had all dreamt about over the past twelve to fifteen years, almost an obsession, had now finally become a reality.

Moments of ecstatic happiness - they were giggling at anything and everything any one of the three said or did. Even Gerry's attempted witticisms were, for once, wholeheartedly acknowledged with laughter. The second bottle of champagne was opened within less than ten minutes after the first. The three of them were almost uncontrollably loud, so much so they did not initially hear Linda's mobile phone ring.

'Ignore it, Linda,' they jointly told her as the phone continued to ring.

'Och, it may be yet another person wanting to offer me stacks of dosh for five minutes promotional work,'

283

howled Linda, immediately followed by Drew and Gerry laughing loudly in unison.

Linda suddenly went silent with the phone still lodged to her ear. The smile had vanished in a flash. She still wasn't saying anything. Gerry and Drew's laughter also died into silence prompted by intrigue at Linda's dramatically altered facial expression. Eventually Linda spoke into the phone, 'Is this a wind-up?' Soon afterwards her mobile phone was put down on the table in a dismissive gesture that saw it slide over and fall onto Drew's lap.

'Who the *fuck* was that then?' demanded Drew.

'It was Fred. Fred Shiels. He's just had contact from the Tennis Association about the tablets he'd been prescribing to me. It appears a recent urine sample I gave just before the semis last week has proven positive to having traces of a banned substance. He said they had been trying to get hold of me, without success, so they phoned him as he is down on their database as being registered as my doctor.'

There was a protracted pause before Linda continued, 'Shiels is now trying to say that I took far too many of the tablets he was prescribing in too short a space of time. An absolute minified trace of some substance called THG has been allowed to build up in my system. He says it is evident from the basic stats from the extracts he was given over the phone from a toxicology report now in the hands of the ILTA.'

'Fuck me, Linda - what does all this mean?' Drew asked.

'Shiels seems to believe I'll be banned. He says he doesn't know precisely how they operate in the tennis world, but if it was an athlete, then the ban would almost certainly be for life these days.'

'Shit,' spat out Gerry.

Linda's phone rang again.

'Maybe it's someone gonna tell me it's all been a bloody windup, eh?'

In fact, it was Toni Darton from ISI. It appeared Linda could after all do wrong in Darton's eyes. Darton made it pretty clear that the drug claim, if true, would be catastrophic for ISI, as well as Linda. It would mean termination of the legal contract that had been signed only a few days earlier and because of the nature of the breach of the terms and conditions of the contract there would be absolutely no compensation payable to Linda.

Linda felt she had no choice but to relay the continuing doom and gloom to Drew and Gerry, 'It seems from what Toni's just said that even if the drug allegation is proven false on any subsequent appeal, the prior bad publicity is something that would probably still make ISI walk away from me, without notice, and terminate the contract. I suppose they can't afford to be remotely associated with any drugs scandal.'

Gerry instantaneously and bizarrely burst out into laughter, but it was almost immediately tinged with tears running down his left cheek. That then quickly developed into him struggling to stop the constant flow of tears from both eyes. In fact, he was soon sobbing in an undignified and uncontrolled manner.

Neither Linda nor Drew had ever seen Gerry cry before, let alone in such an obvious display of emotion. There again, they were unaware that Gerry, on the previous day, had been served with legal papers by his wife's lawyer regarding gross criminal damage, fraud and forgery and she was demanding a divorce settlement that would financially cripple Gerry. His hitherto saving grace from financial ruin had been - or so he thought - the contract signed with ISI that would have in its own merit, over the next few years, guaranteed him a secure and comfortable standard of living.

There was complete silence.

There was prolonged silence.

There were quite possibly intermittent flash-backs going on appertaining to an unplanned pregnancy dilemma, kidnapping ordeal, drug abuse, forged legal contracts, unsolicited lesbian encounter, physical beatings, murder investigation, racism allegation and intimidation, ball-girl blackmail scandal, soccer glory, share investment fraud and corruption, bribery, financial ruin - even memories of some highly entertaining tennis played in between.

And then finally, *finalement,* there would soon need to be some thought given to Ian Girot's nearly completed unauthorised biography, for which he had already received a huge advance fee from a leading publishing company.

Girot's uncle and aunt, Monsieur et Madame Bonneau, would be très pleased.

'C'est la vie……………..pal !'

Gordon Kidd (aged 61) alive and well with some golf trophies won during the 2012 golf season.

He no longer plays tennis. And has not done so since playing at Hillpark LTC 1962-1973. Although it happened a long, long time ago, nothing except vivid, happy memories remain of Hillpark and the then tennis members.

www.ingramcontent.com/pod-product-compliance
Lightning Source LLC
Chambersburg PA
CBHW020948260626
47169CB00006B/1884